CURSE OF DRACULA

IMMORTAL SOUL: PART TWO

KATHRYN ANN KINGSLEY

Copyright © 2020 by Kathryn Ann Kingsley

First Print Edition: August 2020

ISBN-13: 979-8-65555-684-3

ASIN: B089S53NSP

KATHRYN ANN KINGSLEY

All rights reserved.

No part of this book may be reproduced in any form or by any electronic or mechanical means, including information storage and retrieval systems, without written permission from the author, except for the use of brief quotations in a book review.

This is a work of fiction. Names, characters, places, and incidents either are the product of the author's imagination or are used fictitiously, and any resemblance to locales, events, business establishments, or actual persons —living or dead—is entirely coincidental.

ACKNOWLEDGMENTS

As always, thank you to my editor Lori for keeping me on my toes. It seems with every new book comes some new word ruts.

To Kristin, for studiously reading these things and giving me a smack upside the head when I go in a bad direction.

To my increasingly patient husband for putting up with the hours it takes me to do all that's required when one publishes a book.

And thank you to you, readers, for keeping me going.

1

Vlad Tepes Dracula stood atop a building in the city of Boston, the barely born and fledgling city of the new nation that had made such a noise upon its arrival. The youth was reflected in the optimistic industry and mindsets of those who lived here.

Humans were meant to build. To aspire. To reach for the sun.

And he had taken it away from them. Snatched it from the sky and pitched the city into the night.

He reached his arms out at his sides and felt his darkness stretch. He would devour the very metropolis like he would take a life. His nightmare, now released, would spread through the Earth and air like a plague.

He had tried to warn Maxine. He had tried to warn the hunters themselves. But no one ever listened. No one could fathom what it was that dwelled inside his soul.

I am not a vampire. I am far more, and far worse, than that. Within me beats the black heart of all that would splinter bone and pick their teeth with the remains.

I am the river spring from which flows all cruelty on this Earth.

And it was cruelty that made me.

He wondered if those who cursed him so long ago could have even fathomed what they had wrought upon the living. Their faces were lost to him, as were the details of the event itself. He understood only in vague terms as to the why, the when, and the how it had all come to pass. It did not matter. It did not change the simple fact that he was death incarnate.

Yet never allowed to die.

He could bestow that gift upon others, and he did it with both joy and disgust. It mattered not—it did not change the hunger that boiled over in him. The hunger that could change the world around him to the whim of his dark dreams.

The crimson moon had usurped the sun, and with it came his creatures. Demons and monsters he had created over the course of his long "life." Beasts of warped and mutilated forms that put the ghouls to shame for their lack of creativity.

And the city would know such pain because of the actions of hunters who sought to save it. The actions of one hunter in particular.

Alfonzo Van Helsing had come for revenge. It blinded him to the deal that any sane man would have taken. Any man whose mind was not clouded by hatred would have seen it a bargain to spare the life of a city in return for a single mortal woman.

A woman who wanted to be at his side.

That was...until he soaked the ground in blood. Now, all bets were off.

He watched in idle fascination as a few of his creatures

tackled a man on his horse on the street below. The monsters took both rider and steed to the ground. They screamed in agony as teeth tore into flesh and began to rend them asunder without any care for their suffering.

He supposed that was not true. His creatures cared very much for the suffering of their victims—they enjoyed it greatly.

As for himself?

Watching the gore play out beneath him?

He felt nothing at all.

DEATH CAME to the city of Boston on crimson wings. The sun had been plucked from the sky and replaced by a moon the color of blood, shrouding the city in its unnatural light.

But that was not what horrified her the most. It was that the sounds of birds, once happily chirping in the trees or soaring on summer air...had been replaced by screams. The sounds of mortal souls caught in terror and pain joined with a chorus of inhuman howls that joyfully called out their bloody victories.

Death had come on crimson wings, and it had a name—*Vlad Tepes Dracula*.

But Maxine suspected she remained largely to blame.

She pressed her back to the wall of her living room, shivering uncontrollably. A bone-deep chill had taken the summer breeze from the air and was already quickly seeping into her home like a poison. She could feel it beneath the surface of the ground and sense it all around her. A curse had been unleashed. A plague she had thought she had understood. But oh, she had been very wrong. The vampire had asked her if she could eat her steak and kill the cow. If she could face down the hypocrisy of her ignorance and still embrace him.

She thought she had known the answer. And now she knew she had been mistaken.

Fear was consuming the city. Fear and the lust for blood, and it crawled over her like swarming insects. Her empathic gift was overrun by it.

How often in her life had she been accused of being cold and austere? Too many to count. It was not because she wished to be such—it was simply because there was no other way for her to survive. By tuning out all her own emotions, all that dwelled within her heart, she could ignore that of those around her.

It was the only way to keep from drowning in the tide. Always around her, like the very air itself, thrummed the emotions of humanity. Every ounce of lust, of joy, of love. Every speck of agony, of grief, of hatred and loss. It was always around her.

She pushed it all away to keep herself sane. To keep herself whole. To keep from sinking to the bottom of that sea and becoming consumed by it all.

But now a storm had come to her shores. A terrible nor'easter that battered at her windows. She could not fight nature. And nature had come with the singular intent of tearing her shutters free and forcing her into the waves.

Death.

Pain.

Fear.

Suffering.

Agony.

She could feel in her heart what it was like to watch a loved one be torn to pieces. She knew it because someone nearby was experiencing it in that very moment. When she

Curse of Dracula

shut her eyes, teeth were sinking into her flesh. Sharp, dagger-like things crunching through bone like she was made of nothing more than twigs.

Maxine twitched as she felt claws tear out her throat. She put her hands to her own throat to ensure that it had not truly happened. But she could almost—*almost*—feel the wet blood pour through her fingers as cackling, broken-faced monsters devoured her alive.

Limbs were being torn from bodies with wet-sounding pops. Heads were taken from shoulders. Eyes from their sockets. Again and again, more and more, agony flooded into her. Her city was dying, and she was on a sinking raft in a sea of blood.

She was struggling to keep her breathing even, but it felt too quick and shallow.

She loved the creature who caused this. Or she thought she had.

Now all she knew was a primal panic that triggered something in her deep and intrinsic to her species—*run, survive, escape*. But there was nowhere she could go. She was trapped. Both by the Vampire King who had unleashed his wrath, and by the chain that bound her wrists and kept her tethered. A prisoner to the three people responsible for dragging her into this mess in the first place.

The vampire hunters.

They were ignoring her, arguing and shouting at each other. Alfonzo was pacing around the room. Bella was sitting with her head in her hands, and Eddie looked as though he was attempting to pull out his own hair. Their anxiety did nothing to ease her own overwhelmed emotions.

She wanted to sink to the ground and weep. She wanted to cower and hide. But she was trembling. Her legs itched with the need to run from the wolf in the shadows. But where could she go? Where could she hide, even if she could free herself from her chains and escape the three hunters?

I am naïve. I am a fool. I thought I could see the whole of him. I thought I understood what he was. Now, how many will come to pay the price for my idiocy? I let him in. I let him get close. Looking down at her bare hands, they were shaking like the rest of her.

"This is your fault!" Eddie was still shouting at Alfonzo. "You should've given him Maxine. Even if he was lying, it was worth the chance that he wasn't. You didn't tell me he could take out the sun!"

"Because I didn't know he could. But we've prepared for this. This is the war we were expecting to fight. Nothing has changed."

"No. No, we aren't prepared to fight a war. I, for one, never got told we were facing down a man who could destroy an entire city with his mind. You never sent me that little note. And besides that, you know what else has changed? We could have stopped it, Al. We had a chance. And you *fucked it up!*" Eddie was frantic in his anger, his voice higher pitched than usual.

Maxine sank to the ground, sliding her back down the wainscoting. Her dress and the chain pooled around her feet. It was not the only chain she wore. The monster that had unleashed the chaos she felt burning in her mind was the same one who held her far less physical leash. The one that connected to her mind and her soul.

The one she had welcomed in. The one whose hand she had willingly taken. The one whom she had allowed to woo her and win her. "This is my fault…" Her murmur, which she thought was too quiet for them to hear, broke through the argument the two men were waging. She shuddered, her body covered in a cold sweat.

"What, Maxine?" Eddie prompted her gently.

"Are you all right?" Bella asked.

No. No, she very much was not. The fear of all those in the city was consuming her, like a deer that had fallen to a wolf's hungry teeth. It was drowning her, and she did not know if she could survive the tumultuous waves.

So many were dead or dying.

So much pain.

And it was all because of *her*.

She could have stopped this. She could have stopped him, if only she had been strong enough to try. She had held his soul in her hands. Instead of casting it into the void like she should have, she cradled it to her chest, selfish and self-centered in her need to be embraced for the first time in her life.

Tears streamed down her cheeks, and she did not care enough to wipe them away. All she knew was blood on her hands and beneath her nails. Sticky and hot. She could taste it. But there, mingled with the fear and the agony, was hunger. Joy. Need. *Pleasure.* "This is my fault," she repeated numbly.

Lust for blood clashed with the pain of being torn to pieces. Prey and predator, victim and violence, and she felt both at once.

And I could have stopped this.

She was shivering. The city was dying, the city was feeding, and there were both teeth digging into her and the sensation of sinking fangs she did not own into supple flesh. She wanted to retch.

"No, no, Maxine..." Bella sank down close to her. The young huntress reached for her hands but stopped. She didn't dare touch Maxine's bare skin. And for that, Maxine was exceedingly grateful. Instead, Bella chose to place them on her knees over her dress. "You are not to blame."

"But I am." She curled her hands into fists and pulled them closer to herself, dragging the chain across the floor.

"No. Dracula has done this, not you. He has killed these people. He has attacked the city. You have done none of this."

"But I...I could have tried. I could have attempted to stop him." She looked up at the younger woman. Bella was so pretty —so full of life, so seemingly innocent. And her life was likely to end here in this war. None of them would survive this, she was certain. Alfonzo, Eddie, Bella, they would all die. All because of her selfishness. "I could have tried to destroy his soul."

"What? How?" Alfonzo walked up to her.

"The same way I could destroy any of you, were you foolish enough to touch me." She couldn't meet Alfonzo's gaze. She looked down for lack of anywhere safer. She needed the pain to stop. She needed the sound of the screams to go away. She ran her hands into her hair and gripped the strands in her fists, pulling them tight, trying to use that to give her something else to focus on.

"You can destroy his soul," Eddie said through a heavy exhale. "Fuck." Now he was the one pacing the room. "Oh, Hell, Maxine."

"You can kill him." Alfonzo was watching her keenly. Something close to madness glittered in his eyes. Something that scared her a great deal. "You can kill him *for good.*"

"I..." Maxine didn't know what to say. She only knew that she wanted to crawl into a dark place and hide. Somewhere far, far away from the hunters, the vampires, and all the death that cried its warpath outside her door.

"Then I'm going to make sure you get that chance." Alfonzo leaned down and picked up the chain that ran to her wrists. He wrapped it around his palm a few times. "I'm going to make sure you're going to want to do it when you get there. Bella. Eddie. Get your things. We have a war to fight."

"No, I—"

It didn't matter what she said. The crusader had his goal. Alfonzo smiled down at her, and there was no friendship in his expression when he did. "We have a war we can finally end."

———

Dracula stood upon the roof of his temporary home, still lost in thought. Now his new fortress, it was the city's library. By the looks of things, it had recently opened. The paint smelled new, at least to him. But his senses were keener than most. Either way, this building was now his. It was his in the same fashion that all the rest of the city now belonged to him.

The reproduction gothic church that stood across from his home would have an amusing new use. He had plans for it already. What an odd and curious human behavior—to build new places in the fashion of the old. It was an attempt to cling to their past as though it were somehow better and grander than their future.

The past is only ever lesser. What may come is all that will ever give us hope.

He looked down at the corruption spreading through the streets and alleys of the young American city. He had unleashed his curse in full. He had become an unwelcome disease that had taken hold of the center of this little outpost of humanity.

"You are a plague upon your house. You will be a plague upon the world." He remembered those words spoken to him so long ago, when he could feel the grit of sand in his teeth and taste unwelcome and bitter blood in his mouth. *"You will be alone forever."*

He drove away the unwelcome memory with a growl. His beloved empath had dredged up several preserved corpses from the bottom of the bog in his mind. It was disconcerting.

A sign proclaimed this place "Copley Square." He could not care less. The sign that once stood proudly in the center of the plaza beneath him was now twisted and bent by some terrible nightmare. And a nightmare had come, indeed. He watched his power spread, the shadow consuming all that it touched.

The sound of screams hung in the darkness of the never-ending night.

It made him smile.

This city had thought it understood fear when he had turned the moon to blood. Now it would know true pain. It would know true death.

It, like Maxine, would know what kind of demon he truly was.

"Master. Is this…is this truly wise?"

Ah, Walter. The vampire was a rare direct child of his blood, one of the few strong enough to withstand the kind of power his kiss brought. One of the few creatures with the mental capacity to handle immortality for longer than a few hundred years. Or so he hoped. Walter was also forever attempting to play the role of the conscience that Vlad had given up a long, long time ago.

"It is certainly not wise. It is anything but. Yet it will happen regardless. Where is Zadok?"

"Where do you think?"

It was rare that Walter was sarcastic with him. He must truly have annoyed the redhead with his decision to finally wage his war and claim this city. His question had, in truth, been a pointless one. He knew precisely where the illusionist was—off in the mayhem, wallowing in the slaughter.

"Fetch him from his revelries. I have something important he needs to do."

Walter sighed heavily.

"Is this an inconvenience for you?" Vlad turned to look at the other vampire with a raised eyebrow.

"No, my Lord. Forgive me." Walter placed a hand to his chest and bowed his head. "It is not my place to speak against you."

"It is always your place to speak freely. You disagree with what I have done."

"Yes."

"Good."

Walter looked up at him, red eyes that matched his own betraying the younger vampire's confusion.

Vlad turned back to the city. "What I am doing here is cruel. Thousands will die. It is wrong. That is...entirely the point, I'm afraid."

"I fail to understand."

"I know. Fetch me Zadok."

"Yes, Master."

And with that, Walter was gone. He watched the red-winged bats soar off into the sky in search of his more hedonist kin. Zadok was in all ways a difficult creature. But for what was to follow, he would play a very important part.

The Frenchman was loyal and valuable for his skills. He was worth the irritations he brought with him.

Most of the time.

Vlad watched as his disease spread throughout the city around him, growing wider with every passing second. The city would be his within the hour. Creatures stalked the shadows and the skies. Twisted abominations hunted their prey. Some resembled their previous condition of humanity to various degrees—and some did not.

By the time the clock struck midnight, the humans would be left only in pockets, sheltering for protection. They would be hunted down for sport. Only one would be spared.

One would be left to wander. Accompanied by his enemies as she may be, it mattered not to him. They would fall in time. But he had one mission for her in all this death—observe and learn. He would come for her in time.

While he was master of the hunt, how it ended would be hers to decide.

You met me in a dream. Now we shall see how you fare with my nightmare.

2

THEY UNDID her chains long enough to allow her to change into something more appropriate than the opera gown she had worn last night. She pulled on a dress meant for gardening, not for refined society, and pulled the laces of the bodice tight in the back.

Society is dead. No one will care if you do not wear a proper corset. She pulled on a pair of black silk gloves and did her long, dark hair up in a braid. She could not help but linger as she tied the bit of leather string around the end of it. Vlad preferred her hair worn loose. She cringed. Placing her hands down on surface of the vanity in front of her, she struggled with herself.

There was no resolving her turmoil. Not now, perhaps not ever. She left her hair braided and pulled on one of her fall coats. The weather had taken a sharp turn, fading from the balmy warmth of the summer into the chill of early winter. She did not know where the hunters planned on leading her, but she knew it would require her to be out and about in the city for a good length of time.

Comfortable shoes, a coat, and she was ready to go.

Go *where?*

To her death? To his? Or to both?

Still, the echoes of the dead and dying plagued her mind. The city was wounded. Many were likely now lost to the claws of the creatures that hunted the streets. The rest might be hunkered down in their homes, terrified and alone. They could not understand what was happening. They could not understand why.

The sun had been robbed from the skies. What else could they do but cower? Life had ceased its pattern. There were but a few constants in this world, one of them being the rise and fall of the very sun itself. But now, like every other shred of normalcy, it was gone.

All because she dared to love the creature who had stolen it from the skies.

She needed quiet. She needed silence from those around her. She would not get it. When there was a furtive knock on her door, she could sense that the hunters had grown impatient. "I'm coming," she called. The light nature of the knock and the gentle soul across the wooden barrier from her revealed it was Bella.

Each of the hunters had a unique feeling. They burned bright from each other. Bella was sweet, light, and loving. Eddie was curious and resilient. Alfonzo was determined and headstrong. She found herself, despite everything, caring for each of them. They were only trying to do what was right.

She also wondered if she had not been deceived as they had claimed. If her mind had not been corrupted after all. Separate from Vlad's influence as she was, caught in the tide of the stinking death and fear that surrounded them, she could not help but doubt the love she had for him.

Which was the lie?

Curse of Dracula

Which was the mistruth?

Maxine opened the door. "I am ready," she murmured to the young girl. That itself was a lie. All she wished to do was cower in the safety of her room and wait for the storm to pass. Wait for the demon himself to sweep into her room, gather her up into his arms, and take her to where she would be safe from such strife.

But she had never been one to turn her gaze away from that which was unpalatable. She was a creature born to bear the suffering of those around her. And, in her own right, it was her responsibility to experience every drop of blood as though it were her own. The city had fallen because she lacked the strength and conviction to try to destroy the monster when she had the chance.

No. She was not ready.

But she would march out those doors all the same.

When she reached the bottom of the stairs, Eddie stood with the length of chain in his hand. He looked at her, sheepish and apologetic as he always was, and held out the shackles. "Sorry, ma'am."

Shutting her eyes for a moment, she held out her wrists to him. "It isn't your fault, Eddie."

"I know. Still feel like shit for it." He clasped the shackles around her wrists, clicking them into place. He slipped the key into his pocket and picked up the end of the chain to wrap it around his hand a few times.

"I would ask to be set free, so that I might defend myself. But…I have no means of doing so. I am helpless."

"Far from it." Alfonzo grunted as he peered out the patterned glass that framed her front door. "Something tells me the monsters that hunt the streets won't hurt you."

He was likely right. If the creatures obeyed Dracula, then

she probably had little to fear from their claws. But it was, in the end, the same trap.

For something whispered to her that the things that haunted the usurping night were nothing but extensions of the man she would have willingly invited into her bed had the hunters not attacked them. She had kissed him. She had embraced him and had believed, like the child that she was, that she understood him.

No. She had only fallen victim to the lie he had told so many others. He had only shown her a facet of himself, the piece of the whole that she had wanted to see. *Or perhaps this* is *his way of showing you the rest of him. What if you can weather this and love him still? But how would that ever be possible?*

Alfonzo opened the door, brandishing his sword, and strode out into the darkness of the night with not an ounce of fear in his step. Bella followed him, the holsters along her body filled with the daggers and knives that on a moment's notice she could use to fill the air around her. And beside her, Eddie the deadly marksman. Holding Maxine's leash.

No matter what she did, she would either become a prisoner or a corpse.

It wasn't until they reached one street over that she pulled up short. It looked as though a river had tried to overtake the cobblestone streets. Liquid ran between the stones, filling the gaps between them like grout. Wet and viscous, the substance shone in the gas lamps that were lit and now burned an unnatural, ghastly green tone.

It was not rainwater.

It was blood.

Bodies littered the sidewalk, strewn where they had been discarded. Some with huge chunks torn from their sides, some missing limbs. Eaten, abused, and tossed aside like broken toys. She covered her mouth with her hand, trying not to be sick, as if by that method alone she could hold back the bile that threatened to jump up from where it belonged.

But the chain was tugged, and she was pulled along behind the three hunters who acted as though the mayhem and slaughter were nothing out of the ordinary for them. Perhaps it wasn't. She really had no concept of with whom she was dealing.

Step by step, avoiding the rivulets of blood as she walked on the raised portions, they progressed through the city.

They walked from street to street, heading closer to the center of the city. It was slow going. Carriages were overturned, and debris blocked their path. Several buildings looked like they had been demolished by something enormous and torn to pieces, blocking the roads. But everywhere they went, there was death.

He has done this. This is what dwells inside of him. This is what he has unleashed.

After maybe half an hour, they came across their first "living" creature. She could not say that was what it was at all. It was a long, gangly thing. Its skin was purplish in tone, yet sallow and decayed all the same. Its face was distended, as though someone had dug their fingers into a skull made of clay and dragged it forward, uncaring for the pain it might cause the recipient.

She could not even tell if it had eyes or simply sockets pulled out of proportion. Most important was its enormous set of teeth. Fanged, sharp, and rowed like the shark jaws she saw on display in the natural museum of science. Tattered flesh hung from its jaws, stringy and damp.

They had interrupted its meal.

A meal that had once been a man and was now little

more than gore smeared on the sidewalk. Emotions roared through her. *Fear. Terror. Madness. Hunger. Bloodlust. Joy.*

A shake of the chain at her wrists jarred her back into the moment. "Don't run, Maxine."

She nodded weakly. She didn't know if she even could. Backing up, she found a lamppost to lean on. The cold iron helped ground her. The rest was a blur. She heard the monster screaming. She heard gunfire. The sound of steel on stone. Alfonzo and the others shouting to each other, coordinating an attack on the monster.

Death.

The joy of it. The fear of it.

It was too much.

She felt faint. Her breathing was short and shallow. The world was starting to grow fuzzy and strange. She was too hot and too cold. Sinking down to the ground, she shivered uncontrollably.

The darkness that reached out for her was far preferable to drowning in this sea of agony. She let it take her without a fight.

———

VLAD'S ATTENTION was not on the hunters who tangled with the beasts who came from the shadows to fight them. He knew they would likely dispatch his creatures without too much trouble. This wasn't about killing them—not yet. He would have his revenge, but, for now, he was content to simply wear them down.

Standing on the rooftop of a nearby building, his focus was on the poor girl in the black coat, leaning on the streetlamp. Her head lolled to the side. She had fainted. Concern wrenched his heart. He wanted to go to her, to cradle her in his arms and sweep her off to some dark and silent place.

But he could not.

Not because of the hunters. He could take the opportunity of their distraction and abduct her now if he wished. No. Sadly, a grander game was to be played. One that would test his darling Maxine. And if he were fortunate, it would not break her.

"What's wrong with her?" Zadok asked from beside him. The Frenchman was standing with his weight all on one foot, his hands shoved into his pockets.

"Think on what this war has done to the fabric of this city. It has become an ocean of blood. The dark tide has swept her under its waves."

"Why don't I go take her back?" Zadok looked up at him, yellow eyes catching the light of the red moon. "They will never even know I was there."

"She must learn what I am."

"Uh...huh," Zadok said slowly and looked back down at the warring hunters. "You earned her love, and now you want to earn her hatred, and see which one wins, is it? You really do want to spend your eternity alone, don't you? I suppose I cannot fault you for childish games, lest I be the pot and you the kettle. But this is foolish, even to me."

"For once, I fear I agree with him." Walter spoke from nearby for the first time. "I do loathe it when you put me in the position to side with him. The three of us could end them right now."

"Be glad, then, that I do not care for either his opinion or yours in this matter." Vlad smirked, despite their prattle. "And no. We do not attack."

Walter sighed, clearly disagreeing with his plan. Vlad understood his annoyance. The tactician in him screamed to be done with it quickly. Three hunters could not defeat him and his two strongest children, no matter how talented the humans may be.

"This is not about victory. This is about defeat. I will have them broken at my feet, not only in body, but in soul. I will have them beg for mercy before I let them die."

"Ah. I see. They've gone and made you angry." Zadok cracked his neck audibly to one side then the other. "If you want to play with your food, fine. What's the next step?"

"They are strong when they are together…but they are merely human. They draw strength from their sense of solidarity. Shatter it however you see fit."

Zadok grinned. "Gladly." He dissolved into a swarm of rats that poured over the side of the building on which they stood, scrabbling down the brickwork and away.

There were two very good reasons he assigned Zadok the task of tearing the hunters apart at the seams. One, it was Zadok's gift to lie and deceive. And two…he would take great pleasure in the act. There were many adages referring to the fact that a job was not work if it was also a joy.

"Was that wise to release Zadok to his own means?"

Dracula did not look to his second-in-command as he spoke. He did not take his gaze off the girl sitting unconscious on the ground. How he wanted to go to her. But it was not yet time. He would comfort her in her dreams, and that was all he would allow himself for the moment. "Certainly not, no."

"Then why do it?"

"To deny the artist his canvas and paint too long is to drive him mad. Some hungers are not so easily fed as others." He gestured idly at a monster in an alley that was quite contentedly ripping the flesh off a young woman it had run down. She was still alive, although her gagging cries of pain revealed it was only for the moment. "And Zadok has a talent in such regard. He will destroy them from the inside out. And when he is finished, when they split, then we will be done with them."

"And what of the girl?"

Vlad smiled sadly. "Her fate is hers to write. Not mine. She has learned my kindness...now I shall have her learn my cruelty."

Walter was silent for a long time. "You love her. Why put her through such agony?"

"Do you remember what you endured before I agreed to turn you?" It was only then that he looked at his second-in-command. Walter's face was drawn tight and cold with the memory, but there was a flare of fresh pain in his red eyes. "And you understand now why I did it."

"You test her mettle, then, to see if she is strong enough to survive you." Walter grunted wearily and rubbed a hand across his eyes. "She may hate you for this."

"It is likely. I will deserve it if she does. But I would have my hopes shatter and not atrophy. If she will loathe me, I would have her love die in a blaze of glory, not wither and fade as she comes to slowly be disgusted by my true nature."

"Master, may I speak frankly?"

"Of course."

"Do you think you are worthy of love?"

Vlad flinched. He paused for a very long time before responding, debating whether he should speak the truth. But if Walter was not trustworthy, no one was. "I am not sure."

Walter let out a thoughtful hum. "So that is what this is about." He stepped to the edge of the building. "Very well. I will go along with this. I can only pray to the gods in Hell that at the end of this farce you find your answer once and for all." He exploded into red bats, soared up into the sky, and was gone.

Vlad laughed.

The hunters had finished dispatching the monster they had found. Eddie had gone to Maxine's side and was now shaking her shoulder, trying to rouse her. She jolted awake, thrashing in a panic. Eddie stroked her covered arm, trying to soothe her. Vlad watched as someone else gave her the comfort he wished he could provide.

His heart ached for what he was going to force her to suffer. But it was a path he must walk. He would not keep her sheltered from the truth of his soul and let her love only a facet as so many others had done. Like the cards in Maxine's tarot deck, he chose to be whatever they wanted him to be. Oh, his former lovers would always say they knew him for what he was, but it was always a naïve lie.

It was a fate she had begun to share. But he would not spin that falsehood for her. After all, they had made an accord, hadn't they?

She would be forced to see all of him firsthand.

Will you love me when all is said and done? Or am I beyond all salvation?

3

Eddie pressed a flask into her hand. Maxine unscrewed the top and took a sip. She didn't even care what kind of alcohol it was. It didn't matter. She screwed the cap back on and returned it to him, nodding once in thanks.

"I threw up the first time I saw a real fight," Eddie said with a helpful smile.

"It wasn't that." She rubbed the back of her neck slowly, feeling the tightness in the muscles. "I don't even think I saw much of it."

"What's wrong, then?" Bella was also standing nearby, her brow creased in concern.

"It's the whole city." Alfonzo's tone was dark and flat. He was wiping the blood from his sword. "Isn't it?"

She nodded as she pushed herself up to her feet with Eddie's help. She was a little woozy and leaned back on the post for balance. The city was now quiet. The screams had died down, leaving only an eerie silence.

"You can feel all of it. The screams, the pain, the death. You can feel the monsters too, can't you?" Alfonzo sheathed his sword into his holster. "Can you keep going?"

She nodded again weakly even though she felt sick at the idea. She didn't have much of a choice. "I will be all right." She would need to learn to swim in this new tide. "I was caught off guard."

"Good." Alfonzo was watching her, his expression stern. "Do you realize now what he is? What he *really* is?" He jerked his head to the street. Bella and Eddie took the cue, and they started walking.

"I think I am learning." She pulled her coat tighter around herself as she followed them. Once more, she did it because she had no choice. Eddie was still holding the end of her chain. "Is this still necessary?" She lifted her hands to gesture at the links that joined her wrists. "I have nowhere I can run."

"I'm sorry," Alfonzo replied without looking at her. He was already scanning the streets, keeping an eye out. "I wish I could trust you, but you lost that chance when you sided with him."

That was fair. This was a fate she had made for herself. Her decisions had led to this moment, and now she would suffer for it. They walked around the remains of the giant abomination that they had felled. The horror of it was another piece of the scenery of death that had been painted with such a broad brush around her. It was only another body in the mangled pile. Another victim of the corruption that had been unleashed.

And it seemed as though even the buildings themselves were not immune to the plague that Vlad had brought. Walls now twisted in at odd angles or stretched up farther than was natural. Windows and doors were bent out of proportion.

She knew this city well. They were only a few streets away from her home. But she had no inkling of an idea of

Curse of Dracula

where she was. Signs advertised roads she did not recognize. Part of it was still Boston, but part of it was somewhere else —somewhere older.

One of the old Roma in the camp she traveled with used to tell her stories of Bucharest, Prague, and the beautiful cities of Eastern Europe. How the stones used to create the structures were shaped differently than they were here. How they were rougher, more unevenly shaped, and how it gave the structures so much more character than in America.

America simply lacked the age, and was more interested in growing quickly than growing correctly.

The spires and the ironwork seemed somehow both ornate and worn smooth by time. Like a memory of a craftsman's labor. She had never seen the streets of older places other than in paintings and galleries.

But this place *felt old*.

More than that...it linked together in odd and unusual ways. Two buildings that had seemingly nothing to do with each other blended together. It was unnatural. It was eerie. And it was disturbingly familiar. Not because she knew the buildings, but almost as though she could recognize the architect.

She wondered if she traced her fingers over the stones of the nearest building she would not see that throne room in her mind's eye. If she would not hear the vampire's words echoing through her mind.

If she might not feel his hand on hers, asking for her to dance.

It is not Dracula's army that has been unleashed.
It is Dracula himself.

This was not her city any longer. Nor was it any other. It was a dream made manifest...a nightmare. *His* nightmare had come to share itself with the living and devour all that it could.

All this lived within him. All the monsters that stalked the shadows that she could sense watching them were somehow part of him. Creatures of a fiction he had composed. No—children of a god who had rewritten reality to suit him better.

This is what he is.

She paused to gawk in horror at the sight of several bodies impaled on a fencepost. Stacked on top of each other, one at a time, like meat on a skewer. Fresh blood dripped from them like rivulets on a fountain, and all she could feel was the fear that still echoed from their cooling corpses.

She did not have long to dwell on them.

A voice cut through the unnerving silence.

"Greetings, hunters! My Master bids you welcome to his new empire."

She cringed. She knew that voice. *Zadok.*

———

"Be quiet, Mordecai." Walter's patience was wearing thin. Dangerously thin. He only had so much of it left to go around, and he did not want to waste it on the incubus. The captain of the vampire's demons had chosen to stroll about in his natural shape, his gray-purple skin contrasting sharply with his blond hair and black horns.

"No. No, I will not. I have a vested interested in this."

Correction—a whining incubus.

"If you wish to speak to our Master, then go do so." He pinched the bridge of his nose. "Do not take up your arguments with me."

"He won't listen to me. He's too distracted." A long tail

curled around his ankle. Far too personally. "Maybe I can convince you... hm?" The incubus purred. "What'll it take for me to convince you to let me join Zadok in his game?"

Walter glared at him and saw only amusement in the demon's purple eyes. Mordecai smiled playfully with a twist of lush lips decorated with a silver ring in the center of the lower one.

"Do not touch me."

Mordecai hummed. "Poor boy. You're so *frustrated*. I can let you vent some of that if you want. I can make it good for you." His form shifted into that of a fully nude woman, palms tracing up over her stomach to cup her own breasts. "Is this better?"

Walter snarled and grabbed a fistful of "her" hair and slammed Mordecai facedown onto the table. The illusion shattered, and the demon howled in laughter. "Oh, I knew this is how you'd like it! I pegged you for the angry fuck."

"Be silent, you cretin."

"You know how you can be certain I'll leave you alone? Let me go join Zadok. You can command my demons as well as I."

"Why are you so intent on the hunters?"

"I have an interest in this, I told you. Will you let me up now? Or do you want to fuck me after all? You can if you want to." By his tone, Walter knew it wouldn't be a high price to pay for the lascivious creature.

Disgusted, Walter threw the incubus away from him. "Enough."

Mordecai staggered and nearly fell, landing against the wall. He swished his long tail around behind him, frustrated but amused. He smoothed a hand over rakish blond hair surrounding the two black horns that twisted up and out of the strands.

"What interest do you have in them? No lies, and no games, demon."

Mordecai sighed and stretched languidly like a cat before folding his arms behind his head and propping himself up on the painted wallpaper. "The girl. I danced with her at the Master's gala. Now, I want to *dance* with her."

"You're a child."

"I haven't stopped thinking about her, Walter." The incubus's brow furrowed. "That's never happened to me before. I can't even fuck right. I'm too distracted. I have to have her. I *have* to. I have this awful itch that I cannot get rid of."

"I did not need to know that, although I cannot say I'm surprised you have caught a disease."

"That's not what I meant! I meant, like, an itch *inside*. Maybe once I rut her a few times it'll go away. Please, Walter. Please."

Walter shut his eyes and prayed for patience. He clearly needed more than he already possessed to survive this idiocy. He was to be surrounded by lovesick children while they were at war... at the whim of a lovesick child, not that he would ever say so to Dracula's face. The American armies would arrive shortly, and the city, while not large, needed to be secured and managed. The surviving humans would need to be rounded up and penned before the creatures that grew from the shadows destroyed them all in their hunger. And now he had a *lovesick incubus* to cope with.

As always, his work would be easier to accomplish on his own.

"Fine. Go."

"Thank you! Oh, thank you!" A kiss on his cheek, marked with the press of a metal ring, sent Walter snarling in a rage and raking a sharp-nailed claw through the air. But the incubus was already gone.

Walter forced his nails to retract and growled low. He had nowhere to spend his fury. It was a pointless expenditure of energy. Sitting down at the table, he pulled over a map of the city and began to plan.

Someone needed to.

"They're all children."

Looking up at the interrupting voice, he shook his head and turned back to the map. "Yes. They are. Hello, Elizabeth."

The woman had appeared sitting on the end of the table, a glass of red liquid in her hand. She was beautiful, with chestnut hair and surprisingly warm-colored skin. She had all the hallmarks of a youthful thing.

But it was a careful façade. She was a dangerous monster —one of their strongest elder vampires. While she was one more step removed from their Master's blood than he was— the product of a sire Dracula had made directly—she was no less frightening for it. Beneath the sweet and charming exterior was a cold and calculating fiend.

"Boys. Tempt them with a sweet prize where they might lay their seed, and they lose their minds." She sighed and reached out to pull a few pieces of paper over to her, scanning them quickly. "Bees cannot resist a flower in bloom. Well," she eyed him, a playful glint in her green eyes, "most can't. How is our dear uncle fairing? Does he have his new pet back?"

"No. He wishes to test her strength of will versus his horrors." He ignored her flirtatious expression as he ignored all her advances. He had withstood them for three hundred years since she had answered "Uncle" Dracula's call to serve him. He had no intention of cracking now.

She could not be trusted.

Elizabeth laughed and lay back on the table, draping herself across the papers and notes without any care in the world. "The fool. He cannot simply allow himself some happiness, can he?"

"No."

"Sounds familiar." She winked at him. "Like father, like son. Try not to be too much of a hypocrite, Walter. You wear it poorly."

"He is not my father. Nor is he your uncle."

"The humans measure their names by blood relationships. Why shouldn't we?"

"It's childish and sentimental."

"I suppose, then, he would be my great-uncle and you would be my true uncle. And that would make my advances on you quite revolting, wouldn't they?" She smiled. A painfully thin and practiced expression. "Oh, well. No matter."

Gods in Hell, I redouble my prayer for patience. "Why are you here, Elizabeth?"

"To help you! Left all alone to round up the humans and to defend our new home from the rest. You will need assistance. And I am quite brilliant, after all." She toyed with a lock of her own chestnut pooling around her head.

He did not bother arguing the last point. It was true. She was a manipulative mastermind, and that was precisely why he did not, nor would he ever, trust her. But he did need the help. He was never one to place his pride before logic. Even if it did mean he would have to put up with her smirking commentary.

Better her than the alternatives of Zadok and Mordecai.

"Very well, Elizabeth."

Curse of Dracula

She sat up from where she was lying and smiled wickedly. "Good. Where do we begin?"

───────

Zadok.

Maxine sighed drearily. "Damn it."

The vampire smiled at her and placed a hand to his chest and bowed. "Wonderful to see you too, my lady."

Eddie raised his gun to fire at the vampire, who seemed entirely unalarmed by its presence. And for good reason. Maxine reached out and put her hand on Eddie's gun and lowered it. "Save your ammunition. He is not really there. He is a mirage." She could not sense any soul or emotions coming from the apparition.

"Very good! I would hardly be so foolish as to stand here before three capable hunters. Don't think so little of my intelligence. And I *am* called the Illusionist, after all. I have not come for a duel, regardless."

"Then go away, fiend." Alfonzo had his sword in his hand all the same. He rightfully didn't trust the vampire, illusion or not. "Unless you fight us, we have no business with you."

"Oh, but I have come to welcome you to our new city. This place is ours now, make no mistake. I come with an offer to you. Give me the Master's new prize, and the rest of you may leave here alive. Turn back, hunters, and save your own lives."

"No." Alfonzo's tone left no room for discussion.

"Very well. But I'm afraid you will not get much farther into our city than this."

"You cannot stop us. We will fight through whatever you put in our way."

Zadok chuckled. "Therein lies the naivety of mortals. You think you can simply punch and slash your way to Dracula. You will make it not an inch closer if he does not allow it."

"What do you mean?" Alfonzo growled. "Speak plain."

"Ask Maxine. She understands." Zadok pointed at her with a dark smile. "She can feel it."

She pulled back half a step. Alfonzo didn't look at her; none of the hunters did. They knew better than to take their eyes off an enemy.

"What is he talking about, Maxine?"

"This...this place isn't Boston anymore. It's something else. It's as though..." She looked off, trying to sort out her words through the hum of the city around her. Then it came to her. The reason everything was so very *loud*. It wasn't simply the death and the destruction. It was something more than that. "It's as though this place has become one of the creatures itself. It is as though it... is alive."

"Yes! Very good!" Zadok seemed honestly proud of her. "You are so wonderfully clever. How I wish you could be mine. Ah, well, *c'est la vie*, my dove. Maybe in another life." He sighed dreamily. "And you are very correct. My Master's plague stretches to far more than flesh and blood. He has claimed this place as his. He commands the very brick and mortar of this city. You will wander helplessly in circles, my dear sweet hunters. In time, you will wear yourself down."

"You're lying," Alfonzo snapped.

"We shall see." He shrugged idly. "I needn't attack you. I only need to watch you burn your candles low. And when you admit the trap you are in, that is when I will come for you. But my offer stands. If any one of you wishes to turn back and leave this place and spare yourselves a painful death—you will walk out of the city limits unharmed and with our blessing."

"Never." Alfonzo snarled. He stormed forward and swung his sword through the air, intending to cut the vampire in half. But it passed harmlessly through the illusion. "Face me!"

Zadok was still smiling. "Why?"

"Fight me with honor!"

That inspired the vampire to laugh. "Honor. What a charmingly mortal notion. Honor. Dignity. Fairness." He scoffed. "These are concepts created to keep you trapped within a spider's web. They are constructs you build around your society to try to ensure that those with morals play within their pens only to be fed upon by those without such trivial philosophies. Abandon them, hunter, and see yourself plainly for what you are—a bloodthirsty thing driven forward only by the need for revenge."

"You're lying."

"Am I? Once again, I think we shall see." Zadok took a step back then folded a hand at his waist and bowed low. "My offer stands. Oh, and dear Maxine? I nearly forgot. My Master sends you his love."

Alfonzo went to swing his sword again, useless as it was. Zadok vanished in a blink. But his laughter echoed in the air. "Walk your feet bloody for all I care. Prove me wrong."

Maxine was shivering again. She was trying desperately to keep from falling into another fit of panic. She had to try to keep herself together. She had to try to be strong. *The city is alive. Well...as alive as Vlad may be.* It was all around her. Zadok was not lying. If this thing served its master in the same way all the rest did, it could keep them wandering about for days.

But she also knew it would not stop the hunters from trying.

"Hey, uh, Al?" Eddie interrupted the silence.

"We are not turning back."

"No, that's not what I was gonna ask." Eddie shifted uncomfortably. "All your books. All the Helsing legends. Um. Did any of them mention anything about a whole city turning into a giant, bloodthirsty monster?"

Alfonzo's shoulders slumped. "No."

Eddie groaned. He summed up nicely, and with a perfectly crass choice of words, her exact opinion on the subject. "Oh, good. We're fucked."

4

THEY WALKED for hours among the twisted streets and the dead. And as the vampire had warned, they seemed to make no progress despite their march. Boston was not that large a city. By this point, she should have been able to walk from her home in the Back Bay to the waterfront and back. But with no landmarks she could identify, she couldn't even say which way they were headed.

Only that it seemed to do no good.

They marched. And with every hour, warped creations that seemed birthed from nightmares dogged their steps. Maxine did not know that she would ever become adjusted to the sight of them.

One creature had eyes that seemed to cover every inch of its body. They opened and shut in undulating waves. When it died, it had burst into flame that glowed a bright blue and reduced its remains to ash. Which was for the best.

There were enough bodies.

When they were too tired to continue—or they claimed to be out of pity for her aching feet and slowing gait—Alfonzo had chosen a home and knocked. He shouted for whoever was inside to open the door, and that they meant no harm. No one answered, so he kicked the front door in. Thankfully, no one was home. Nor were there corpses littering the floor.

She sank down onto a sofa in the home's drawing room. Eddie took up a spot by the window, keeping watch for if they were being pursued. Bella went to scrounge for food while Alfonzo searched the building for trouble.

"Do you sense anything?" Eddie asked her.

Tiredly, Maxine shook her head and resisted the urge to lie down on the sofa. Barely. "There is no one here. I feel nothing but the…" She didn't know how to describe it. "The noise."

"Noise?"

"The city is loud. It…is wearing on me. I'm sorry." She ran her hand over her face.

"Nothing to be sorry about, ma'am. None of this is your fault." Eddie sighed. "I know you say different. But I'm not going to blame you for not destroying him even if you had the chance."

"Why not? Alfonzo seems eager enough to do so."

"He's had it rough. He doesn't mean to be so, well, mean." Eddie shifted to half-sit on the window frame, peering through the blinds as he searched for trouble. "He's only doing what he thinks he needs to."

"But why don't you fault me for not destroying Dracula?"

"I don't want to wish death on anybody. Not even him. You didn't know he was going to do this. Fuck, we didn't even know he was going to do this. Sorry about my language."

"It bothers me none. Honestly, it doesn't. And, yes, I knew. At the very least I had a suspicion."

Curse of Dracula

"But it isn't the same. I don't believe in killing people because they *might* do something."

"I agree. But now that it has come to pass, it has to end."

"Will you help us, then? Really?"

She nodded. "I have to do whatever I can. So many are dead. So many more will die. I cannot let that happen if I can stop him." She looked up as Bella walked into the room carrying a tray of food. She was starving. Bella handed her a plate of fruit, cheese, and bread, and she had to stop herself from annihilating it. "Thank you."

"Of course."

Alfonzo returned and began unhooking his belts and putting his weapons down on the table. "We will stop here for a few hours to rest. I'll take first watch. Eddie, second. Bella, third. We all stay in this room."

Oh, thank God. She did not question why she was not on the list of those to watch out for demons. She was still not to be trusted in his eyes, and she could not blame him. She knew there was nothing she could do to win it back.

The room was quiet as they ate. She finally gave in to her exhaustion and lay down on the sofa, pulling a pillow under her head. There was enough furniture in the drawing room for them each to have somewhere to sleep, but the floor would have been the same to her.

Sleep came for her quickly.

Her dreams were not empty.

She was suddenly standing on a balcony, overlooking a vast forest and mountain range. It had snowed recently. The moon was full and crimson and cast the white surfaces in brilliant hues of reds and maroons. The air was cold, and even in her vision her breath turned to mist around her. It was breathtaking.

A hand settled on her shoulder, and she jolted at the contact. Whirling, she was not surprised at who she saw standing there, towering over her. She knew his face this time. He was looking down at her with a tired and beleaguered kind of acceptance. His breath did not fog as hers did. He had no warmth of his own. He was dead, after all.

She took a step back from him, wary and unsure.

Wordlessly, he turned from her and walked inside through a large, ornate door. The architecture reminded her of his throne room—twisted and terrible, filled with screaming faces and mortals being consumed and taken by monsters. It was not merely decoration; it was a warning. A promise to all those who saw it. *This is the fate that awaits you if you stay here.*

But now she knew she could never leave. She would be dead either when Alfonzo saw fit to kill her or the vampire would take her life. There was no surviving this ordeal; it was only a matter of when and how it happened.

Death was inevitable.

And so was her going inside.

It was freezing, and she shivered. Vision or not, dream or not, she wasn't going to suffer in the cold out of childish spite. She walked inside and shut the door behind her. He was standing by the fireplace, a poker in his hand, nudging at the fresh log atop the stack. It was comfortably warm in the room, that kind of soothing heat that only came from a fire.

"I will ask you but the once," she began after it was clear he was not going to start the conversation. "And only once. Stop this insanity now."

"I will end it in time. Once my armies have been fed.

Once the lust for blood has been quenched, and I have all that I have come for. I will take it all back into myself and retreat to some distant shore as I have done before, and as I will do again. Humans shall retake this city and will whisper of the legends of the time the skies went black and darkness came for them. In time, it will be nothing but a myth. Explained away by some terrible plague."

"Vlad...please. You have done enough to prove to me that I was a fool. No more need die." She walked slowly across the carpeted floor to approach him, keeping her distance. Not that it would do her any good. He could move faster than she could see, and this was his home. He was the master here.

"You think I have torched this land for your sake?" He sneered. "Do not flatter yourself. You wander my world because I wish you to see who I truly am, but the destruction I have wrought was in the workings long before I knew you. I have been in this city for two years."

"What?"

"I have lain in wait. I have seeped into every pore, every water work, every shadow of this city. My creatures were a warning to the wise to escape before I unleashed the rest. Did I delay a few days when I met you? Yes. Would I have taken up my armies and departed if the hunters returned you to me? Yes. But they did not, and here we are." He placed the poker back in the rack with the others and leaned his hand on the mantel, watching the flickering flames as they sputtered and gained purchase on the untouched lumber.

"And what is to become of me?"

"That is for you to decide."

"How so?"

"Will you still love me in the end, or will you come to

despise me instead? Will you look at me in disgust as you did just now upon the balcony?"

"I..." She began to argue, then stopped. He was right. She went to make excuses, to tell him how many he had killed, but it was futile. He knew. And they paled in comparison to all the suffering that lay in his wake. He was a wrathful god. "Then...kill me. Do not make me endure this."

"No. You will not die until I allow it."

"Then I will have Alfonzo—" She gasped in shock as her back met the wall. He had slammed her there, and pain bloomed across her shoulders. She could not pay it much heed, for his hand was around her throat, threatening to squeeze. It tightened but did not cut off her air.

"Do not *dare* speak those words!" His voice was a snarl as he glared down at her. "You belong to *me*. You live by my grace, and you will die by my mercy, not his."

She placed her hand to his wrist and felt his tepid skin. She didn't try to pull away. Even in a vision, it was as though he were really there. "I can destroy you," she whispered.

"Then do it, little empath. My Lady of Souls. Do it. Tear me from my cage and thrust me unto the void." He bared his teeth, fangs extended. "Deem me unworthy of this world and your love and do what no one else has ever managed to accomplish. Free me from my curse."

She hesitated. "Please. I don't want to do this."

"Decide, Maxine. The choice is yours. This is the fork in the road before you. The point of no return approaches. Kill me...or obey me."

She placed her other hand on his chest and felt him burning there. She was not certain if she could destroy him from a dream.

But she was unwilling to even try.

Tears streaked down her cheeks. His anger faltered and

Curse of Dracula

faded and dissolved into a weary sadness. He released his grasp on her throat and moved to wipe her tears away. "Forgive me, Maxine."

"Do not make me do this."

"I have no other choice. I know you do not see it yet. But you will." He crooked a finger beneath her chin and tilted her head up. "I love you. And I will have you love me in return. All of me. Walk the streets of my pain, my darling. And when you find me at the end of it, I will accept your judgement on my knees. I will bow to you like a slave and take your forgiveness or wrath with a joyful heart." He leaned down, ghosting his lips over hers. "But not until I have decided you have suffered enough."

And with that, he kissed her. It was harsh. It was passionate. It was needy, and it was full of love, lust, and *greed*. She moaned against his lips, unable to stop herself. He undid her. All her surety, all her resolve, cracked and shattered under his first strike like a shield made of ice.

Hands scooped her by her thighs and lifted her up the wall to his height. She was left with nothing to do but to cling to him, startled, as he forced her legs to hook around his waist. Fearing the fall, too startled to fight it, she crossed her ankles behind him. His hands slid up her stockings, rolling her dress to her waist.

His lips did not leave hers. They did not relent. He kissed her deeper, tilting his head to the side, her new height easing his access to her.

Stepping in, he pressed himself to her. He was there at her core, already eager for her. It made her gasp and whimper. She broke the kiss, needing to fill her lungs with air. She was trembling.

He chuckled at her reaction. "Once the hunters abandon you—and they will, my sweet, mark my words—I will come for you. Then I can complete our dance." He once more mimed the action she knew he wished to do to her, if there were not so many layers of clothing between them.

She arched her back. It felt so good. Each time he pressed against her it sent a thrill through her body. A hint of pleasure she could only dream of—things she had only stolen from the minds of those she had touched.

The feeling of him crashed over her like a wave, like velvet and satin and like wings in the night sky. The creature she had fallen in love with had not changed. He had simply grown more complicated. He had warned her of the things that lurked in the shadows of his mind, and she had been foolish enough to think she had understood.

He growled low in his throat. "But I will not come for you yet. I will have them fall from grace. I will break them, one by one, until they lie weeping and shattered at my feet. I will tear the wings from their backs and their halos from their righteous heads." Still he kept at his tempo, driving her mad with his teasing despite his terrible words. "I will make them leave you, frightened and afraid, and know that they have sealed your fate. Then I will use their desecrated flesh to decorate my home. Perhaps I will even add them to my ranks."

And despite his gruesome threats, her body did not stop begging for him. She clung to him, whimpering each time he leaned into her, tilting his hips up to hers *just so*. "Please, Vlad—"

"Please, what? Release you? Take you here and now in this dream? Would you have me spare them, or do you prefer I kill them sooner so we might be joined in the flesh? What is it that you wish for? Say it, and it shall be done." When she was silent, he purred his next words. "And therein lies my game, my love. You do not know that for which you wish. And until you do, you will languish in this nightmare of my creation."

He tilted her face to his once more, and his breath washed over her lips, no longer cold, but hot. Spurred to life by his desire for her. "But while we wait for you to make up your mind, my sweet princess—my Lady of Souls—know that you belong to me. And the instant they leave you behind...I will come to claim that which I own."

His lips crashed against hers again, devouring her, making good on his words of possession. And in his touch, she crumbled. Overwrought, her mind sank back into the darkness.

5
———

Mordecai leaned forward and kissed Zadok's shoulder. "You're too kind, my old friend."

"Who am I to stand in the way of young love?" The vampire chuckled. "Go. And now we're even."

"Your debt is paid, yes, yes, and all that."

"Mmh, one thing. If you come up out of her for air, mind if I cut in? She is such a pretty thing."

"If there's anything left, of course. If she's half the hellcat I think she is, perhaps we can have her together."

The vampire waved his hand to dismiss the incubus. "Go. You'll have this one chance."

———

It was Bella's turn to take watch. She was standing by the window, idly twirling a dagger between her fingers. Eddie was so tired that he had nearly fallen asleep standing up. Poor boy. Alfonzo was lying in the corner, his coat tucked under his head. She always knew when he was sleeping. The snoring was a pretty good indication.

It made her smile. No matter the chaos, no matter the death, or destruction, or the end of the world—it didn't matter. Alfonzo Van Helsing snored like a lumbermill. And to travel with him meant she had to become inured to it or reach the level of exhaustion where she ceased to care. Even the poor empath Maxine was too tired to wake from her sleep, no matter the noise.

Bella looked over at the woman and frowned. Her heart broke. She was at the mercy of everyone else's needs. First the vampire's hunger, then Alfonzo and his search for revenge. Maxine seemed like a kind, compassionate woman. She did not deserve the fate that was forced on her. Either in her gift that left her unable to be touched—at least by natural humans—or in the morbid and dreadful future before her.

It was clear to her that Maxine loved the vampire. Alfonzo and Eddie might miss it. Alfonzo for his disbelief that such a thing was possible, and Eddie because he did not know what real love looked like. But Bella could see it for what it was. It was tragic to watch Maxine's first real hope for a simple connection with another be dashed.

Bella's heart broke for Maxine.

But broken love was something with which she was familiar. Her gaze traced back over to Eddie. Guilt stabbed at her, seeping into her like a poison, making her hate herself. Eddie loved her. She knew he did, for he had said the words aloud. Yet she did not feel the same for him.

But why not?

She *should*.

He was sweet, kind, young, handsome, and her dear friend. They traveled together. They fought together. She trusted him with her life. But no love bloomed in her heart for him. She searched and searched and found none. She worried if she dug much harder through the turf, she would destroy the roots of the friendship they shared in the process.

It made her feel lesser. It made her feel disgusting. What was wrong with her that she could not embrace his love and return it with her own? It was a great mark of shame on her soul.

Souls.

Funny things, those.

Bella looked back to Maxine and wondered if the empath knew of the unrequited love that Eddie bled out upon the floor every time he turned to Bella. She assumed so. And she also assumed Maxine was dignified enough not to speak of it.

How many secrets did the empath know? How many unknown and tragic things lived inside her mind? Maxine seemed so much older than she was in years. There was a grief in her eyes, as if she had seen far more than a person should have been able to witness in such a short span of time.

"Help!"

Someone screamed from outside. A man caught up in panic. She whirled to the window to see if she could see the source. There was someone running down the street, tripping over his own feet in his eagerness to escape. Creatures were at his heels, snarling and biting.

"Quick! Everyone, wake up!" She didn't pause in her rush to the door as she shouted for the others to join her. She didn't wait to see if they followed, knowing they would be close behind. She burst out the door and raced toward the man, summoning her knives and daggers to fly forward and strike the monsters chasing the gentleman up the street.

They screamed in pain as her knives bit into their hides,

Curse of Dracula

propelled by her abilities. Several of her blades punched straight through their flesh, sending blood gushing out of the wounds left behind.

She held her hands out at her sides, commanding the knives to obey her. They swirled about the creatures, ripping them to shreds until there was barely anything left. Only bits of blood and bone on the sidewalk.

"By God. Oh, holy Hell," the gentleman wheezed. He was leaning heavily on his knees. His head down, coughing to fill his lungs. "First monsters, and now flying knives? You aren't going to kill me now, are you?"

"No. I saved you."

"What a relief." He didn't lift his head. "I suppose I should panic about the impossibilities later." He coughed. "I do not know who you are, or how you did that, but I must say, I'm quite grateful."

Bella smiled. "It isn't any trouble." She paused as she looked him over. His voice sounded familiar. Something about him struck her and told her that she had seen him before. When he lifted his head, she gasped. She knew him indeed.

"Bella?" the man asked in disbelief. He straightened and ran a hand through his blond hair in an attempt to smooth it back. He did not need to worry. He was still impossibly handsome. His lavender eyes were still breathtaking, even if he looked disheveled and out of sorts from having run for his life.

"Mordecai?" She took a step toward him.

"What are you doing here?" he asked and closed the distance between them, eagerly pulling her into his arms.

She embraced him tightly, her body nesting so wonderfully with his. It felt like home. He smelled so good. She pushed away the errant thoughts and tried to focus. He had asked her a question, after all. "My friends and I are trying to stop this madness."

The man gaped. "I suppose I should have to ask my dance partners more explicit details about themselves in the future. Hello, yes, how are you, where are you from, can you wield a terrifying and deadly power?" He shook his head. "I should be terrified. But I find the sun is missing and the streets are overrun with monsters. I suppose I am simply grateful it is you who has saved me. Can your friends also wield flying knives with their minds?"

She laughed and pushed a step away from him but found her hand still lingering in his. She did not wish to let him go. "They cannot, but they are dangerous in their own right. They—" She looked back toward the house and realized no one had come down the stairs to join her. She blinked in confusion. "They should have been right behind me."

"They're still asleep, I'm afraid."

She looked back to him. He was still smiling, but something had shifted. Just barely. His eyes were no longer blueish violet. They were *purple*. And something about them shone and glinted like a jewel in the light. Luring her deeper. Calling her in.

And she was helpless.

Fear gripped her suddenly as some kind of snare wrapped around her mind. She whimpered, feeling like a trapped child.

"No, no, don't be afraid, my beautiful. It's all right." He shushed her gently, reaching up to stroke her hair tenderly and to tuck a stray strand behind her ear. It didn't help the panic that was rising in her mind. "The vampire illusionist owed me a favor. Your friends are all still quite soundly dreaming."

Curse of Dracula

When he traced his knuckles over her cheek, she leaned into his touch. She didn't know what drove her to do it. She didn't mean to. She hadn't wanted to.

She was screaming in her mind, but nothing came out. Something else had risen to take its place. Something deep inside her, primal and low, had roared up and taken over.

It saw what glittered in his unnatural eyes and heeded his summons.

Monster. He is a monster!
This is wrong!

She was fighting as hard as she could, but she was helpless. And that scared her more than anything else. But those eyes...they had her in their snare like a metal trap around the leg of a deer.

"Don't be scared, my angel. I have you. You're safe." He leaned down to place a slow kiss to her forehead. "I will take care of you now."

Finally, she managed to force her words out of her throat. But they were strangled and broken. "My friends, they—they'll come for me—"

"I'm afraid they won't even notice you're gone." His voice was a low and sultry purr. It resonated through her body, and something hot coiled deep inside her. "They won't know what's happened for quite some time. Now...kiss me, my sweet." He tilted her head back to look up at him.

The sight of him cut through her panic like the ring of a silver bell. Something in her struggled, fought, then...let go. She was left basking in what she saw. Chiseled and handsome, it was as though someone had painted before her the most perfect man she could imagine. He was her deepest fantasy brought to life. An impossibility she could not believe could possibly exist.

She could have sworn her heart stopped.

Mordecai smiled *for her.*

"You are one of them," she whispered. "You're...you're—"

The jaws of a beast had come from nowhere at all and sank deep into her soul.

The man in front of her had found her weakness. His inhuman eyes glinted with the promise of safety. Of a warm fire on a cold night. "Yes. I am. And so, I will greet you again, in truth. I am Mordecai, Captain of Dracula's demonic army. Hello, gorgeous one. I have been waiting for you."

"I..." Bella tried to take a step back, but he took her hands, lacing his fingers into hers, and pulled her back to him. She could not find the strength to resist. Her body heated under his gaze, and something dangerous—sinful and wonderful—pooled in her core.

His gaze raked down her body then back up to her face. He pulled her into his arms, and she did not push him away. His hand pressed to her cheek, eager to touch her. "So innocent...so tender. So *ripe.*"

Something pulled her under the waves. Something grasped her, invisible and terrible, and consumed her. Her mind struggled like a fish caught in the talons of an eagle.

She was prey.

She had always *been* prey. She had been such a fool to think otherwise.

And this creature...this creature was her predator.

This was right. This was as it should be.

When his fingers grazed over her neck and cradled behind her head, she fell into his embrace. She melted, surrendering to it completely. It was sudden and inexplicable, like being taken by the tide. It was rushing her out into the deeper ocean, and there she knew she would drown. She floundered, struggling to free herself, but it was inevitable.

Curse of Dracula

Wicked thoughts crashed over her. Things she wanted to do to him. Things she wished he would do to her. Her body was burning in desire, instant and inarguable. He was controlling her—this was wrong! She tried to push away, but she had no strength left in her body. "No, please…"

He shushed her as he gently stroked her cheek, cradling her into his chest. "Don't be afraid. I won't hurt you. I will never hurt you." His lips grazed over her ear. Bella shuddered and reached out to touch him. He let out a dusky, heady, and inhuman growl as her hands traced up the lines of his throat to his cheek, exploring him as well.

He was every prince from every novel she had ever read as a child. He had burst from the pages of her imagination, and every part of her cried out for him. She had known it when he had danced with her, but she had not wanted to accept the truth. Now that she knew it, she wanted him no less.

"This is wrong," she whispered. "You are wrong. You are not real."

"I am very real," he answered, ghosting his lips over hers. "I am as real as anything you will ever have."

It was as though her body were aflame. His hand on her lower back threatened to trace farther down, and that was all she could think about. But still, her mind struggled for freedom. "What…what are you?"

He smiled. His breath was hot where it washed over her. "Incubus."

A demon of lust. Of course. He would feed on her and consume her. She had been so naïve to think the only creatures that walked this nightmare would drink her blood. This creature wanted to drink something very different indeed.

And she found she did not wish to run from him.

"This is wrong," she insisted.

"By whose standards? Why should pleasure be shamed? And oh, what ecstasy I can bring you."

It was only then that she realized they were no longer standing on the street. They were standing somewhere else—indoors—a comfortable room, with a gently flickering fire. He moved her back and unclasped her cloak, letting it fall beside them. Before she could speak, she was lying on a chaise lounge, with him over her.

Everything was moving too quickly. She could barely keep track of what was happening. She felt drunk. Like everything was just a bit blurry. God help her, her hands were dug deeply into his clothing. "Am I really this weak in the end?"

"You are not weak. And this...this is not the end." He brushed the fabric of her skirt up around her waist. Suddenly, he was teasing at the dance that her body wanted him to fulfill. "This is the beginning."

She felt the hard, inarguable presence of him there. Promising. Teasing. Begging. "You are a demon. A monster. This is what you do. I am only one of"—she broke off as he pressed against her again—"one of many."

"And what is the fault in that? I have so much love to give."

"It isn't love..."

"Demons may love. Oh, we love the fiercest of all. Why should I not love as much and as many as I can? You could do the same. You could have made those two men you travel with very happy."

"I'm not a harlot—"

"Harlot, slut, whore..." He sighed. "Your culture has so many words for a wanton woman. But what about words for men? There are none. If your friends wished to take twenty

Curse of Dracula

women in a day, they would be lauded for their virility. If you took twenty men, you would be shamed. Where is the justice in that?"

She did not have an answer for him. There was none. She tried to shake herself free of him, tried to knock loose whatever control he had placed over her. But with each teasing caress, she descended deeper and deeper into his grasp.

He leaned down to kiss her, and her last bits of strength shattered.

It felt so good.

He felt so good.

This was safety. The end of struggling. The end of having to fight the darkness that had always threatened to consume her. It was calling her home. He would keep her safe. He wanted her. *No!* She broke away from the kiss, tilting her head away from him. "You're lying to me."

"Lying? You think what I feel for you is not real? What I feel for you is more real than anything else in your life has ever been. More permanent. I will *always* want you. Give to me, my beautiful, gorgeous, delicious creature."

Somehow, at some point, her clothes had disappeared. She was not sure how or when, but suddenly they were gone. She lay naked beneath him. Turning her head away, she was ashamed once more.

But his moan brought her attention back to him. He was looking down at her, not in disdain, not in triumph, but in *worship.* "Look at you…how can you be embarrassed by this? This body, gifted to you?" His hands trailed up over her. "This is divinity. This is the only God I need to know. This is the only God you need to embrace. Let me fall to my knees at your temple."

Her hands no longer twisted in the fabric of his coat,

they traced over naked flesh. She caressed his sculpted muscles and was eager for more.

Her legs were up on his thighs, and she felt his hot skin beneath hers. She could not help but let her eyes trace down between them. The sight was so lurid, so profane, it took her breath away.

"I can give you everything you have ever needed, Bella." He kissed her throat, hovering over her as he tortured them both with his teasing movements. "I can give you a home. A family. Love. Pleasure. You belong here with me. But I cannot do this unless you ask me to. You belong here, you know you do. Say it. Call me home to you, and I will give you all you need and more."

Perhaps if she had just kissed Eddie, slept in his arms, and surrendered to his love for her, she would not have been so weak in the end. "Is your name really Mordecai?"

He smirked. "There is power in a name for my kind. We do not give them lightly." He leaned down to kiss her again, searing, tender and passionate all at once. It made her want to beg him for more. To kiss her harder—rougher—to not be so gentle with her. As he broke away, he whispered, "I gave my true name to you the moment we met. You pulled it from me. I could not bear to think of you crying out any other."

This creature over her said she belonged here with him. But it was wrong. "I can't…"

"I want you for my bride. I have never mated another. I have never made another soul to match mine. But I feel you —I need you, Bella. Be mine. Say it…I beg you."

An incubus wanted her for his mate? Oh, God above, how she wanted him to sink into her depths and release her from this suffering.

She wanted him.

Curse of Dracula

She wanted the simplicity he offered.

All other concerns fell away in the face of the simple, easy truth.

"Do you really want me?" She could barely breathe.

"More than you can imagine. Do you want me?" He never faltered in his slow, unwavering strokes, but not yet ending her torment and driving himself inside. "Do you want to come home?"

Yes.

She did.

Something in her crumbled and surrendered. She couldn't fight it anymore.

She arched herself up into him. "Take me."

6

Maxine awoke and rubbed her hand over her face with a small grunt. She had never had so many visions in such a short span of time in her life, all thanks to the Vampire King. It was an exhausting thing to suffer *before* the nature of the dreams came into play, let alone after taking into consideration that he was an intense individual at the best of times.

But something told her she would not have any opportunity for real rest anytime soon. Not until she was dead.

"Bad dream?"

She jumped at the closeness of the voice. Bella was sitting on the edge of the sofa next to her, smiling down at her. Glancing over, she noticed both Eddie and Alfonzo were asleep elsewhere in the room.

Something instantly felt odd.

Maxine pulled herself up, edging away from Bella to sit at the far end of the sofa. "I'm all right." She watched the other woman silently for a moment. There was definitely something…awry. Something that did not feel right. Then, it hit her. Her eyes went wide.

"There it is." Bella lifted a finger to her lips and shushed her. For a split second, her eyes flickered yellow before they returned to her normal tone. "I wondered how long it would take you to figure it out." She smiled again, although this time a bit more wolfishly than before. "You're certainly not a disappointment."

She went to stand, and "Bella's" hand caught her gloved wrist and pulled her back down. "Now, now, don't be so hasty."

"Zadok, let me go! Alfonzo—Eddie—"

"Oh, shush." She—he?—laughed. "I'm not going to hurt you, silly girl. They are trapped inside my illusion, so don't bother screaming. They can't hear us right now." The other woman's hand tightened around Maxine's wrist. "Stop making a fuss, or I will have to rethink how nice I'm being right now."

Maxine watched Bella's form in wary fear. She knew the feeling of the soul beneath her hand, even through her gloves. She pulled her wrist away from him but obeyed and stayed seated. There was no point in running. She was useless in a fight with something like an elder vampire. "What have you done?"

"Hm? Me? I've done nothing."

"If Alfonzo and Eddie cannot wake, please drop the illusion. This is extremely unsettling."

"As you wish." Bella's form melted and shifted, changing into that of the smirking yellow-eyed vampire. He placed a hand to his chest in mock insult, crossing one ankle over his knee casually as he reclined next to her. "And I'm hurt you think I have done anything to dear Bella."

"Where is she? How did you get past the wards they placed to protect the house?"

"So many questions!" Zadok laughed and leaned his head back on the wood frame of the sofa to watch her through lidded eyes. "She is not here. She was taken by another for safe keeping. As for the wards? Simplistic mortals. They do not think holistically. Bar me from the doors and windows all you like, but they did not place wards beneath the ground."

She pondered his riddle for a moment before she made a face. "The sewers?"

"Mm. Not exactly the most…elegant way to travel." He grimaced. "But effective. I grew up in the gutters, I'm afraid. It's a smell I'm accustomed to."

That was both sad and disgusting. "Is Bella dead?"

"No. Nor does her warden have any plans to kill her. That might change if you do anything foolish." Zadok's knowing smile never wavered.

Ah. So, that was his game. She sighed. "How long do you plan to masquerade as Bella in their presence? And to what end? Why have you not simply killed Eddie and Alfonzo?"

"The latter directly involves the former, I'm afraid. Death is too simple an end for our Master's enemies." Zadok shrugged. "I think it's foolish. I would rather scatter their brains out on the walls. But he wishes to have his revenge, and, I live to serve. As to what my game is, I think you do not wish to know."

"What do you mean?"

"What good would it do to spell out the pain they are going to suffer? None. It would only upset you and do no other good. You cannot stop what will befall them."

"You speak as if they will not succeed."

"They won't." Zadok's expression turned oddly sympathetic for a moment. "And you know I speak the truth. One of them has already fallen. The other two are inevitable." Zadok reached out to touch her where Alfonzo had punched her but pulled short as she flinched away. The bruise on her temple likely still stained her skin. "He will not allow them to walk free if they choose to continue. If they turn away, my offer still stands. But you know they won't."

"Do you want them to leave here, or do you want them to die?" She wasn't sure what inspired her to ask the question. She thought she knew the answer, but the flash of regret in his eyes had made her question if there was not more beneath the vampire's salacious personality than met the eye.

Zadok turned his gaze to Eddie. "That one is young. He does not deserve what will happen to him." He turned to Alfonzo. "That one is a waste of air. He is consumed by zealous and hypocritical hatred." He sneered. "I'll enjoy watching him suffer. But the boy? The boy should be spared. I hope he turns away from this place. But I know his type—he won't."

At least his cruelty wasn't universal. "I do not know how I will walk beside them and pretend I do not know what has come to pass, Zadok."

"You have heard every lie spoken to you by every creature you have come to meet, have you not?"

"Yes, and?"

"Then I expect you are quite talented in the art." He stretched, and she heard his back pop as he did. "I am not concerned."

She sighed. "What has become of Bella?"

"Our Captain of the Guard has taken her. Our personal lord demon." Zadok snickered, finding something very funny.

"What?"

"You do not wish to know." But still, he did not stop chuckling.

"This time I think I do."

"She is with Mordecai. He is an incubus." Zadok cackled loudly, unafraid of waking the two men in the room. "Oh, I wish I could be there to watch!" Maxine moved to stand, but he dragged her back down by the wrist once more. "No, stay."

"That is disgusting. She is being raped, and you expect me to—"

"I promise you, it is anything but rape." Zadok smiled. "She has merely been freed from the chains she was trained to wear by society. And if he is half as interested in her as it seems, she is being treated like a *princess*. That boy is quite talented."

It sounded like he spoke from firsthand experience. She blanched and looked away. Not that she had any issue with men cavorting with each other. Really, it was simply that Zadok was involved. "Wait." Then she remembered. "Mordecai. The man from the dance?"

"Indeed. He saw her then, and he has been *insufferable* ever since! He will not shut up about her. The constant whining was going to drive me insane. I don't think you understand how miserable an incubus can be when denied." He grunted.

She paused for a long while and looked off, her heart breaking for Bella. "Promise me she is not suffering. Whatever fate she shall befall, promise me she is not afraid or in pain."

"Not unless she's the kind of lady who likes it." Zadok purred, his voice sultry as he traced his hand up her arm. Maxine pulled out of his grasp. Even if his touch was over her clothing, she wanted none of it. "Are you?"

"I rightfully wouldn't know."

"Then I hope our Master soon finds out."

"I do not enjoy speaking about these matters with you."

"Why?"

"You are revolting."

"Mmh, you don't mean that." He watched her with an idle smile. "You are made uncomfortable by me and the things I say in the way all proper ladies of your age are. You will come around in time."

"How does Vlad suffer you?"

"He likes me well enough." He scratched at his shoulder absentmindedly. "Most of the time. Then again, he occasionally tears my arm off for sport. Now that I think about it, he never does that to Walter. I've always suspected the old bastard plays favorites."

She tried not to laugh. She couldn't hide her smile as she looked away.

"Tell me, Miss Parker. What do you wish might come to pass? How do you want all this to end?"

"Why are you asking me?"

"I wish to know if Master Dracula is in danger. If you are a threat to his life—and ergo, likely mine as well. That is why I am here. And to get away from Mordecai." He grinned. "I did not wish to listen to him whine as he jerked himself off for the *fourteen-thousandth* time because Bella was not yet his."

She tried not to feel sick. "I did not need to know that."

"That is how an incubus whines, darling. How else did you expect?"

"I am not well-versed in the social behaviors of demons."

"I expect you will be before long. Now, come. Tell me. What do you wish for?"

"I want the hunters to survive and to leave unharmed. I do not wish ill upon them."

"Not even Alfonzo?"

"I understand him. Even if his methods are harsh and I do not agree with them, I understand him."

"How can you understand someone but not agree with them?"

"I am an empath." She looked over to Zadok and found him watching her, quite puzzled. "And that you do not understand the difference between seeing the reason behind someone's actions and agreeing with them might be why Vlad keeps tearing your arm off."

Zadok laughed. "Fair enough. What else? What about *you,* my dear? All you have spoken of is the fates of others. But what do you wish for yourself?"

"That which I would desire for myself factors little to none into my own fate, vampire. I am always a product of others—their memories, their emotions, and their desires. What I want does not matter."

"I am asking you all the same. If you do not know, that is all you have to say." He grinned, a coy and fiendish expression. "Do you love our Master?"

"I do. I did. Until this." She gestured at the window. "Now, I am not so certain. I was naïve to think I truly fathomed what he was, and what he was capable of unleashing."

"You still love him. You simply need to come to terms with what you see. And I am sure he is willing to give you as much time as you need to do so. He is a patient creature. Far more so than I."

"I wouldn't have guessed."

He was clearly unfazed by her sarcasm. "Do you want to love him? Do you want to be at his side for all eternity? Or do you want to wrench his soul from his chest and destroy it like all the others you have touched?"

"I do not know. I...do not wish to hurt him. But I will not let this city burn if I can stop it."

Curse of Dracula

"I suppose that is fair. And I think when the time comes, you will need to decide which you care about more. And I do not pity you for it. I am a man of simple pleasures and simple needs."

She watched him for a moment. "No. You merely like everyone around you to believe that. You hide behind your callousness, your shallowness, and use it to mask your pain, don't you? Tell me, Zadok—who hurt you?" She smiled snidely. "Or is the list too long?"

He laughed. It was not what she was expecting. But he seemed honestly entertained by her comment—no, not entertained, pleased. "You are wonderful! Truly you are. I see why the Master adores you so. Who hurt me, my little dove? Everyone. Everyone in this God-forsaken world. I take my pleasure when and how I desire it in exchange. And I desire very much. But!" He slapped his hands on his legs and stood. "You should be sleeping. The Master would be very cross with me if he learned I was not allowing you a good night's rest with my prattling. I have to keep watch, after all." He tugged on the bottom of his vest, and as he did, his form shifted back to that of Bella.

"Do you honestly believe you can trick them? Even if I do not give you up, they know her. They have traveled with her for years. How do you think you might hide from them?"

"Simple. I am a woman." The false Bella smiled. "No one notices a woman's moods, and if they do, they explain it away to her nature. She is an accessory to them, nothing more. Even Bella."

"Even if what you say is true for Alfonzo, Eddie loves her. He will see the change."

"No, I do not think he will." Zadok-Bella walked over to where Eddie slept and nudged him with her foot. The sleeping hunter did not wake, caught up in the vampire's illusion. "Eddie does not love her. He merely thinks he does. He loves the *idea* of her—the beauty and purity that traveled at his side for so long."

"You're wrong."

"Perhaps. Perhaps you are right, and he will see straight through my charade." Bella smiled a sickly-sweet expression. "But if I am wrong and he does not notice? What then? Are you willing to wager a bet on it?"

She shook her head silently. No, she wasn't. Because his words were true. Eddie's love for Bella was not a lie. But it was shallow.

"Oh, but—let's wager anyway. I do so love a game. Come now, what is a silly bet between friends?" Zadok executed a perfect imitation of the girl. Her voice, her tone...everything. Zadok was a good actor, and it was clear he had been observing her. "We are friends, aren't we, Miss Parker?"

Perhaps Alfonzo and Eddie *wouldn't* notice. "This is cruel, Zadok."

"Ah-ah." She ticked a finger back and forth. "I am Bella, remember? You will play along, or the real girl dies. Now. Let's wager. I bet I can go...oh...two days. Two days and nights like this without them noticing anything is amiss. That is, if you do not interfere. What do you think?"

Two whole days? Without Zadok slipping up? It seemed impossible. She was going to curse herself for this later. "What is on the line?"

"If I am right, then I want you to touch me." At her disgusted noise, he grinned. "Not like that. That's not how I want to touch you—simply hand-to-hand. I want to feel what the Master feels. I want to know why he loves you. I want to know why everything is worth putting in danger *for you.* Why he lets someone who can destroy him walk this world. I want to know why I have been banned from ripping these stupid mortals limb from limb and being done with it. I want you to press your palm to mine, and I want to understand."

"I could destroy you. I might do it accidentally. I might do it willingly."

"I know. I don't rightfully care. Now, what do you want in exchange? If I lose, what do you want?"

Maxine paused. She didn't know. She shook her head dumbly.

"A favor to be named later, then. I wouldn't worry overmuch about deciding your fee too soon. I doubt you'll win." The false Bella sat on the edge of the window and took up her watch of the street outside, farcical as it was. "Sleep well, my dove. I will see you in the morning. At least the sun will no longer rise to trouble me."

Maxine did not know how she was expected to sleep in a room knowing an imposter had taken over Bella's post. But she supposed he was truly no more or less a friend to her than Alfonzo or Eddie. Eventually, she lay down and shut her eyes and tried to let sleep come back to her. Slowly, exhaustion won over her reluctance and troubled thoughts.

It did not matter who was in the room while she slept, human or vampire. She was to spend the rest of her days a prisoner.

There were only two variables left to resolve. Who held her chain…and how long she would survive as their slave.

7
―――

Vlad should not have been surprised.

When he walked into the room to speak to Mordecai, the eldest and the captain of the demons in his armies, he should not have been annoyed to find him as he was—lying sprawled out on his back on a chaise lounge, fully naked.

He was an incubus, after all. He was wearing the guise of a beautiful mortal man with short blond hair and a trim build. He was wearing the shape of a man plucked from the very fantasies of the woman who was between his legs, her head lowered to him, eagerly worshipping his body with every ounce of passion she owned.

Vlad should not have been surprised, but now he was a little impressed. Not at the act, but at who Mordecai had as a partner. He recognized the girl. Bella, the vampire huntress. "I believe I told Zadok to deal with them."

"Hello, Master." Mordecai picked his head up from the back of the lounge briefly to greet him with a lazy smile. He was basking in the affection. "The Illusionist and I came to an arrangement. I hope you're not angry."

"I should have expected this would come to pass after

Curse of Dracula

you danced with her." Vlad sighed. "No. I am not angry. Nor am I terribly surprised. Did she fall to you easily?"

"I would say so. She is such a perfect little thing." He groaned and reached down to stroke her hair. The woman was intent on swallowing him whole. "Will you look at that? Oh, Bella...yes, please, a little more." He groaned again and tilted his head back, shuddering as the woman succeeded in her goal. "Oh, yes, Bella—like that!"

Impressed, and perhaps a little jealous. Vlad shook his head, walking to stand by a window and look down at the dark city below. "I am surprised she did not give you trouble. She seemed a willful one."

"Willful, yes. But she yearned to be free. She wanted what I could give her. Anything but the chains she wore to those two idiots she called friends. One look at me, and she fell into my arms. She struggled so briefly. Now I can barely contain her. I think lust is her true nature. She has so much of it to give."

"I am surprised you have not drained her." Incubi and succubae were much like vampires in that they could choose whether or not to harm their victims. It seemed that he had not touched the girl. Usually, when he found one of the demons feeding on their prey, the mortal would be mindless and empty-eyed as though they had taken opium. "I would have expected you to kill her."

This girl, who lavished his body, was neither numb nor limp in his arms. She was clearly in his thrall, as was to be expected, but she was acting very much of her own volition. The girl had not looked up at Vlad, despite the foreign voice in the room. She was so focused on the demon beneath her that she did not even know there was anyone else in the room. Such was the way of an incubus' magic. They kept their victims enamored only to them and what they wished to see. Bella would know nothing of the world around her that Mordecai did not wish her to.

"I think I will keep her with your permission, sire."

Vlad shrugged. "Keep her for as long as you wish. It seems she has much fire for her to give you."

"No. I mean I wish to keep her permanently."

That drew his attention back to the incubus. He turned and looked at the demon with a raised eyebrow. "You wish to take her as your bride?"

Mordecai was smiling dreamily down at the girl. He did not answer for a moment, instead moaning and tossing his head back. He grabbed the girl's head in his hands and pressed himself into her to the hilt. His body twitched and spasmed as he spent himself into her eagerness.

Vlad rolled his eyes and waited.

Demons.

When the moment subsided, the girl crawled up the length of Mordecai's naked body and collapsed into his arms, snuggling into his chest. He wrapped his arms around her tightly, cradling her. "Sleep, beautiful Bella. You need your rest."

She was already unconscious.

As the girl went under, his form changed. He shed the mortal shape and took the one Vlad was far more accustomed to seeing—his true one. Mordecai stretched like a sated cat. His pale blue-gray skin was not the most significant change. That credit was given to the black horns that curled away from his temples and the tail that now swished beside him.

At least he had donned clothing. Little more than a loincloth that draped over his waist, but it was better than nothing. Vlad was hardly a prude. He enjoyed lust more than any of the other sins, including wrath. That said, if he had

Curse of Dracula

the option to actually converse with someone while they were naked or clothed, the choice was clear.

"You want to claim her?" Vlad repeated his question.

"I do. If she will have me." He sighed and looked down at the naked girl in his arms, her rosy skin a far cry from his strange coloring. His long tail curled around her leg covetously. "I will have to free her from my spell to ask her. I would have her gaze on me such as I truly am and understand what she would become. She will reject me, I am sure."

"Have you ever tried before?"

"I have never felt the need."

"For what it is worth, I hope she accepts you." Vlad turned back out to the moonlight and let out a breath. He had his own hopes for the future that might lay in the arms of a mortal girl.

"How goes your hunt? What a delicious thing that Maxine is. Think you might consider sharing?"

"No."

"Come, now, not even a trade for a night?"

"No, Mordecai."

"How about all at once, then?"

Vlad growled angrily in response.

"Oh, well. But perhaps you are right. Once she tasted me, she would likely never want you again," the demon teased.

Vlad laughed and shook his head. He knew the creature was only half joking, but he took it for the good-natured goading that it was meant to be. His thoughts drifted over Maxine. He wondered how she was faring. Though the sun had not risen, he knew the morning had still come. They would be on the move once more.

"Where is Zadok?"

"Oh, here is the clever bit. He has assumed the form of Bella in order to better tear them apart from the inside." Mordecai chuckled.

Vlad sighed. It was a dangerous ploy, but he knew the Illusionist did not like a game that came without risks. He also did not enjoy the idea that Maxine was left alone in the watch of his most unpredictable general outside of his direct supervision.

But that was how fate had played out. Replacing Bella was a brilliant ploy, Vlad had to admit. It would be all the more beautiful when they realized she had been missing for days. It would be so easy to kill them. But he did not simply wish them violence. He wished them *suffering*, and such was a gift he had learned to masterfully craft many years ago.

And oh, the terrors he had planned for the Helsing mortal were truly breathtaking. The girl behind him might be a useful tool, if she embraced Mordecai and chose to become as he.

"Is this love, Master?"

"Perhaps." Vlad shook his head and looked back out the window.

"It's terrible. It's frightening and putrid. It hurts me in my heart when I think about her rejecting me. I despise it so very much. I think I can't live without it."

Vlad shut his eyes. "Yes. You are in love."

Mordecai grunted. "Damn it."

They had been walking for hours. Maxine, Alfonzo, Eddie…and "Bella." As they marched, they passed bodies left bent and broken wherever they had been discarded—or whatever had been left of them. Even more alarming than the piles was when there was nothing left, only blood, oozing down walls and across sidewalks, dark but shining in the crimson moonlight.

The moon that never moved, never set, and never gave way to the sun. As the hours ticked by, it remained the constant watcher hanging high in the sky overhead.

She had hoped Zadok's farce would last a few minutes at most. But it seemed the vampire was an exceptionally good actor. Or his commentary on Alfonzo's and Eddie's views of Bella as a commodity and an accessory rung far truer than Maxine would have wished. Perhaps some of each.

Either way, she walked beside "Bella" on their trek through the city. The vampire-turned-huntress had asked to be the keeper of her chains for a turn, to spare Eddie the responsibility for a few hours, and the young boy had agreed.

It had taken every ounce of Maxine's will to keep from protesting the arrangement. She would have no issue with Bella being the one to hold her "leash," and therefore it would raise suspicion if she balked at it now. She only spared the vampire a few sidelong glares when she was certain no one was looking.

Meanwhile, Zadok was clearly pleased as punch to stand close to her, smiling, pretending to whisper to her like they were two girls at school. "Six hours we've marched. Not even a bat of an eye from either of them. And I haven't exactly been quiet," Zadok whispered in Bella's voice.

It was true. Bella was a talkative, chipper thing. And Zadok mimicked it easily. He was also very careful to avoid topics that which might require reference to previous knowledge of their lives and travels together. And when something did come up, he danced around it like a prizewinning performer.

It was like watching a master at work. This was clearly not his first time playing this game.

Bella snapped her fingers in the air as if she were struggling to recall something. "Oh! Eddie. Do you remember that time we fought the…oh, oh, what was it? The big one."

"The flesh-beast in Rio."

"Yes! That's it. Ugly thing. Oh, Maxine, you should have seen it. It was like…" Bella paused again thoughtfully.

Eddie was too eager to cut in and provide his own take on it. "Like someone had glued a hundred corpses together. All the ugly bits too. What brings it up?"

"I'm telling Maxine about all our travels together."

Eddie snickered. "Messy. Our travels have been messy."

"All of you be quiet. We make enough of a racket as it is." Alfonzo was at the lead of the line, as he always was, his hand on his sword hilt. It rarely left it.

"They all know where we are," Bella chimed. Her tone was eerily chipper despite the topic. "They've taken the city. We're only allowed to walk around because they're letting us."

Alfonzo sighed. "I know."

"And we haven't gotten any closer to the center." Bella seemed a little too comfortable with what she was saying. Maxine elbowed "her" in the side and shot her a glare as if to ask her what she was doing. Bella smiled back at her beatifically. "She" was very much doing this on purpose.

"I know." Alfonzo's shoulders raised for a moment, before they went slack again. Whatever was upsetting him, he decided it was not worth worrying over in the moment. "We keep going."

"That's why I'm making conversation, is all. We have nothing better to do than walk."

"We haven't even seen any other monsters," Eddie

Curse of Dracula

pointed out. "They could be attacking us. But they aren't. Why?"

"Tiring us out." Alfonzo finally loosened his grip on his sword. "If they know we can't get any closer...they'll let us walk in circles."

"Hm. Maybe they're trying to convince us to leave," the false Bella said thoughtfully.

"We aren't leaving. They're only giving us the option to walk out because they're threatened about what we'll do if we stay. We almost had Dracula... but *Maxine* got in the way." Alfonzo turned back to glare at her. She couldn't deny what had happened. She looked down at the ground instead. "So, we keep marching. We keep going. We will find a way past whatever spell they've cast."

Bella sighed. "I think it might be better to leave. Get our bearings. Call for reinforcements. I'm sure the army will be here soon, and we could have some assistance." The false huntress made logical points. But that was her goal, wasn't it? To get the hunters to splinter and divide? The easiest way to do that would be to approach it from a purely rational stand.

"She's got a point, Al," Eddie muttered. "I hate to admit it, but retreat makes sense."

"No. We keep going."

So they did. For another six hours.

Right until they wound up exactly where they began. They looked up at the same house they had slept in the previous evening, and all of them groaned in dismay. Even Bella.

Zadok was quite a talented actor indeed.

"Rethinking the idea of retreat?" Eddie shoved his hands into his duster pockets.

"No." Alfonzo stormed up the stairs to the house and

shoved the door open, sending it smashing violently into the wall.

Eddie followed the older man with a shake of a head, leaving Bella and Maxine standing on the sidewalk.

Bella smiled at her sweetly. "Day one. Check." She hopped up the stairs and looked back over her shoulder. With a tug, she yanked on the chain that still remained tethered to Maxine's wrists. It pulled her forward a step. "Come on now, sweetheart."

"Don't do that."

"This'll be the only chance I ever get to have you on my leash." Bella winked. "Let me have my fun."

With a heavy sigh, Maxine shook her head and walked after the vampire. She climbed the stairs and paused next to Bella, casting her a woeful glare. "This will not end well, Zadok. Mark my words."

"Mm...I thought you weren't psychic."

"I don't need to be to see what is coming."

"One more day, and I win our little bet. One more day, and this'll all be over, anyway."

"What do you mean?" Maxine took a step back from the vampire masquerading as the huntress.

"Oh, shush. I'm merely saying it will be by the end of day three that I break them down. I promise you." Bella gathered up the chain that had pooled on the top stair and began to wind it around her hand. "I do think I very much like having you on a leash, little dove. Are you sure you wish to choose the Master over me? I can be so very kind...so giving."

"Enough." She glared at him—her—whichever. "The answer is, and forever will be, no."

Bella rolled her eyes and let out an exasperated sigh.

"Fine. Well, we might as well eat with the two fools then get some rest, hm? I get to watch you while you sleep."

"I dislike you. Deeply."

Bella grinned, a cruel and feral expression on otherwise sweet features. "I know."

8

Dinner had been awkward at best. They did not dare use the stove for fear of attracting the creatures they all knew were purposefully avoiding them. But it was better to be cautious, even with the eerie silence and the wards Alfonzo had placed on the home the day prior.

The wards that had clearly been broken by Zadok if he could traipse in and out without worry. She still shuddered at the idea of the vampire coming up through the sewers to invade the house as a swarm of rats. She tried not to dwell on it. Nor did she want to dwell on the fact that he was still sitting there in the room with her, masquerading as the blonde huntress, carrying on idle conversation and eating a plate of dry goods, cheese, bread, and some fruit they had managed to find in the house's pantry.

Maxine thought it best to stay quiet. No one seemed to care. Alfonzo and Eddie weren't cruel to her by any means, but neither were they her friends any longer. She had betrayed them, and they had responded accordingly.

So, it was with mild surprise that she was dragged into

the middle of their growing debate as to what to do about their current predicament.

"What do you think, Maxine?" Eddie was sitting by the window, a revolver in his lap, watching for any trouble on the streets. But there was none outside but the dead who lay where they had been abandoned. They were not moving. For the moment. She did not fault the man his caution. "Should we retreat? Or keep going?"

"I..." She looked up to see Alfonzo and the false Bella also watching her, waiting for her answer, although for two very completely different reasons, she suspected. *Poor Bella. I do hope she's all right.*

"She sides with the vampire," Alfonzo grunted and ripped off a piece of bread from the partial loaf in front of him. "She can destroy him, but she won't."

"I have not decided. I don't want to hurt him. But this... what he's done cannot be allowed to continue."

"What do you plan to do about it, then? Say he were here, right in this moment, what would you do?" Eddie asked. The young man was much less judgmental in his tone, and for that, she was grateful.

She shook her head. "I imagine I would beg him to stop. To take us from this place and go somewhere he and his creatures would not do so much wanton damage. I expect I would fail. Then I would be forced to decide whether I truly stand behind my convictions to stop him. I do not know if I can."

"Why?" Alfonzo threw down a hunk of bread, and it clattered off his plate and onto the table in front of him. "How can you be so docile? So gullible? You say you wish to stop him, and in the same breath say you do not think you can. You are the first person perhaps since the dawn of our kind who can stop him, really stop him once and for all, yet you waver! Is it because he can touch you? Because you want him?"

"No—"

"Then tell me *why,* Maxine!"

She shrank back against the sofa cushion at the man's rage. She understood it. She did not begrudge him. "I am a fool. I understand this. I find myself devoid of all the moral fabric I had once believed I contained." She looked down at her gloved palms and something in her heart cracked. Something she had been trying to shore up against the storm since this all began. She was exhausted, and it was all wearing her down. She could only hold the shutters closed for so long before the wind shattered the glass and tore through her.

"Why do I hesitate to kill him, Alfonzo? Why do I not know if I can look him in the eyes and dash his very being upon the rocks?" Maxine lost the war with her tears. She swiped at her cheeks irritably, hating to show weakness in front of the hunters and the vampire. But it did not truly matter. It was only what was left of her shattered pride. "Because I have seen the stars that he knew and which are long forgotten to the world. I have seen the deserts he has walked. I see the eternity that stretches behind him and the one that waits, and I hear the pain that echoes in his heart. Because I love him! That is why."

She walked from the room, dragging the chain behind her. She did not care. She went up the stairs and found a bedroom there that would suit her desire for somewhere dark, quiet, and empty. She walked to the window and slumped down onto the ground. Leaning on the wall, she cried.

For the first time since the hunters had knocked on her door with that damnable brooch, she let herself feel her

Curse of Dracula

own grief. Her own sadness. Her own tragedy. Rarely did she ever experience her own emotions. She was always so inundated with those of others, she became accustomed to ignoring what she felt.

But now, it was too much.

She did not know how much time had passed when there were quiet footsteps behind her. She had stopped crying at some point, the tears having run their course and gone dry. Now she sat there, empty and hollow.

"Eddie would have come, but I told him it was better for ladies to speak of such matters, and he quickly agreed." Zadok—as himself—sat on the floor behind her. As unnerving as the illusionist vampire was, he was much less so wearing his own face and using his own voice than masquerading as Bella.

"Please, leave me be, Zadok. I do not think I can withstand more of your goading." Her voice sounded ragged, strained, and tired. She must have been sobbing. She didn't quite remember.

A hand settled on her shoulder over her dress. It was gentle and unassuming. It was meant to be comforting. "That is not why I have come."

"Then why?" She jolted in surprise as another Zadok appeared sitting in front of her, shimmering out of thin air. It was an illusion—a copy of the man at her back. But this one suffered no threat of her touch. He lifted his hand to her cheek. Cold as a vampire's must be, but feeling no less real than anything else.

He brushed away what must have been still-drying tears and shifted closer to her. "I cannot hold you in truth, my dove. Nor can I bring you to him who would wish to comfort you. But I cannot leave you here suffering alone."

"Why?" Tears threatened to come anew, and she pulled

away from the phantom. She went to turn away, but he tutted and turned her back to face him. "Why do you care?"

"Because it is so rare that others care for creatures such as I. That anyone might dare love us, let alone him. You are a rare thing, meant to be treasured, not dragged through the muck and mire as you are now." Before she could react, Zadok's illusion pulled her into a hug. He tucked her head under his and held her tightly to him. He smelled of cologne. "You show such compassion for others. I wish to show some to you. Accept it, stubborn girl. Do not bring yourself suffering merely because you are under the bullheaded opinion that you somehow deserve it."

She let the tension slack from her shoulders. For once, he was being sincere. She could sense him at her back, the *real* him, and knew he was not lying. There were no insidious games beneath this show of kindness. Just a gentle sadness.

Caving to the illusion, she let him hold her. "I don't know what to do," she whispered.

"If it were up to me, I would stab those two mortal idiots, leap into my Master's arms, and accept his eternal kiss. I would want him, and you, to be happy. If I also had my way—and this *is* my fantasy, after all—you would be so very grateful for my compassion you would spend a night in my bed. Or a week. Or a month. Oh, Hell, how about a year? Dream big, I say."

She shouldn't laugh. She shouldn't. But he pulled one out of her regardless. She knew he was perfectly serious, and knew he was also trying to cheer her up. "You're an ass, Zadok."

"Yes. I am. And sometimes people love me for it. Now. Come. Stand up. There is a bed there, perfectly soft and usable, and you are here slumped on the floor like a petu-

Curse of Dracula

lant child." His illusion stood, taking her with him, and urged her toward the bed. "Rest. Our Master will find you in your dreams and comfort you properly."

His hand slapped her rear.

And she rounded and slapped him across the face. Or rather, she tried. Her hand passed through thin air. The illusionary version of him vanished and left only the real one leaning on the wall, smiling at her with that fiendish expression he was always wont to have.

He shrugged idly. "Do you blame me?"

"Yes. Now, go. I do not wish to spend another night knowing you are staring at me while I sleep."

Pushing himself away from the wall, he threw up his hands in mock frustration. "Oh, yes, make me stand in the hallway like I am your royal guard. Very well. Suit yourself. Far be it from me to have earned any leniency just now."

"Here is your leniency. Take the chair." She pointed at one by the wall. But when he shot her his playful smile, she suddenly wore one of her own. Damn him. He had succeeded in his game of cheering her.

"Yes, my *mistress*," he purred as he plucked the chair from its spot and walked outside. He plunked it down across from the door, and as she watched, his shape changed to that of Bella. It was still alarming and unnerving to see. She turned, gave a deep curtsey. When she spoke again, Zadok's voice was once more the blonde huntress. "Sleep well, my dove. Send our Master my regards."

"He is not my master."

"Mmhm." And with that, the false huntress shut the door.

With a shake of her head, she lay down on the bed over the sheets but under the blanket that had been folded at the base. There was not much of a feeling of the previous owner left lingering to bother her. Perhaps this had been a guest bed.

Maxine tried not to think very hard about what had become of the tenants of the house before Vlad had come and released his ruin upon the city.

They were likely dead amongst the bodies out front, after all.

Her exhaustion spared her any more gory and tragic thoughts. She embraced sleep as it came for her with welcome arms.

———

Bella awoke with a long yawn and stretched herself out. She was utterly cozy. Totally and perfectly comfortable. It was that kind of softness that came with sitting by a warm fire, or after drinking the right amount of wine.

Where was she?

What had happened?

She remembered the poor cursed city and its fleeing residents. She remembered the man from the gala who had swept her off her feet. A beautiful, impossibly perfect man. Then…flashes of memory, nothing more. But what she could recall made her body heat, like illicit dreams. But she knew better. She could picture herself twisting in his arms, feeling him buried deep inside her, bring out feelings and emotions she had not even known she was capable of experiencing.

Pleasure. Joy. *Real* joy. Tangled up in a creature who brought her to that peak of the world again, and again, and again.

It had not been only in her dreams. He had been real.

Very real. And the things he did to her—the things they did together.

Incubus. Demon. Monster.

She was his prey.

He had opened his arms to her, and she had fallen into them like a naïve child. Was she really so weak as to surrender to him as quickly as she had? She could remember the feeling of him kissing her, his lips all over her body, of him delving inside her—and her body responded to the memory as if it were still happening.

It gave her the answer. Yes. She truly was that weak. She had avoided that kind of contact with a man for so very long. It would have only caused complications in her life. It seemed her abstinence had come back to haunt her with a vengeance.

She had been prepared for violence. For a battle. For blood drinkers. She had, like an idiot, not been prepared for the warfare they might wage on her in other ways. She had fallen to the incubus. He had ravished her body, and she remembered begging for more.

Am I truly so depraved?

Something smelled divine. Something warm, wonderful, and sweet was calling her away from her troubled thoughts. She snuggled closer to it instinctively, wanting to find shelter from her guilt. Whatever was beneath her let out a hum of appreciation, and she froze.

"Good morning, sweetheart."

9
———

THE SOUND of his voice ran up Bella's spine like fingers. Sultry and smooth. She jumped up, tripped, staggered, and fell onto something far less welcoming and hard.

Wild-eyed, she looked around to try to understand what had happened. She was lying on a cold stone floor; that much she figured out rather immediately. It was quite alarming due to another fact—she was entirely naked!

Something was twisted around her ankles. It was a blanket made of the pelt of some dead animal. She snatched it up quickly and covered herself.

"Funny creatures, you mortals are. Modesty before safety? How does that make any sense at all?" A voice chuckled. "Especially after what we've already done. And done again. And done some more."

Finding the source, she was without words. He—the incubus Mordecai—was spread out on a bed. She must have fallen from it. The idea of having been sleeping so blissfully in his arms made her cheeks burst into flame.

She blushed also because he too was completely nude.

Curse of Dracula

She had robbed him of what had been covering them both. He was on full display. *Full* display.

She looked away sheepishly.

He laughed. "You take your eyes off your enemy? Why? Is the sight of how much I desire you so troubling that you would rather be vulnerable to attack?" She heard him shift, and she saw out of the corner of her eye that he was lying down fully on the bed, sprawled out like some great cat. "I am not going to hurt you. I promised you that, and I meant it. I don't lie as a point of pride."

"You're an incubus. You feed on—on—" she stammered uselessly. She couldn't even say it.

"On lust? On fucking? Yes. I do. Do you feel drained? Do you feel out of sorts? Do you even feel *sore?*"

No. She didn't feel any of those things. And seeing as she now could distinctly remember him entering a part of her body that no man should have any natural inclination to enter, she moaned in dismay and curled up into a ball, burying her head in her hands.

"And, trust me, you should be sore after what we've done."

She remembered begging for it. *He was controlling me!* But why did it feel as though he had only pushed her down that hill? Just the memory of what he had done made her shiver—and it was not in disgust. She wanted to hide from it all to avoid it.

"Don't make that face. I know that face. It's regret. I would love to take it away from you, but I won't. I can't without making you more upset later."

"What do you mean?"

"I'm not influencing you right now. I won't. Not ever again." Mordecai rolled over onto his stomach, and only then did she find the bravery to look up at him. He was lounging with his arms folded and his chin on his wrists. He was smiling at her dreamily. "I've freed you from my influence."

"But…why? I don't understand. I'm your enemy."

"No, you're not. You're anything *but* my enemy, sweetheart."

"You serve the vampire."

Mordecai shrugged. "He isn't your enemy either. You made him that way, not him."

"I don't understand…"

"He gave you three the chance to stop all this. All you had to do was give up the young mortal empath, and all those lives would be spared. It was your zealous hatred that caused this. It could've been avoided."

"I…it was Alfonzo's choice, not mine."

"You're his servant, then?"

"No!"

"Mmhm."

"Does Dracula never command you to do anything you disagree with?"

"Oh, all the time. And I voice my concern. And I am his servant. You're proving my point."

"No. I'm not Alfonzo's servant. I'm not his slave, or his—his anything. He's our leader."

"But you do everything he says. And when we gave you the chance to turn around and leave and spare your life, you chose not to."

"Dracula must be stopped."

"No, that is not what you're after. You believe Dracula must *die*. You could have stopped him. It's violence you want."

"N…no."

"I don't think I'd like to argue with you. There are much nicer things I'd like to do."

Her cheeks flushed again. "Stop."

"Stop what?" Mordecai yawned and half-shut his eyes while he watched her. Something about him remained constantly sultry. Part of her wanted very much to crawl into the bed next to him and ask him to show her all the things he had done to her once more when she was clear-headed and could really enjoy them.

No! "Stop it."

He laughed. "You're so flustered. I can't stop anything if I don't know what you're talking about."

"Stop lying to me!"

"About what?"

"Controlling me."

"First off, it's not 'control.' It's influence. We can trigger the lust a person feels and compel them to act on it. I can't make you do anything you don't already want. We aren't an all-powerful race, trust me. I can only make you ignore the part of your mind that screams that you *shouldn't*. Second, I'm not doing anything at all. I'm only lying here, talking to the most beautiful girl I've ever seen."

She stood from the floor and wrapped the fur blanket around her body. "Let me go."

"Mmhm. Skip over that and right to the next thing. I see how it is." He puffed out a sigh and pushed himself up onto his elbows.

She tried not to look at his bare ass. She tried. She tried so very hard. But it was so perfect. She failed spectacularly and looked away entirely, deciding the stone wall of the windowless room they were in was a far better option. "Let me go."

"Not until Master Dracula has what he wants. Then you're free to leave if you wish."

"What...?" She looked back at him again in surprise.

"If you didn't think I'd let you go, why did you bother asking?" He laughed. "You mortals! Such silly creatures." He rolled onto his back to watch her upside-down with his head draped over the edge of the bed. "You want a reason to be upset with me."

She looked away from his nudity once more. "I did not think you would have the kind of honor it would take to grant it, but I saw no harm in asking."

"You weren't asking. You were demanding. Just a point of fact, but it's fine." He stood, and she shrank away from him as he walked up to her. She kept retreating until she had backed into the wall. He stood a few feet away from her but came no closer. "Master Dracula will keep the city in this state until his business with Miss Parker is concluded one way or another."

"I thought he was here to create an empire."

"Until he met her, yes. Now he has other motives. He hasn't spoken them aloud to us, but they're plain to see. He wishes the girl to either love him or kill him. I'm not sure he entirely minds which she picks." He was still fully naked, and fully proud, and she kept her eyes dutifully turned away.

"Why?"

"That's his own business, not mine. I have my own matters to attend."

"And what is that?"

"I've been told to either kill you or keep you out of the way until his game is over. I've opted for the latter."

She chewed her lip. She dreaded to ask the question, for fear of the answer. But she needed to know. "Why?" If she was going to be maimed or tortured, she had every right to—

"I love you."

That broke her out of her goal of keeping her gaze away from him. She looked up at him in wide-eyed shock once more. There was a deep and...honest warmth in his odd purple eyes. He was watching her with a tender smile.

"You're...you're lying."

"I'm not!" He put his hand to his chest in hurt.

"You say that to all the girls—"

"Not just girls."

She cringed and tried to ignore his salacious, wicked grin. "—to all the *people* you...you..."

"Fuck. Say it, Bella."

"No."

He snickered. "I bet I can get you to say it."

"Stop it."

He laughed and took a step closer, and she shrank back. Without her weapons, she was helpless. She had her gifts, but she couldn't see anything in the room on which she could work her telekinesis to do any real damage at all. The bed was too big for her to budge. There was next to nothing else in the room, and she figured whatever bits of furniture or bedding she could lob at the incubus would only annoy him.

"Don't be afraid of me...please don't. I love you. I want to protect you. I will never hurt you. Think what you will of me, but I am not lying. And I certainly do not say those words to my prey. Never once have I said them to another."

He reached out to touch her face, and she flinched. She was shivering as he traced his fingertips over her cheek. It sparked something in her that she couldn't understand. She wanted to lean into him—she wanted to embrace his words.

She wanted to believe him.

Terrifyingly, she really rather did. She was so tired of fighting. So tired of the constant struggle she had known her entire life. Always running, always battling, never experiencing the better things in life. Like love. Like sex. Like *belonging* somewhere. "You don't know me." She was grasping at straws now. "You can't love me."

She needed to keep herself from giving in to him. Giving in to everything he offered her.

"Don't I know you? From the moment I looked into your eyes, I saw a beautiful heart. One so full of life, even though you surround yourself with death. You danced with me, talked with me, stood with me and spoke of the world you had traveled and seen. Such love for humanity, despite all its flaws. I see in you a heart wider than the sea. One I would happily drown in, if you would but let me swim the waves."

His hand slipped to hers, and he gently took it. She did not know what to do. She realized she was trembling. His words shook her, left her reeling and uncertain how to react. No one had ever spoken to her like that before. Not even Eddie. He lifted her hand to his lips and kissed her fingers slowly, one at a time.

Eddie had told her he loved her one night and had gone to kiss her before even waiting to hear her reply. When she had pulled away from him, he had acted crestfallen and frustrated with her. He had held a grudge ever since. Their friendship had deeply suffered for it. Despite any insistence that he did not hold it against her, she knew he did.

But never with Eddie did she feel like this.

This pull.

This draw.

This *desire*.

It was making her dizzy. She swallowed the lump in her

Curse of Dracula

throat and tried very hard to ignore the response he was drawing from her body. It didn't feel like the hypnotism he had placed over her before—no, he was right. This was entirely her fault. Her face was burning. Her cheeks must be crimson. Need was pooling low in her body, boiling and unexpected. It was a forbidden fruit she had never tasted and a poison to which she had no resistance. "What do you want from me...?"

"Mmmh, besides the obvious?" His hand holding hers moved down to his lower abdomen, dangerously close to something else. She squeaked and yanked her hand away. But she had paused there for a moment before she realized it. A moment too long. He grinned and took a step away from her, holding his arms out to his sides as if to display all of himself to her. "I want you to be my mate. My bride. My one and only."

"But you're...you're a..."

Mordecai sighed dramatically and stared up at the ceiling as if asking God for patience. What an odd concept. "Mortals." He looked back down to her. "Do you know anything about my kind?"

"I know that you...you—"

"Fuck," he provided helpfully with a grin.

"—to feed on mortals. You kill them. You—you—" She stopped in horror as she realized the word she was about to use had new connotations to her. A flash of memory washed over her. Him, buried down her throat. Her, moaning and begging for more.

"Suck?" His smile looked like it was going to split his face in half, he was so amused.

She let out a groan of dismay and put her palm over her face. It smelled like him, and she moved it away just as fast. "—People dry."

"Besides that. What do you know?"

She was silent for a long moment. "That's all there is to know."

He scratched the back of his neck. "I would point out that you're being rather narrow-minded in your views of race and culture, but...another discussion for another time. Yes. We fuck to feed. That's true. But that's different from *love*, Bella. Certainly, as innocent as you clearly are, even you know the difference."

"Simply because there is a difference, doesn't mean there should be."

"Ah. Ah, there it is. There is your burden. Explain. Why?"

"Because...sex should be about love."

"Mmhm. So, if you wanted to crawl into that bed with me, and have me ride you until you screamed my name like you did last night, again and again until you fell asleep purring like a kitten in my arms, that's wrong?"

"Yes!" Her face was warm again—or maybe she hadn't stopped. She wanted to huddle in the corner and hide away from it all.

"Wrong of me to do it? Or wrong of you to enjoy it? You *did* enjoy it, trust me."

"Both!"

"Why is it wrong for you to have enjoyed your time with me?"

"Because it is. It's impure. Improper. You're a monster. You hypnotized me, coerced me into doing terrible things."

"Terrible? Why were they terrible?"

"Because they're sinful!"

"Sin. Yes. Right. And are you harmed? Are you wronged? Are you at all injured? Did you not enjoy what we did?"

"But...you defiled me."

"Define 'defiled,' please."

"I...what?" Bella shook her head. He was so confusing. She wanted to curl into a ball and weep. She did not want to be stuck in this strange argument with a demon. But he seemed intent on continuing the conversation. "No. I won't bother. You're goading me."

Mordecai folded his arms across his chest as he watched her with a raised eyebrow. "Fine. Did I take your innocence? Your first time?"

"No."

"Who did?"

"I...I had too much to drink in a pub, and—and it isn't your business."

"Someone took advantage of you. And are they a demon and a monster?"

"It was my fault for what happened. I should not have drunk so much."

Mordecai put a hand over his face and groaned in dismay. "We have so much work to do, you and I."

"What do you mean?"

"You are so *backward* in your thinking! I swear this society has ruined your species. You blame yourself because some drunken piece of shit bent you over a barrel. What he did is far worse than my crime."

"You hypnotized me!"

"I did no such thing. I compelled you. There is a difference. I cannot make you act against your desires. If you did not want me, if you did not want what I offered you, you would have been unaffected. Otherwise we incubi and succubae would rule humanity, don't you think?"

"Then...then what I did was wrong. What *we* did was wrong."

"Says who? Who will judge you for such things? Your friends? Society at large? The Church?"

"Yes."

"Your body is their commodity, then? They own your flesh?" He huffed. "My mistake. I didn't realize I was impinging on someone else's property. My apologies to Alfonzo, Eddie, the Church, and all the other mortal men in the world."

"Well, n…no—" She looked up at him, confused. "I don't belong to anyone."

"Don't you? If you belong to yourself, and you enjoyed me, then for what reason are you ashamed? Do you love the boy Eddie? Is that it?"

"No!"

"He clearly loves you."

"I—I know."

Watching her stammer, he tilted his head curiously. "And you don't feel for him in return?"

How on Earth was she standing here trying to defend herself to an incubus? "I don't. I feel terrible about it, but I—"

"Why? I never understood that particular social defect. You poor mortal women are supposed to keep your bodies locked in a cage, but your heart is free to the first person who asks for it. And if you don't grant it to them, it is *you* who are supposed to feel grief? How are you the villain here?" He sighed. "Your race is evil to make you feel such a way."

"We are not!"

"Explain to me how your heart isn't the world's commodity, then." Mordecai shook his head, as if disappointed. But not in her, perhaps. "You cannot fuck when you wish since your 'purity' belongs to the world. You feel as though it's your fault you don't love every man who wants to crawl in between your legs, but if you let them, you are labeled a whore. You are shamed either way. Your world is cruel to your gender, Bella. Your society wants to keep women like pets. Subservient and docile. Slaves to their wants. How is that not evil?"

"Don't you keep me here for that same reason?"

"Oh, if you want to play with whips and chains, sweetheart—I will be there with literal bells on." He winked, and she looked shyly away from him again. He had a wicked sense of humor, and it made her squirm in a way that was, well, shameful. "No. You're not here so I can break you in to being my good little mare. I'm keeping you here so neither I, nor anyone else, will have to kill you. Dracula knows you're here safe with me, and he condones and approves it."

"He…approves?" That didn't sound like a positive to her, but it was also confusing.

"He wants me to be happy. He also doesn't enjoy pointless murder, believe it or not. If there's a way to spare your life that still serves his ends, he prefers it over putting you in the ground."

It was her turn to scoff.

"I said believe me or not." He walked up to her slowly, carefully, as if he were afraid he would scare her. "My kind mate once in all our immortal years. Once. We get to pair ourselves to one other soul in all our time. If one dies, the other will never find a second. It is a soul bond forged out of love. Not fucking. Although there is a lot of that involved."

She wailed and shut her eyes.

He laughed. "Sorry. You are so stunning when you blush and hide away so bashfully." His voice was close to her, and she felt the warmth pouring off his body. "Do you know how my kind are made?"

"No."

"Two ways. We are either born or bred. I was born here on Earth to my proud parents. My mother was born a succubus. My father was made into an incubus when he fell in love with her and agreed to lay his seed in her womb. As he did, he became as I am."

When his hand slid along her stomach over the fur blanket she wore, she nearly jumped out of her own skin. She looked up at him in shock and horror. "You didn't!"

He laughed hard and leaned his head down close to hers. "No, darling. Unlike humanity, we do not work that way. You are not with child. You have to want it. You have to ask for it. You have to love me first."

Before she could react, he was resting his forehead on hers. He was so close. He smelled of spices and something sweet. She should push him away. She should shove him, fight him, punch him. But instead, she was trembling and clutching the fur.

He leaned down a little farther, and his hot breath washed over her cheek. She shivered despite his warmth and the blanket.

His words had left her reeling. *I am not the property of the world. I am not. He is wrong.* But he made so much sense. And his nearness was doing terrible things to her. Things that felt so good. He tasted like freedom—like bliss. Like there might be another way to live.

Another life that wasn't the one she spent trapped in the chains her friends and society itself made her wear. "I shouldn't…"

"Shouldn't. What a stupid word. It means nothing here. Do what you want. What you *can*." He closed the distance then, pressing her to the wall with his body, his lips claiming hers. The noise that left her was not one of protest. The kiss was slow, sensual, and skilled. So *very* skilled.

He teased her, slowly letting up from the embrace before kissing her again, and again, but it was never enough. It was never deep enough. When he pulled from her the next time, she chased his lips with hers, and he let out a low, pleasured and praising hum.

It was then that he gave her what she wanted. What she needed. He pressed her harder against the wall, tilting his head to the side to turn the kiss from one that was sultry into one that was nearly bruising. His tongue flicked at her lips, asking for entry.

Asking. Not taking.

Not taking like she wanted him to do. It would be easier if he did. It would cure the debate that raged in her mind. But he seemed intent on only taking what he was offered, the *bastard.* She parted her lips, and he moaned as his tongue slipped in to dance with hers.

He kissed her until she thought she would have no brain left in her head to give her such turmoil. It was what she needed. But then, it was over, and he pulled his lips away from hers, his chest heaving, his body—all of it—pressed to hers.

"I want to dance with you again, my beautiful Bella."

Suddenly, she wanted to drop the fur pelt. She wanted the pleasure to chase away the guilt.

Purple eyes glittered as he watched her, lidded and dark with desire. "There is no judgment here. No sin. No shame. Don't be afraid."

Fear.

That was what it was, wasn't it? Deep at the core. She was afraid of doing what she wanted, for fear she might like it. For fear that everything she had come to believe had all been a lie. Morals. Society's expectations. Sin. God. Her friends. Her fight to uphold what was "right." She wanted to cling to what she had spent so much work on upholding, as if that condoned it.

Bella never considered herself to be a coward.

But then again, she had never been free enough to find out what else—who else—she was.

She dropped the fur blanket and let it pool around her feet.

Suddenly, she was lifted up the wall, her legs wrapping around his hips. He held her up by her thighs, and he was there at her entrance. Ready, but waiting. He was gazing at her still, searchingly, needing her to give him permission.

Yes, oh, God above, forgive me. She leaned in to kiss him, unable to form the words, wrapping her arms around his shoulders to support her weight as he moved her down the wall and himself deep inside her, stretching her, filling her, bringing her happiness. Their sounds of bliss mingled as did their bodies.

Her dreams were once more reality.

And she did not wish to wake.

10

Maxine found herself standing in a throne room and knew she was dreaming. She gazed up at the magnitude of it and felt so very small. So inconsequential. That was the point of places like this, wasn't it? And none were so effective as this, with all its twisting horrors and crimson tapestries. The fires that blazed in the caldrons that hung from the tortured gargoyles did little to warm the chill air around her.

"Come here, Maxine."

The voice carried easily without trying. It was so deep, and the room was so cavernous. She turned to see Dracula sitting on his throne, looking every inch the austere and aristocratic creature that he was. It was pointless to avoid him, and she did not even know if she wished to try. As she walked to him, he held his hand out to her. She gave him her hand. He gently pulled her forward and guided her to sit on his lap straddling him, the black fabric of her dress pooling around them.

Even perched on him as she was, he remained inches taller. She bowed her head to his chest and fought off the urge to cry once more. Vlad wrapped his arms around her, his palm stroking up and down her back soothingly. He was a murderer, but she could not help the feeling that this was where she belonged. Her fate was tied to him, one way or another.

"Zadok sends his regards," she murmured.

He chuckled, a low, deep rumble that vibrated in his chest. "Is he behaving himself?"

"As much as I think he is capable." She smiled faintly and looked up at the vampire, meeting his crimson gaze, and suddenly wished to kiss those pale lips of his. She tried to keep herself distracted. "I think there is more to that lout than meets the eye. He can be oddly sympathetic."

"Only sometimes. Only when there is something worth sympathizing with." His fingers whispered across her cheek before stroking through her hair, combing it, his sharp nails grazing her scalp. It was wonderful, and it lured her into shutting her eyes. He repeated the motion, and it was as though he could solve all her woes by that one gesture alone. "You are an easy thing to love, my Maxine."

"It seems that is true among vampires."

"Mortals rarely pay us anything more than hatred. Someone who might look upon us and see the souls that we still own is a jewel worth treasuring." He pulled her closer until her knees touched the back of the throne.

She let her hands rest on his chest, her fingers tangling in the fabric of his vest and coat. "I do not know what to do, Vlad."

"I know. I wish I could decide for you, but I cannot."

"End this massacre. Take me somewhere far from here. Please."

"You must see the extent of who I am. Once you have done that, once you truly understand and have chosen, we will go wherever you desire."

Curse of Dracula

"Have I not seen enough?"

"As much as it pains me, no, you have not. You wish to turn away. You wish to live in willful ignorance. You must watch the hunters fall."

She cringed and bowed her head. "Please, don't force me to watch their fates play out. I do not think I can bear it."

He hugged her to his chest. Her tension melted, enjoying the smell of roses that seemed to accompany him, and the strength in his broad frame.

"You shall see my kindness and my cruelty in equal measure until you decide which half you prefer to accept is the greater part of the whole."

"I fear they are equally matched and I will spend the rest of my years wandering in this purgatory you have made for me, weeping over the death you would create only to let you kiss my tears away."

"I see no problem with this." At the dismayed noise she made, he chuckled. "Forgive me, my love. I have an ill sense of humor. This is why I do not joke at all."

"What has become of Bella? I do not trust Zadok's words."

"Nor should you. Bella is alive and well. The creature that commands my demons has her safely stored away. I believe he means to court and woo her to his side. Once this is all concluded, if she wishes to go, she will be freed unharmed. But I suspect she will fall for him as he has for her."

"I suppose I cannot rightly judge her."

"No." He kissed the top of her head. "I suppose not."

"Will you spare the other hunters?"

"Helsing dies here. The boy might live if he chooses to. I have no grudge with him."

"I worry what he will do to save Bella once he learns of her fate."

"So be it. It is his right to toss away his life if he wishes."

She took in a slow breath and sighed it all out at once, trying to relax. It was easier than perhaps it should be, with the feeling of his soul touching hers, and his arms cradling her to him. "I hope Bella is enjoying her time with the incubus."

"Oh, she is. I assure you. Mordecai did not rise through the ranks because he was inept. And I assume he is a far better lover than he is a tactician."

"Promise me one thing, Vlad?"

"If I can, of course."

"I find myself oddly jealous of her. If I must die in all this, please let me not die a virgin."

He laughed, clearly deeply amused, and with the crook of a long finger, tipped her head up to meet his as he leaned in to kiss her. One hand cradled the back of her neck as the other pulled her hips to his, letting her feel the outline of his need against her body. His embrace was bruising, eager, and full of the passion she felt roaring away inside him.

When he broke away from her, she was breathless, her head reeling. She wanted more of it. She wanted him. But she wanted it to be real—not trapped in this vision.

"That is one wish I am eager to grant you, believe me." He ran his tongue along the line of her lower lip, swollen as it was from his kiss. "Zadok's work will soon be done. The hunters will soon fracture and split. And when they abandon you—and they will—wait for the clock to strike midnight. Then I will come for you, my love, and I will quite happily grant your request...as frequently and as ardently as you might desire."

Her face grew warm at his words, but it was not the only

Curse of Dracula

thing that was suddenly heated. She kissed him back, surprising herself with her own furor. But her heart was aching. She needed him to soothe the wound she had been dealt, even if it was by his own hand.

He growled, a sound that was both predatory and inhuman. It was not a sound of displeasure—anything but. It was the sound of a wolf ready to sink its teeth into its newest kill. It was a sound of approval, that whispered the word *mine* and threatened all the ways he would claim her.

If only things were so simple.

Vlad ended the kiss and sighed drearily. "As wonderful as this is, I fear I must go. I have business to attend, and I feel Walter calling me. And you, my dear, must rest. You have a trying time ahead of you. Both in what you must witness and what I fear you will have to endure when I have my hands on you once more."

He kissed her, and it was with the feeling of his lips on hers that she drifted back into the emptiness of her sleep.

———

Morning came, and Maxine marched anew with the three hunters. Well, two hunters and one vampire, as the case was. She was somewhat more put together than she had the night prior, although it was difficult to feel worse.

No one spoke to her. Not even "Bella," and she was glad for it. It was one of the few small favors they could give her. Eddie had taken up her chain and walked beside her, and she had nothing to say to the young man. She had nothing to say to any of them.

The carnage they passed had changed, although the buildings had not. Perhaps *changed* was not the right word—but many of the bodies she had seen the day before like grotesque and horrifying road signs were now gone. Missing. Either they had been eaten by predators or…they had gotten up and walked away.

Neither idea was comforting.

The air was chill, and her breath turned to mist in the air despite it being July. The world was forever painted in the muted tones of red and crimson, with little adding any kind of contrast to the bleakness. Or the hopelessness.

"Do you think we should leave?" Eddie asked her quietly, trying to keep Alfonzo from hearing. She did not know why he bothered. The city was silent. There were not even the howls of demons and monsters to trouble them. "Honestly?"

"I do not know how you might succeed. I do not see a path forward for you that does not end in ruin. I have only begun to truly understand the enormity of who Dracula is, and as much as I loathe to admit it, the odds of success are slim."

"They aren't if you decide to destroy him," Eddie pointed out as if she didn't already know that.

She pulled in a breath, held it, and let it out. She had nothing to lose by telling them the truth. "Vlad wishes me to decide whether I shall embrace him for what he is or try to kill him. I do not yet know the answer, or if destroying him is even truly possible. He intends to force me to walk this carnage and see it with my own eyes until I decide. He will not let me—or any of us—progress any farther than we have already walked unless I do so alone."

Alfonzo pulled up his steps abruptly and turned to face her. "What?"

"He wishes me to judge him. I do not think he will let me do so until you have left me behind. He has reiterated the threat that Zadok issued. They intend to split you apart.

Curse of Dracula

I would rather this not come to pass. I want you to leave this city. I want you all to leave. I want you to save yourselves before it's too late and I have even more blood on my hands."

"No. I am going to find a way through this illusion, and I will drag you to the foot of that vampire's throne." Alfonzo stormed up to her, and she froze as he fisted a hand into the collar of her coat and dragged her to him. "You said yourself you love him! If I do not ensure that you kill him, you are too weak to do what needs to be done."

"Al, enough. Back off." Eddie put his hand on the older man's arm and tried to tug him away.

Alfonzo whirled to face the younger hunter and shoved him back with a sweep of his arm. But he released her in the process. She backed up as far as she could, but the chain that tethered her to Eddie ensured she could not go far.

"You are not in charge, boy." Alfonzo was not done with his angry rant. "And I have had enough of your soft-hearted whimpering. Both of you." He glared at Zadok-Bella, who only raised her hands as if to say she wanted no part in this. "We keep going. We find a way through this. We take her to that wretch, and we do not stop until she tears him apart!"

Hatred. It poured from the older hunter. Hatred and loathing. There was no arguing with that kind of zealous blindness. There would be no convincing him. She let out a wavering breath. The vampires would have their way. The hunters would be torn apart.

Alfonzo began walking once more. Reluctantly, Eddie followed, pulling Maxine along with him. Shaking her head, Maxine cast a baleful and knowing look at the form of Bella who walked close beside her.

The false huntress only smiled sweetly and shrugged as if to say, "*I told you so.*"

Bella awoke once more in Mordecai's arms. Although, this time, she had willingly put herself there. She stretched and lifted her head to look up at him. He was asleep. The lines of his face were smoothed, and he looked peaceful. Happy.

Almost *innocent*.

That wasn't possible. The things they had done together had proven that to be quite clearly a lie. And they had indeed done them together. With each round, with each embrace, he gave her the chance to turn away and protest. But she had thrown herself into his affections headlong and seemed to find a fire in her that answered his own.

She had enjoyed it.

There was no denying that.

Guilt pulled at her, trying to tug her down into the world of regret. Just because she could now accept his affection and her willing part in it did not mean it was "right."

His words echoed in her mind. What was right? What was to say she was not living in a backward way of thinking as he claimed?

Perhaps it was her opportunity now to choose which world she wished to live in. Hers...or his. She ran her hand along his chest, exploring the warm expanse of it. He was muscular but not bulky. Warm, and soft, with the promise of strength underneath. Strength she'd tested and used several times over.

He felt so good. She never knew it could be this nice to have someone beside her, beneath her, and in every other way she figured a man and woman could know each other.

His face bloomed in a slow smile. "Good morning. Or evening. Or whatever time it is."

"I am sorry to wake you."

Curse of Dracula

"You're sweet." He yawned, stretched, and wrapped an arm around her to rest a hand idly on her lower back. "I was awake."

"Have you not slept?"

"Hm? No."

"Why not? Do you not trust me?"

He paused as he opened a purple eye to peer at her both mischievously and sleepily at the same time before shutting it. "If I fall asleep, my charade will fall apart, and I fear this will all be for naught."

"What do you mean?" She pushed up onto her elbows. He was lying on his back, still stretched out like a damn cat. There was something deeply feline about him.

"This is not my true appearance. I have taken the shape of what I can sense you would desire the most. It is a gift my ilk has mastered." Purple eyes were watching her now with a surprising amount of sadness.

She sat up and gathered the blanket over herself. More out of the chillness of the air and less out of modesty, she discovered. She had already shown him every part of herself that he could witness without gutting her open. He did not seem offended. He was lying there with a hand across his bare stomach, his other toying with the edge of the blanket by her knee. Now she was curious. "Show me."

He furrowed his brow. "I had hoped to wait. I wanted to give you more time in my presence before I revealed myself to you."

"Why?"

"I had hoped to win your heart before scaring you."

"Are you truly that revolting?" She smiled faintly. She had a hard time believing it.

"Pah. Hardly. But you are a woman of righteousness. I doubt you would take to my demonic self so readily."

"I *was* a woman of righteousness. I am not so certain anymore." She paused and made up her mind. Nodding once, she sat back to give him more room. "Go on. Show me."

Mordecai let out a groan that was partially a whine. "But I don't want to."

She laughed at his childishness. It was more endearing than it had any right to be.

"Fine." He grunted and climbed out of bed. Simply watching him move was captivating. The smoothness and gracefulness to his lithe muscles made her mouth water. It pooled a dangerous fire in her once more, and she tried to shove it away before she acted on it.

He seemed nervous. Shy. He ruffled his hands through his blond hair, mussing it, and turned to face her.

"Why are you troubled? Do you not want me to see your true form?"

"I want you to love me as I really am. Not this, or any other illusion you would ever want me to wear. Oh, and I will happily wear them for you. But…I…" He sighed, resigning himself. "You're right. I…wanted to prolong this."

He sounded so vulnerable as if he were afraid she would say no to him. She watched him and wondered what kind of grotesque and terrible creature he was. Perhaps it would help fight off the burning heat that was pooling in her body, gathering in her core, begging her to give in to her desire.

"Are you ready?"

She nodded.

His body shimmered. It was as though a cloud around him gave away, and the mirage dropped.

She gasped.

He was not hideous. He was not a gargoyle.

He was anything but.

Curse of Dracula

She should be horrified. She should look at a naked demon and find herself repulsed. Instead, she stared in awe. He had grayish-purple skin, grayer perhaps than not. His face had changed and become sharper in the cheekbones and along the jawline. His hair was still blond, but longer, and fell over one of his eyes in a rakish, jagged, and uneven cut. His eyes, still purple, were now far more saturated and unnatural.

He was lean. Long, muscular, and almost elven in his build. Not narrow by any means, but hardly bulky. A tail swished around behind him, the same color as his skin, hairless and tapered. Jewelry ran along it—no, through it—near the end. Piercings. Silver baubles and thick hoops dangled from it like they would from a woman's ears.

That was not his only jewelry. A metal loop ran through his lush, full lower lip, silver against the darker purplish blue. A pair of black horns twisted out of his hair in elegant, graceful curls back from his head. They were carved with symbols and a strange pattern she had never seen before.

Her gaze betrayed her and wandered down.

And found more silver jewelry. Not to mention, it turned out that his horns and tail were not the only thing about him that was inhuman. She gasped and looked straight up at the ceiling. "Oh. Oh, God. Oh, God on high."

Mordecai laughed. If he was offended, he didn't show it. "God's not here right now. Just you and me. Don't be afraid."

It really isn't fear I'm feeling, is it? She wanted to look again. She stared at the ceiling.

He snickered. "Do you want me, Bella?"

Yes. "No."

"Do you want to touch me?"

Yes. "No."

"Are you wondering what it'll feel like to be with an inhuman man?"

Yes. "No."

"Do you want me to never touch you again?"

"No—wait!" She looked back down to him and glared angrily. "That was cheap."

He was howling in laughter, and he flopped down onto the bed on his back and watched her with sultry, heavy-lidded eyes from his vantage point by her knees. "Sorry. You're too much fun."

She wanted to know what it would be like to be with him. He looked so foreign—so inhuman. She wanted to experience every inch of him.

And he could clearly tell by the warmth in her cheeks what she was thinking as he smiled at her. "There isn't anything wrong with desire. There isn't anything wrong with love. Let me love you, Bella. Let yourself see if you can feel the same for me. When all is said and done, and Dracula's game is through, if you don't love me, I'll let you go. Unharmed. I vow it to you."

"How can I trust you?"

"I gave you my name. My true name. I did it because despite my teasing, I trust you. My bright-eyed, beautiful, kind-hearted vampire hunter."

"I..." She looked to him and was unable to look away. His true appearance lit a fire in her that she hadn't even known existed. *I am going to Hell, but I find his real form more beautiful than the illusion.* There was something honest about it—about him. She looked into those eyes, a far more vivid purple than before, and couldn't see a scrap of a lie.

She saw a fiend, a demon, a playful thing...a beautiful thing. And in those bright purple eyes she saw love.

"Do you really love me...?" Bella asked him breathlessly.

Curse of Dracula

"Beautiful creature," he breathed. He rolled over and got up onto his knees beside her. "I love you more than anything or anyone I have ever known." His hands, which sported black nails, traced tenderly over her body.

She gasped. He was so warm to the touch—much warmer than a normal person. It sent her eyes drifting shut as he stroked his palms over her, cupping her breasts and gently caressing them. She couldn't help but let out a small moan.

Following her own desires and instincts for once, she pushed his shoulders, sending him falling onto his back. He let out a startled noise but watched her, wide-eyed and awed, as she shifted to straddle his thighs.

I don't have to deny myself this.

He was squirming at her ministrations as if he had never known the touch of a woman before. He rolled his head back, his mouth open, revealing that his top and bottom canine teeth were a little too sharp. Also revealing that he had another piece of metal in the form of a bar through his tongue. Now she was imagining what he used it for. *Oh.* She pointed down at him as if lecturing him. "No illusions. No control."

"None, sweetheart," he said through a heady, blissful moan at her touch. He was writhing beneath her, clearly overcome by her touch. "This is real."

Real.

So much of her life had never been that. The people who took her in from the orphanage, her childhood, all of it —it all seemed to fall away so easily as the façade that it truly was. Society's expectations. Death and horror paid to her by a monster, only for her to turn around and pay their kind more in return.

All of it was a lie.

This was real.

"Oh, Bella..." he said through a breathless sound. "I love you."

As she pressed her body down onto his, as he delved inside her in all his demonic glory, she tilted back her head and cried out his name.

11

Walter was pacing. He did not pace frequently. Only when it was called for. And in this moment, it was required. He had too many problems to solve all at once. The American army had already rallied and was on its way. Humans needed to be corralled and monitored, fed and cared for enough that they could be sustained.

And there were three—*correction, two*—hunters on the loose in the city, dragging his Master's new prize behind them on a damnable chain. The Captain of the demons had not come up for air since taking the female huntress as his spoil of war. Zadok was indisposed dealing with the remaining two. And Vlad was often nowhere to be found.

Walter was once more on his own to strategize and defend the newly taken city.

Mostly on his own.

Honestly, he wished he were on his own.

It was not that Elizabeth was not helpful—she was a malicious, cruel, and calculating creature. She was as intelligent as she was dangerous, and she did not serve in Dracula's higher ranks because she was weak.

She was a distraction.

And he needed to *think*.

"Gather Mordecai's forces to the western border. The Americans are unlikely to request help from the Canadians unless we expand. We should take the scouts that come to garner information on the city. The less information they have on us, the better." Elizabeth tapped her finger on the map. "Here is the major route I think they will take."

"You're likely correct. I doubt they will approach from the water until they get desperate."

She sighed. "This is not a great city to survive a siege."

Walter nodded. "I hope we do not have to withstand one for long. I do not think we will."

"Do you think Uncle means to move us?" Elizabeth blinked at him.

Walter stilled his pacing briefly to face her. He debated how much information to give the woman but saw no harm in it. She was the only one who had expressed interest ensuring that they did not all die from cannon fire, after all. "I think we will stay here until the business with Miss Parker is concluded, and we will move on with whatever prey we have managed to garner before then."

"Huh." Elizabeth looked down at the map then back to him. "Well. Then all these plans are rather much for naught, aren't they?"

"It is not a certainty. He may destroy her, and then we are back to our original goal."

"Which do you prefer?" Elizabeth swung around to face him, her legs draping off the edge of the table. Her chestnut waves were loose around her face, curling along features that were carefully made to be perfect and beautiful.

But it was not uncommon for vampires to look as such. Their survival was based on their effectiveness to hunt, and

Curse of Dracula

if their prey came to them willingly, drawn in by their allure, all the better. A wolf who did not have to chase its sheep was bound for a longer and happier life.

With Elizabeth, he found the practice irritating. Of course, he found her irritating in general. That might have more to do with her constant requests to become his bed-partner and less with her decision to carefully maintain her personal appearance.

He was quite happy that he did not find himself a lonely individual. He did not find himself lacking when he woke up alone. Otherwise, he might have been tempted to give in to her constant banal flirtation.

That was not to say that he did not understand the desire to have a companion. He did not fault Vlad or Mordecai for their distractions. Even if they did come at an immensely inconvenient time. "I would prefer that our Master and the young girl come to an understanding. I wish to leave here. Taking this city is a dangerous ploy with little to gain from it. I would prefer he find his entertainment with the empath and not where it might put the rest of us in danger."

"Well said." Elizabeth leaned back on her hands behind her, watching him with her calculating emerald eyes. They were brighter than would be possible for a human, but if it weren't for her pale complexion, she might pass as a mortal. Far easier than he ever could. Being the direct descendant of Vlad's blood came with benefits and pitfalls.

Being his "right hand" came with even more.

"What do you believe the odds are that he might be successful?" she pondered. "He has taken brides before. They last either the length of their mortal years or one of a vampire's. Either way, long enough for us to leave this place safely once he has her."

"But this is a very different game he plays." Walter walked to the window to look down at the city in its perpetual night. The library they had taken over and begun to corrupt into their own fashion of a fort had once been a beautiful structure sitting near the heart of the city. Now it was full of the odd and twisted angles that came with the corruption of Dracula's power. The hallways and rooms were no longer what they were. Elements remained—such as the walls of books everywhere—but now corridors led to places the building had not formerly contained. Bedrooms, storerooms, a kitchen…a dungeon.

It, like the city, now served its Master.

Like they all served.

Save for one. Miss Parker. "He does not seek from her a bride. He seeks from her an eternal judgement. The girl can see the whole of him in a way that no one else can. Therefore, I do not know what will come to pass. The scales remain balanced. She has not yet condemned him…but she has not yet embraced him either. Who knows what she will think when she ventures deeper into his madness?" Walter shook his head. "I think this will get worse before it will get better."

"Is it true that she could destroy him once and for all? I have heard Zadok whisper rumors that she can rip souls from bodies and send them to the void."

"He believes that if anyone can, it would be her."

Elizabeth swore quietly. "Then we should kill her immediately and end this game."

"And defy Dracula's wishes?"

"To protect him? Absolutely. If he dies, chaos will descend on the rest of us. We might all die as well if the source of our curse is removed!"

"At least you admit your desire to safeguard him is selfish." Walter rubbed a hand over his face. He hated dealing with sycophants. Unfortunately for him, they were more common than not.

"We should go into that city now, find them, dispose of the hunter, and tear off the girl's head. She is only mortal."

"No."

"Why? Do you wish him to die?"

"I am loyal to him. That is why. If this is what he wishes, then I will do all that I can to see it come to pass."

"Which do you prefer to happen, then? That she loves him, or that she tears him apart? You said yourself you believe he cares not which occurs. Something I cannot fathom, but I believe you."

"You do not know what he has endured. He has desired the kiss of death for thousands of years, Elizabeth. We may embrace our end at any point we wish. He is denied such a thing. It is a terrible burden to bear."

"You have not answered me. Do you wish him to be 'worthy of love,' or do you wish him to cease to be?"

Walter paused and debated his answer. Not because he did not know it, but because he did not know whether he wished to speak it.

A hand snaked around his side, and he moved reflexively. His hand snapped around Elizabeth's throat and slammed her up against the wall, his lips pulled back in a snarl. Wide-eyed, she raised her hands in a show of submission and went to speak, but he tightened his grasp, cutting off her air. "Do not mistake my tolerance for your presence as more than what it is, Elizabeth."

And with that, he threw her to the side, sending her sprawling to the ground. He straightened his coat and his vest. Shadows that had unfurled from him in his rage snapped back in place. He did hate losing his temper. It happened rarely, but the infuriating vampiress could pull it out of him with ease. He looked back to the window and down at the city below. "If you do not have anything more of use to say, then leave."

"I see now why you are his favorite." He heard her stand, but he did not pay her the dignity of looking. "Uncle's protégé has such sharp claws. And here I thought you were another marble fixture in the hallway."

"Go away, Elizabeth. I care not where."

"As you wish."

He sensed her leave and let out a long and dreary sigh. This was a miserable game his Master was playing. He prayed this ordeal with Maxine resolved itself quickly. "To answer your question, Elizabeth?" he said to the empty air. "I desire that our Master might find peace...once and for all. Be it in her arms or the grave, it does not matter." He paused and laughed quietly to himself. "Although I know where I would place my bet."

———

Maxine was becoming very sick of walking in circles. If they were making progress, she would feel less like a dog or a cow on a leash being paraded through the streets. But if she was frustrated—then Alfonzo was irate.

Eddie had long since gone quiet, no longer wishing to discuss the decision his leader had made to continue their hopeless trek through the bloody and nightmarish streets. Bella-Zadok was walking along beside her. Each time she glanced at the "woman," she-he would smile sweetly at Maxine. Sweetly and confidently, knowing he was right in his victory. Only a few more hours to go before their circular and pointless march would

Curse of Dracula

conclude, and she would lose her "bet" with the vampire.

She could not quite fathom why he was so eager to touch her and place himself in the very real threat of death, but she did not pretend to fully understand him. He was a strange creature. There was, as she was discovering with all the other vampires she had met, a vacuous pain that lived at his heart, along with a healthy heap of madness. She knew it was likely a product of the number of years he had lived. Immortality must weigh painfully on them.

Walter had turned to coldness to protect himself. Zadok had turned another way. And Vlad...

Maxine looked at the city around her. Although she could recognize the buildings as ones she had passed before, she could only do so vaguely. Each time they came across the same intersection or area of the city, it had changed. Not much, but enough to be unsettling.

Wrought-iron fences were twisted and warped, jagged and sharp, harsh and uninviting in their angles. Buildings seemed to lean in toward the street like ones she had seen in Prague, hunkering close together as if the stones sought shelter and comfort in each other from the poison that was seeping through them.

She wondered if those who made him could have honestly fathomed who and what it was they made when they laid this terrible curse upon him. Or if they knew the world itself would pay the price for their deed.

She pondered who they were, and what had Dracula done so long ago to deserve what they had done to him. Or perhaps he did nothing to deserve it at all. It was possible he was merely served up to be sacrificed to an ancient god. She knew he did not remember.

But there had been flashes of imagery. Memories of

sand, and temples of white limestone and the feeling of the sun burning overhead. She dwelled in her thoughts for the remainder of the day.

More hours, more marching, and they once again wound up right where they began. Back at the house that was becoming familiar to them all. Alfonzo was nearly apoplectic in his rage as he smashed the door in, sending it crashing into the wall. The handle stuck into the plastered surface. The rest of them stood on the sidewalk and listened to the sound of breaking furniture.

Eddie's shoulders slumped, and he buried his head in his hands. "This started off as stupid, but now I think it's insane."

"I think you might be right," Zadok-Bella muttered. "I do not feel as though he is thinking clearly."

"What do we do?" Eddie looked at his false companion. Maxine did everything she could to be silent. If she said anything at all, she knew she might give the vampire up. Then the real Bella would be in grave danger. Maxine would have no more lives on her hands if she could help it.

"We could go our separate way from him," Bella replied thoughtfully. "He will not turn back from this fight, no matter how hopeless it is."

"We can't leave him here. He'd...he wouldn't stand a chance on his own."

"I don't know as we stand a chance if we stay by his side, Eddie." Bella reached out and placed her hand on the young man's arm. His face rose in hope. Zadok was playing on the boy's broken heart. "But we could survive together without him. You and me."

Damn you to Hell, Zadok. Damn you to the pits for this.

And damn Eddie for not seeing through the vampire's ploy. Eddie was smiling at her with such a puppy-dog

Curse of Dracula

expression it forced Maxine to turn away to keep from revealing the game. She needed to hide her face and her look of horror and disgust. She could not have imagined that Zadok could have hidden himself for two days among the people who claimed to know Bella best.

But he was right. Eddie loved the idea of her and clung to the hope of a future with her through all the signs that something might be amiss.

The monsters around her always seemed to be right.

"What's wrong, Maxine?" Bella asked.

The curses she rattled off in her head toward Zadok were colorful and creative. The Roma had taught her well. She was going to give him an earful when this was all said and done. "Nothing. I am tired. There is a cloud in this city of corruption, maliciousness, *and lies*. It is wearing me thin."

"Yeah. It's influencing all of us." Eddie grunted. "C'mon. Tomorrow we'll try to talk sense into Al again. Maybe if the three of us try to convince him, it'll work."

"I don't think so." Maxine turned back to them when she could swallow the urge to punch "Bella" in the face. "Sadly, I think there is little that will sway him from his need for revenge."

"I know." Eddie took off his leather hat to scratch over his dusty hair. He was in bad need of a bath. They all were. "But sometimes it's not about winning, it's about trying. Sometimes that's all we've got to show for ourselves in the end."

And with that, the young man plodded up the stairs after his leader who, by the sounds of it, was still intent on destroying furniture in his impotent rage.

"Who knew the whelp was a prophet?" Zadok snickered before nudging Maxine's elbow. "I did not miss your jab, don't worry. Come on, my dove. Tonight, I win my bet." With that, the false huntress walked up the stairs, carrying Maxine's chains. She had no choice but to follow.

She did not know what she dreaded more—spending another night in the house with the hunters, one of whom was irate, or fishing through the vampire's head for some unknown reason.

They were about tied.

12

THE HUNTERS WERE silent all through dinner and into the evening. "Evening" being only the product of the clocks in the house and Alfonzo's pocket watch keeping the time. The darkness never changed.

Maxine did nothing to try to break the silence or to spark up a conversation. Alfonzo appeared itching to break someone or scream, and she was not going to volunteer to be first in line to either event. She ate the scavenged food and took up her position lying on the sofa by the wall.

Bella offered to take the first shift, and Maxine knew why. Alfonzo and Eddie agreed, and they lay down on their makeshift beds and seemingly fell asleep. Whether they did so naturally or because they had some help from Zadok and his magic, she did not know. It was all the same to her.

The "woman" sat on the ground near where Maxine was lying, her back against the front of the sofa. She patted her dress dramatically.

"Really, I'm not sure how your gender gets anything done. It isn't even the tits that are the problem—yes, fine, they're distracting—it's the damnable lack of pockets that is the real issue here." Bella looked down at herself and picked up the folds of her skirt and dropped them in frustration. "Is this a manner of repression I have been previously unaware of? That if we let you wear comfortable clothing that serves any functional purpose, you might revolt?"

Maxine rolled over to lie on her back, watching the false huntress complain. "It's quite possible."

"It's asinine." Bella's form melted back into that of the vampire's true shape, who stretched and grunted as if releasing himself from constraints. "That's better. That's a world better."

"And you weren't even wearing a corset. I am grateful I haven't had to march through the city in mine, I will admit."

"I am not sure how you are still walking. All Eddie can do is complain about his feet, and he's in sensible footwear. You're in heels."

"It's astonishing what people will learn to accept if they feel they don't have any other option." Maxine looked up at the ceiling. "Zadok…what happens tomorrow?"

"Pardon?"

"Vlad has led me to believe this jaunt around the city ends tomorrow. He has referenced that the hunters will abandon me in this city. You have hinted at the same. What are you both plotting?"

"Do you really wish to know?"

"This time, yes, I think I do."

Zadok shrugged. "As you wish. Tomorrow, I will reveal that Bella is our prisoner and has been for two days. If they agree to leave us and this city in peace, we shall return Bella to them unharmed."

"I cannot imagine Mordecai will agree to that."

"It will not happen, so it does not matter. Eddie will wish to take the deal. Alfonzo will not. He is too caught up in his

Curse of Dracula

desperate need to destroy Dracula to turn away now. It will be what fractures them in half."

Maxine sighed and shut her eyes. "You're right."

"I am a manipulator and an illusionist. This is my game. And with Vlad's assistance, I fear they stand little chance." Zadok leaned his head back and rested it on her arm. There was no need to pull away from him. It was a friendly gesture, little more. She had enough reasons to loathe the man; she did not need to take insult where there was none meant. It was clear he was accustomed to being near to others in a way that she was not. "And then, I fear, comes your part to play in tomorrow's affairs."

"Which is what?"

"We will tell them that the only way they will be allowed to make forward progress into our Master's city is if they leave you behind. The boy will chase after Bella and try to free her. The old fool will hunt down our Master alone. They will both die."

Maxine shut her eyes and knew he was very likely correct in his assumptions. Zadok was, for all his faults, a strong judge of a person's character. He had played the role of Bella flawlessly for two days and skillfully hidden his lie from the two men. And her predictions were, sadly, the same as his.

"You do not wish to argue? To fight me and claim that they shall do the right thing? That they could not possibly be so foolhardy in their selfish needs?"

"No. I have nothing on which to base such opinions. I dread what may become of them, and I may hope you are wrong, but it is merely that—hopes alone. And I have long since learned that when it comes to predicting human nature...optimism is worthless."

"I am glad to end this game. I tire of the charade. Now it

is simply boring. But I do have one opportunity for entertainment left, do I not? I won our bet."

"I never did honestly agree to any of this."

"Oh, come now. Don't be such a sorry sport. Besides—you could rip my soul from my body if you find me so repulsive, no?" He nudged her arm, and when she looked over to him, he was holding up his hand to her. "Where is the harm in it?"

"The harm in it is quite simply this—if I tear out your soul, a piece of it remains within me, forever marking me like a scar. I would have to suffer with a bit of you inside my mind for the rest of my life."

"That explains why you do not simply run about destroying everyone who annoys you." Zadok cringed then grinned. "But mine will not be so much of a scar as it would be a beauty mark, no? Think of it—a little bit of me, following you about wherever you go. How wonderful."

She rolled her eyes. "Why, Zadok? Why put yourself at risk? I cannot imagine you are so curious as to why Dracula has become interested in me that you would put your own eternal existence on the line."

His expression darkened, and he lowered his hand with a sigh. "If he dies...if he truly dies? If you rip him to pieces because you decide he is not worthy of life? Then I will be left alone. I suppose it is possible that I could die as well—all of us, our eternal plague—might fall apart without the source at its head. I think I would prefer that to the alternative. To abandonment."

There was an ache in his words. A hollowness that struck her. She reached out and placed her gloved hand on his shoulder. For all his showmanship, he was terrified. She could sense it burning away like a fire. It was a childish kind of fear. One that cried out for someone to come and make it right. A lonely kind of thing, desperate for an embrace.

He was afraid of being left alone. Dracula was his family.

"I want to know why you're *worth it*."

Maxine took off her glove and offered him her hand. "I will do my best not to destroy you. I am sorry if I do."

"I am not so fragile as those mortal things you killed." He smiled, an expression that did not reach his eyes and left him looking sad more than anything else. "And if I am, then enjoy carrying a piece of me around with you, I suppose." He took her hand.

His touch was cold like Vlad's.

Then it happened. His soul was touching hers.

She pulled in a breath and shut her eyes as his memories crashed over her.

"*Get up, sewer rat!*"

A foot met his ribs. He tasted blood and dirt in his mouth. It didn't matter. He didn't have much else to taste. This time he did not feel a crunch when the foot met his midsection like he did the previous week. He grunted in pain and spat the viscous liquid that pooled under his tongue, bitter and hot.

"*Get up! It's no fun if you don't fight back.*"

"*Stop it, Robin.*"

One of the older boys—one of the stronger ones—reached down and yanked him up from the ground. The world tilted and moved violently as he was pushed. He reeled, crashed into a pile of crates in the warehouse their little pack had taken up residence in. The wood constructs rocked and teetered, but he was much smaller than they were.

He was smaller than most of the other boys, even for his age.

The older boy—Girard—marched forward and glowered

down at him with his best attempt at looking authoritative. "What've you got to show for your day?"

He was supposed to have gathered and stolen. Pickpocketed and lied to bring back a haul for the others. But it had been a terrible day. It had rained throughout the entirety of it, and the markets were bare of the foolish aristocrats who kept their belongings tucked in the easily pilfered outer pockets of their coats.

Zadok could only shake his head. He had nothing. He had come back emptyhanded.

And that was a sin.

A sin he had to pay for.

"Then you know what happens." Girard sneered as he undid the fly of his pants. "Turn around, sewer rat."

This was his punishment. He deserved this. It was better than being alone.

Anything was better than being alone.

He turned and bent over the crate. This was not his first time being scolded in such a way.

He doubted it would be his last.

"No! Don't leave me—please, please don't—" he cried as he watched the carriage roll away. He chased it, tripping over himself. His aching ankle, sprained from the beating he had been given, was useless. He landed in the dirt and the muck and the ruts left behind by the wheels of those with money and privilege.

How he wished to be like them.

Fancy. Rich. Clean. Popular. Beautiful.

But he was a servant. An orphan. A homeless man who had scrubbed pots and risen through the ranks of the local lord in an attempt to secure himself some manner of safety, of security, of family.

The lord's daughter had taken a shining to him. He did clean up well, she said. She had brought him to the garden one night, pulling him along by the hand, and had begged him to touch her. She had spread her legs, rolled up her skirt, and displayed herself to him like a fruit on a branch, begging to be tasted.

And so, he had.

And the lord had found out about it when she was with child.

She was to be taken to a local doctor to "dispose of the infection." When he had screamed and raged over the destruction of a life that belonged to him, as well, the lord had seen him beaten low and driven to the middle of nowhere and left for dead.

To rot.

To ruin.

Perhaps he should die like this. In the gutters and the dirt where he was born.

It was dark when he heard the wolf howl in the distance. The moon was high in the sky when teeth tore into his throat. Not those of an animal—but those of a man. Cruel and harsh. He thought he had desired death to greet him. He thought he would welcome it with open arms. But standing there at the precipice, he fought back. He wanted to live. *He wanted to fight for each new breath as the one that followed might be denied to him.*

His fervor caught the monster's attention.

A bloody wrist was proffered to him, and he drank from it greedily.

It tasted like home.

Ash. *That was all he saw. Ash. Not the room, not the note upon the dresser, not the others standing about him weeping for their loss.*

Only ash.

His Master was gone. The sun still streamed from the

curtains, pooling on the carpet, painting it in shades of blue and black. The fire that had consumed his Master had done great damage to the thick and expensive covering.

Numbly, he walked to the desk and picked up the note that lay upon it. He did not read every word. He did not need to. He knew what it said.

It expressed sorrow, reluctance, but a need to go. A lack of desire to keep living. It was what notes like these all said. It was empty of real meaning and real regret.

Zadok crumpled the note and left to pack his things. His Master was dead. His family was once more gone. But there was another, an eternal one, whispered in lore and legends and spoken of even amongst their kind like the King of All who Died. A dangerous and powerful thing who had been denied true death long ago.

He would find this King of Vampires.

And he would kneel at his feet.

He would find a home that could not leave him. Someday. Somehow.

MAXINE SNAPPED out of the visions with a gasp and sat up. She was shaking like a leaf. Those visions and more crashed through her mind. A life of loneliness, of fleeting pleasure both taken and given, and a life of seeking a place to belong.

Her heart was pounding in her ears, and it took her a long time to steady her breathing. It was only then that she looked to Zadok, wondering if she would find him empty-eyed upon the floor, staring up at the ceiling only never to see it again.

But he was not a shell of a creature. He was crying. Silently, tears of crimson ran down his cheeks. Vampires could cry, it seemed...and they did so in blood. It was only fitting. She slid down onto the floor beside him and, reaching up her bare hands, slowly brushed the tears from his cheeks. She did not care for how they might stain. She reached out and gently gathered him into her arms. Wordlessly, she pulled him into an embrace.

He sobbed, all tension fleeing him as he chose to lie in her lap. She stroked his hair slowly, shushing him. Trying to do what she could to soothe his pain. Pain she now understood firsthand.

If she killed Dracula, he would be alone again.

"I am so sorry, Zadok..." she whispered. "My platitudes are vapid and bland, I know. There is little to be said for things that have been suffered. There is little condolence to be said to those whose lives have been like yours that does not feel insipid. But I am here, and I...I am sorry."

His yellow eyes shut, and he lay there in her embrace, his fingers curling into the fabric of her skirts like a child hugging a pillow. They stayed like that for some time in silence, with her gently stroking his hair.

He pulled in a deep and wavering breath before letting it out in a rush. When he spoke, his voice was haggard and strained. "Thank you. I understand now."

13

Bella was lounging against the headboard. She had pillows arranged behind her, but she was sitting upright, thinking over the creature who was lying half in her lap like a giant cat. Mordecai—the incubus, a thought that still seemed to hitch her thoughts every time it occurred to her—was asleep. His head was in her lap, horns and all, and he was draped over her right leg.

His tail had wound around her ankle several times, holding on to her as if that part of him was concerned she might wander off. A tail, with its jewelry at the end, that seemed to have a life of its own. He swore it acted of its own whim and on instinct most of the time. She now knew in a very personal sense. Oh, the terrible things he had done with it during the night made her cheeks grow warm. The terrible and *wonderful* things he had done.

She began stroking his rakish, unevenly cut blond hair. It looked like someone had tried to cut it with hedge sheers, but it suited him all the same. Slowly, she kept stroking her fingernails gently along his scalp. The gesture had lured him

Curse of Dracula

to sleep, and now it seemed to be doing quite a good job of keeping him there.

She was touching him like a lover.

We are lovers.

She had taken him into her body willingly. She had been the one who had climbed into bed with him. He had not coerced or blackmailed her. He had merely pointed out the faulty reasoning behind her adherence to her shame. The darkest thing he had done to convince her to sleep with him had only been to point out that she had no reason to feel guilty for it.

That wasn't to say that what had followed had been innocent. Not in any shape of the imagination. Bella had been free for the first time in her life—cut loose of all the expectations of the world around her. For all her life, the whispers of the desires of others had stung her psyche.

Be a better orphan.
Be a better woman.
Be a better hunter.

But not with Mordecai. With him, she could simply be. He put no expectations upon her. He seemed utterly grateful to receive whatever she might pay him, kindness or otherwise. And she decided she was unwilling to treat him poorly.

He was so attentive. So intuitive. He knew what she wanted before she did. She supposed that was his instinct, after all. She smiled faintly. He was an incubus. A demon of lust sent to prey on the weakest part of mankind.

It could all be a trick. He could be seducing her slowly, seeking to make the moment he finally devoured her lifeforce the moment he also shattered her heart. But there he was, lying—rather undignifiedly, she might add—in her lap, hugging her leg like it were a stuffed toy and he a child.

He was smiling in his sleep.

He was *happy*.

And it was because of her that he felt so.

It made her smile as well. She knew she shouldn't enjoy him. He was a demon from the pits, and she was a hunter. She was sworn to rid the world of things like him. *But I was not taught the whole truth. That they can love. That they can wish for families. That their lives might have meaning beyond the death and ruin of mortal men.*

She had been like this for a few hours, if the muted toll of a church bell nearby was any indication. She spent the entirety of it lost in her thoughts and the slow, repetitive movement of her fingers through his hair.

His horns were fascinating. They did not dig into her enough that she cared overmuch. She gave up stroking his hair to run her fingers over one of the ridged black curls. There was writing etched into it, as if it had been carefully carved there. It was a language she could not fathom. One she had not ever seen before.

A demonic tongue, she was certain.

He mumbled, snuggled into her harder, clutching her leg to his chest, and buried his face into her lap. With a whine, he uttered something that might have been vaguely English. "Dn'stop…"

She went back to stroking his hair. He purred in contentment—actually *purred* like a giant cat—and rolled half onto his back to give her more room to pet him.

"You are ridiculous."

"An' you like it." Again, he slurred it so badly in his half-sleeping stupor that she nearly missed what he had said altogether. He yawned loudly, stretched, and draped his arm over her legs, clearly caring little for how much room he was occupying. He clearly liked to take up as much of it as he possibly could.

"I take it you slept well?"

"Haven't slept that good in…mmmh…don't know. You?"

"Not much, I'm afraid."

A single purple eye opened to look at her. "Then I didn't fuck you hard enough." It slipped back shut. "I guess I shouldn't be surprised. I wasn't trying to make it as good as I could. I was trying to be nice."

"Nice?" She shook her head in disbelief.

"I was being a shining knight. I was damnably chivalrous."

That made her laugh, and she squeaked as he pulled her down to lie on the bed next to him. He was cuddling with her again, but this time with his head resting on the pillow of her breasts. "I was your King Arthur last night."

"I think you have been reading the wrong myths."

He grinned. "You're wonderfully naïve if you don't think Arthur ever fucked a girl up the—" She slapped his shoulder, and he broke off his elicit speech with a grunt. "Fine. You and your silly bashfulness. We'll cure you of that yet."

They fell into companionable silence for a long time, before she had the urge to speak again. "Mordecai?"

"Mmh?"

"What's your favorite color?"

"Purple."

"What is your favorite food?"

"Strawberries."

"How old are you?"

"Three hundred and twenty-seven years old." He finally lifted his head, one thin eyebrow lowered as he scrutinized her. "What're you doing, angel?"

"We do not know each other. You claim to love me, and I…know nothing about you. I am trying to rectify that."

"With a list of facts."

"Yes."

"That I could write down for you."

"Yes?"

He sighed heavily and lowered his head. "Mortals. You're a stupid lot, you really are." His tail curled around her leg, higher up on her calf than before. "I enjoy moonlit nights on the black sand beaches of Urn'ala, a precinct of Hell. I love tiger lilies, but flowers make me sneeze in general, so I observe them from afar. I keep cats as pets. What else would you like to know about me, oh glorious comptroller, tax collector of my life?"

"Have I offended you?"

"Oh, hardly. I'm amused." He grinned and placed a kiss to the swell of her breast. Her face grew warm. "If this is what you think love is, I am more than happy to play the game."

"I am twenty. I think my favorite color is blue."

"You aren't sure?"

"I've never really thought about it."

He snickered. "Then why did you ask me?"

"I don't honestly know. I thought it was what a person is supposed to know about their lover." She looked up at the ceiling and furrowed her brow. "I find this all very confusing."

"Lover. We are lovers now?"

"I think the last few nights have been quite clear to that effect."

He grinned and stretched over her again, nearly preening himself in his obvious pride. "Lovers. A good first

Curse of Dracula

step. Keep talking. Tell me this checklist of your life. I will take it all with joy."

"I do not much care for flowers either. I think it was because I was never raised with them."

"Oh?"

"I was an orphan. I moved from home to home until one night a band of vampires set upon us. Everyone died, save me. When they came for me…that is when my gift first manifested. I tore one of them to shreds with every last piece of broken furniture I could lift with my mind. The others fled. Alfonzo heard my tale and came to speak to me. I joined up with him, for I did not know what else to do. I did not want to live my life in an orphanage only to be sent to the streets."

"You and Zadok have something in common, then. He was an orphan too, or so he says. I am sorry."

"Thank you." It was an odd thought to have something in common with the blond vampire she had met briefly and mostly in battle. She wondered if she would meet him again on different terms.

She wondered a lot about her future. She did not know what it held for her, but she knew with whom she might want to spend it. What a dangerous thought. She tightened her grasp on him, and he answered it in kind. He turned his head to kiss her collarbone. It made her smile. He likely meant it as an innocent gesture, but the effect it had on her was anything but. "I too love strawberries."

"See? We are meant to be. Destined lovers from the stars for our shared love of red fruit." He held her like he loved her. Really loved her. Perhaps it was not her body he was trying to claim after all.

Perhaps it really was her heart he was after.

She wondered how long she could pretend she had not already given it to him.

―――

MAXINE'S DREAMS WERE QUIET. She barely slept, to be fair. She stayed there on the floor with Zadok, holding him, gently stroking his shoulder. She had put her gloves back on, afraid that too much contact with him might weaken her control. His soul was more substantial than those of the mortal lives she had accidentally destroyed, but hardly as firm as Vlad's. She worried that if she touched him for too long, she might tear him to pieces without intending to.

Finally, he stood and, placing a kiss atop her head, walked across the room in silence. He seemed lost in his thoughts. He retook the shape of Bella, and, nudging Eddie to wake him to take his turn, the vampire lay down to pretend to sleep for the rest of the night.

Maxine had then shut her eyes. She only knew sleep had come for her because Eddie was gently shaking her arm. "It's morning, Maxine. We've got to go."

It was time for all this to end.

In a strange way, she was relieved. She hated this endless wandering—this purgatory within which she had been placed. It would be a relief to make forward motion, even if it was into disaster.

The hunters allowed her to use the water closet to relieve herself before they departed. She ran some cold water through her hair and over her face to try to straighten herself out a little. She assumed Zadok would not wait long before revealing his game.

Maxine and "Bella" were the last to step out the door and down the stairs to the street. The huntress stopped her

Curse of Dracula

with a gentle hand on her gloved wrist. Turning toward the other woman, she watched as Bella took her hand and lifted it to her lips. She placed a gentle kiss atop her knuckles. It was a masculine gesture—one of the few times she let the act slip—and it was a tender one as well.

"Be strong, empath," Zadok-Bella whispered. "He needs you to be strong."

And with that, the moment was over, and the false huntress was once more the giddy young girl, smiling proudly and bouncing down the stairs to the street, holding Maxine's chain in her hand. With a shake of her head, Maxine could do little more than follow.

"You were right," she said quietly to the illusion as she walked behind the pack of hunters. "I think I would have been happier not knowing what was to come."

The blonde girl flashed a cunning smile over her shoulder. "That makes me two for two, hum?"

"I suppose so."

Regardless of which turns Alfonzo chose to take, or which alleyways he decided to duck down, it did not matter. They never made progress. The streets were always the same. Repeating again and again, connecting to each other in nonsensical and impossible ways. It was truly a nightmare. But whose, she could not say. Dracula's, or theirs?

She supposed it did not really matter.

It was around one bend that Alfonzo drew his sword and held it in front of him. Eddie drew both his pistols. Finally, they were not alone.

More or less.

Zadok—an image of him, at any rate—stood in the center of the street facing their way. Ghouls were crouched at his back, jaws dripping ichor and gore as they clung impossibly to the walls of nearby buildings like a spider might do. The hungry creatures gnashed their teeth.

They were all a lie. Even the monsters.

As was the vampire who stood at their lead. "Greetings, hunters! Have you been enjoying my Master's hospitality?"

"Fuck off, demon," Eddie snarled and lifted a gun and pointed it straight at Zadok.

"Now, now, don't be so hasty." Zadok lifted his hands in a false show of harmlessness. "I have only come here to negotiate."

"Uh-huh." It was clear Alfonzo did not believe him. Nor did he have any reason to. "You've come to negotiate only because we're getting closer, aren't we?"

"Hardly," Zadok said through a lopsided smile. Malice and amusement glittered in his yellow eyes. He held all the cards, and the poor men in front of her had no inkling of how much danger they were really in. "Well. If you *two* hunters have not been enjoying my Master's grace, I know of *one* who has."

"You can turn around and—" Alfonzo paused. "Two?"

The illusion of Bella at her side melted away. Before Maxine could warn the two hunters, Zadok stepped forward, a dagger in each hand, and sliced Eddie's back with one and Alfonzo's arm with the other. He cackled and vanished as Alfonzo whirled to swing his sword through the vampire.

Gunfire rang out, but Eddie's shots met empty air.

"Where...where is Bella?" Eddie whirled around. "What have you done with her? Bella!"

"Shout all you want, mortal, she cannot hear you." Zadok appeared again, standing in front of them.

Eddie raised his guns again, but Maxine interrupted him. "Save your bullets. He's another illusion."

Curse of Dracula

"Come here and face me!" the young man shouted, his voice cracking in panic. "Where is she?"

Zadok laughed and shook his head, as if beleaguered by the tantrum of a child. "First, no, I will not face you both. I would be a fool to do so. You are not a threat to me by benefit of your stupidity, not your lack of brute strength. And second, she is nowhere near here. She has been gone for days."

"What?" Alfonzo took a threatening step toward the illusion before he growled, realizing how pointless it was. He pressed a hand to the bloody slash on his arm. Zadok could have killed them both if he had wanted to, but Maxine knew he was under orders to leave them alive to suffer. "You're lying."

"Am I?" Zadok was nearly preening himself. "What say you, Maxine?"

The two hunters turned to her, and her face grew hot. Of course, the vampire would not let her stay out of this. "I... he's right. Bella has been gone for over two days."

"And you said nothing? We had a viper in our midst, and you said nothing!" Alfonzo reeled toward her, lifting his fist as if to clock her again. She staggered back. "You are a traitor, Maxine. To us and to humanity itself! I should kill you here!"

"If I told you and I revealed his game, Bella would die. I wished to keep her alive!" She took another step away from the irate hunter. "He cannot lie to me, any more than any of you. I believe his threat."

Alfonzo snarled and whirled back to the smirking illusion of the vampire. "Set her free!"

"And that is why I have gone and revealed my little game, however wonderful it's been having a chance to get to know you all." He sneered. "My Master extends to you a bargain which I am sure you will understand is quite generous. One that will only be good this once. Leave this city. Turn back now. Abandon your crusade for retribution against Dracula, and Bella will be free to return to you unharmed. We will leave Boston with Miss Parker and relinquish our hold upon this place."

Alfonzo snarled. "Never. I will see his evil driven from this world. I will not rest until he is in the grave! She can destroy him, and I will see it done."

Zadok rolled his eyes and looked over to Maxine with a perfect expression of "I told you so" on his sharp features. He turned back to the hunters. "Do you not wish to discuss it?"

"Al. Al we *have* to save Bella. We should take their offer," Eddie begged.

Alfonzo shook his head. "They're lying. They'd never give up this city. Even if they do, they'll go on to another. We have an opportunity here that I cannot let pass. We stay. We fight. We'll save Bella another way."

Eddie ran his hand over his face. "But…Al. This is asinine. We've walked for days and made zero progress!"

"Then go!" Alfonzo shouted at the younger hunter. "Leave if you are too much of a coward to do what needs to be done. I will take the traitor"—he jabbed an angry finger in the air in her direction—"and I will put a stop to this once and for all. I will make sure she tears his soul from his chest like she should have when she had the chance. I vow to God above I will see it done!"

"You will not make one more step of progress in this city unless my Master allows it, Alfonzo Van Helsing. This city is his domain. He is the only god in this place. Take the bargain, you foolish mortal. Take Bella and leave this place with your lives."

"Al, we should listen to him—"

"Shut up, Eddie!" This time it was the young hunter who met Alfonzo's fist.

Eddie fell to the ground, clutching his head with a groan. Maxine knelt to help him stand back up, holding him steady.

Zadok *tsked* and shook his head. "Very well. Then know this—the only chance you will have to move forward is if you leave Miss Parker behind. The Master has his own plans with her, and they do not involve you. If you wish to seek out your revenge, you will only do so if you release her."

Alfonzo shook his head. "You're baiting another trap. I won't fall for it."

"How many weeks do you want to uselessly crusade around in circles? Hm? How many until you run out of scavenged food and die? We have not even bothered to send beasts to slow you down. We have not needed to. Your rage is impotent, and you know it." Zadok shrugged. "He is willing to let you test your mettle against him…if you abandon the empath."

"She is the means I have of destroying him once and for all. No."

Zadok laughed. "If you want to give her the opportunity to judge him, then leave her! Do you not realize what will happen once you do? She will return to his side, where he wishes her to be. If she deems him worthy of destruction, she may do so."

"She cannot be trusted to do the right thing. She claims to love him."

Zadok *tsked* and shook his head. "You would make her destroy the man she loves in your need for revenge?"

"It isn't revenge."

"Mmhm." Zadok shook his head. "The fact remains as it

was, hunter—leave her, or go not a single step closer to your goal. That is all."

Alfonzo growled and clenched his fists at his sides. He rounded on Maxine. She staggered back, trying to keep distance between them. But it was no use. He was faster and moved with purpose. He grabbed the front of her coat in his fist and dragged her up to him.

"Careful, hunter," Zadok warned. "I am allowed to kill you under one condition—if you threaten her wellbeing."

"You can try," Alfonzo replied even as he glowered down at her. "You listen to me, Maxine. That man is a *demon*. He might as well be Satan himself. Look at all the horror he has created—all the death and suffering." He fished a key out of his pocket and undid the locks at her wrists, letting the shackles and the chain drop to the ground with a loud clatter. "I need you to do the right thing. I need you to."

She nodded weakly. "I will strive to do what is right." She was no more free than she had been a second prior. She had only traded her chains for another more ephemeral set.

There was no use telling him that she was not quite certain what was right or wrong anymore. The line between justice and injustice had become blurred of late. But it seemed to satisfy him enough that he shoved her back from him with the flat of a palm to her chest. She had to scramble to keep her footing.

"Go. Be his harlot. When I find him and whatever has become of you, I will make sure you watch him die."

"Now who is the monster here?" Zadok sighed drearily. "Go, Maxine."

She looked to Eddie and tried her best to smile. "Be safe, Eddie. I'm sorry."

He nodded. "You too. Good luck."

She turned her back to the two hunters and began to

walk. It wasn't even ten feet away when something rumbled in the ground. When she turned, she discovered a wall had appeared behind her. She took a step back and looked up at it in astonishment. This place truly was alive.

And it served Dracula.

She shivered at the cold mist that clung to the air around her. The city was deathly silent. She did not realize how comforting it was to have someone with her—even Zadok and the two hunters—until the exact moment she no longer had them.

Until she was alone.

A clock somewhere chimed one. She shut her eyes. Dracula would come for her at midnight. Until then...she knew not what else to do. He wanted her to witness this place that dwelled inside him.

And so...she walked.

14

Eddie scratched the back of his neck, his nerves on end. Alfonzo was pacing angrily around the middle of the street. The illusion of the foppish asshole vampire was still standing there, watching them with a smug smile. A giant wall had rumbled up out of the ground and cut them off from the empath. Whatever was going to happen to her, he prayed she would be all right. She didn't deserve this shit.

"Your way is now opened. You may proceed." The vampire bowed and extended an arm out to his side. "Oh! I nearly forgot." He straightened. "You will find Master Dracula has taken up the city's library as his new fortress. But dear, sweet, charming Bella is not there. She is in the North End, at the antique church that sits near the hill's peak."

"Why would you tell us this?" Eddie narrowed an eye. "Why would you help us?"

"Two reasons. One, I enjoy watching you idiots get yourselves killed. And two...I was told to." He flashed a fiendish grin accented by pointed canines that were a little too long to be normal. "And with that, I bid you *adieu* for now. Ta!" He vanished in a swirl of smoke and was gone.

"Good. We know where we're going now." Alfonzo started walking.

"Al…I think the North End is that way." Eddie pointed off in the other direction.

Alfonzo hung his head and sighed. "We need to stop him. If we stop him, she'll be safe. If we go to her first, we might lose our chance."

"What chance?" Eddie threw his hands up in frustration. "What the *fuck* chance do we have, Al? None! We've been up fate's asshole this entire goddamn time. I'm not going to that library without her. I'm not."

"Then go save her!" Alfonzo rounded on him, and Eddie backed up, afraid he might get punched in the head again. Being socked one by the older hunter was not a comfortable sensation in the slightest. "Go. I can kill him on my own."

"Can you?"

"Yes."

"How're you so sure?"

"Because I have. Because I *can't* give up." Al shook his head and turned back to walk the direction he had been going.

"I need to save Bella. I…I love her." Eddie knew it was childish, but he didn't have a choice. If he knew he had left her there to rot, he'd never forgive himself.

"I know. Go. I don't care."

Eddie stood there for a long time and watched in silence as Alfonzo walked away and left him standing by himself in the center of the street.

He was alone. For about a second. It was a moment later that he heard a howl from the distance. The monsters were coming for them now.

He sighed and swore quietly. "Yup. Makes sense, I guess. Can't make this easy, huh? Nope. Nope. Why not? Fuck you, Eddie, that's why." He checked the ammunition on his guns and adjusted the strap on his rifle. His rifle wouldn't run out of bullets—enchanted and all—but his revolvers weren't so lucky.

Cracking his neck, he walked in the opposite direction that Alfonzo had gone.

"I'm coming, Bella. God help me, I'm coming."

THE CITY WAS SILENT, save for the sound of Maxine's heels on the cobblestones. She could sense creatures in the shadows, watching her, but she couldn't see them. She could only feel their eyes on her. Their curiosity. But none came close nor ventured up to her.

None dared.

She wasn't quite sure if it was the threat of Dracula's wrath that kept them at bay, or if it was her own strange and inconvenient manner of self-defense that she had in her touch. It was likely both. She tucked her hands into her pockets. She was glad to be free of the weight of the iron links around her wrists, though. She was happy for that much.

The city changed around her, finally breaking out of its repetitive pattern of the same buildings looping over and over again like a zoetrope. Now, the horrors were new and fascinating once more. The twisted buildings and bizarre adaptations of a city she once called home were eerie, but there was a strange grace to them.

"So, *you're* the one who's caused all the fuss."

Maxine stopped and turned. A woman was sitting on a

Curse of Dracula

fence nearby—perched too perfectly on the thin rail to be human. Her ghastly pale skin and unnatural green eyes were another clear indication of what she was.

By God, she was beautiful. Perhaps one of the most stunning people she had ever seen in her life. Chestnut hair curled around her face in perfect waves. Maxine blinked, a little shy about herself as she looked at someone who she knew could have stopped streets—or toppled cities. "Hello."

The woman smiled. It wasn't an entirely friendly expression. "And he's left you out here now for what reason, precisely? The hunters are gone and have abandoned you as he said they would. What is his foolish game *this* time?"

"He said he would come for me at midnight. I think he would like to give me one more chance to see his handiwork." She glanced to a pile of bodies that lay stacked up by one wall. Judging by the smears of blood on the pavement, they had been placed there to clear the street. But by whom, she was not certain. Likely the vampires. She had not seen a single other living human since Dracula had taken the sun away. She gestured to the corpses. "Such a talent as it is."

The woman laughed. "I do love those with dry humor." She slipped from the railing and walked up to her, her emerald dress chosen to match her eyes, no doubt. "I am Elizabeth." She held out a white-silk gloved hand.

"You must go through a great deal of those." Maxine motioned to the woman's hand before taking it with her own in greeting. "White must be terrible for vampires to maintain."

The woman laughed again, and this time it was more genuine than the first. "Indeed. Oh, indeed. Come. Let me walk with you for a time. I would like to know my new sister."

"Sister?"

Maxine could do little but go along for the ride as Elizabeth hooked her arm and began to stroll up the street with her like they were two childhood friends on a promenade in a park. As though the death around them were nothing more than daisies and poppies sprouting from the earth on a spring day.

"I suppose if I were to be literal, you might be my new aunt." Elizabeth smiled wickedly and laughed at Maxine's look of abject disgust. "I do not mean it literally! I prefer to refer to those around me like family. It annoys Walter to no end. I think it disgusts him a little."

"You are a bit insane, aren't you?" Maxine surmised.

"Indeed. I'm sure I am. I think we all are, to a certain point. After living long enough, I'm not sure we have much choice."

"How old are you, Elizabeth?"

"I was born in 1590. I am only three hundred and some-odd years old, believe it or not."

"Only?"

"Zadok is older than I. And Walter is nearly a thousand years old. And no one can quite fathom how old Dracula might be—not even him."

Maxine looked off thoughtfully. "There was sand, and sun, and stone…I think he calls his origin from Egypt or Babylon." She tried to hold on to the memory she had pulled from the mind of the vampire. But it was fleeting like the smoke of a candle drifting through her fingers. She shut her eyes and considered the imagery. But she could see a statue, carved from stone and adorned in gold. It had the head of a jackal upon the shoulders of a man. "No. It was Egypt."

"Oh, my…you *are* what Zadok has said." Elizabeth let out a breath. "Well. I'll be certain not to touch you, then, hum?

Curse of Dracula

The last thing I need is for you to tear my soul to smithereens."

"It seems to me that there is a direct correlation to the age of the soul and my likelihood to accidentally destroy them. I managed to touch Zadok without harming him."

"Was it his idea, or yours?"

"His, believe me. Do you think I would willingly fish around in that madman's head? I ran the risk of having to carry a piece of him inside me for the rest of time. Hardly anything I would seek willingly."

Elizabeth smiled, and the hungry expression in her features faded. It was a real smile that she paid Maxine this time. "Touché, sister. Touché. Whatever did you find in there? I expect a bunch of abandoned sex toys and dust."

Maxine laughed despite her better instincts. The woman had a clever wit about her. "No. I'm sure there is some of that. What I found was more tragedy than I would have expected. I suppose that is the way of everyone who seems a monster at first blush—there is always more lurking beneath the surface."

"What do you mean?"

"I am not sure I should be telling you of his history. It is personal."

"Come, now, what's the sanctity of his past to you? He is nothing but a fiend. Besides...we are to be friends, are we not?" She nudged Maxine in the side gently. "What did you find?"

"He seeks to fill his bed because he does not know how else to matter to someone. He seeks to calm a fear of abandonment." She eyed Elizabeth curiously. "I think you refer to the others, myself included, as kin for the same reason. To feel as though you belong."

"Clever. Very clever. I won't deny it." Elizabeth shrugged

a shoulder idly. "I serve Master Dracula not because I swear fealty to him. I barely even respect the distractible tyrant. I serve him to be around others. Being as we are is…very cold, Miss Parker. Very cold and very lonely. Most of the terrible things our kind is prone to do are out of the desperate need to fill that void."

"Such is what I am coming to learn."

"Save for Walter. I think that frozen bastard enjoys being the way he is."

Maxine smiled, honestly enjoying the conversation with the lady vampire. "No. He simply wants for peace and quiet. He cares not how he gets it. He tires of being responsible for everyone else's madness. Perhaps if Dracula and the rest of you were not always devolving into destroying whole cities or playing games with humans like they were children's toys, he would not glower as much as he does."

Elizabeth hugged Maxine's arm to her chest with another laugh. "Oh, I adore you, Maxine! To think of how much fun it will be to gossip with someone who knows what goes on inside the heads of those around her."

"I am not a psychic. I do not read thoughts. Only emotions."

"Good, then you hear past even the lies that someone speaks to themselves. Even better."

"I suppose."

They walked in silence for a moment among the ruin of the city. Now she could see creatures atop roofs, crawling along the slate and copper on all fours or on their canted back legs. They looked like demons, and they were watching them both. "Do they mean me harm?"

"Yes and no. Some mean any living thing harm. But you? You are an exception. Dracula has made it very clear that anyone who comes near to you with any ill intent will have their insides rearranged and suffer a long and painful death. And the rest? The more sentient types?" She hummed thoughtfully to herself. "No. No, I do not think they do."

"Why not?"

"Now having met you, I think I come to know why Dracula is so obsessed with you as he would turn down this wonderful new chance at paradise." She gestured with her palm up in a wide arc at the city around her. "We have the opportunity to farm a great deal of cattle for ourselves, and he would throw it all away for you. But if you can see into the center of all of us, I can see why. I do not agree, mind you. But I understand."

"What do you think he should do?"

"Snatch you up, take your mind and body until you profess your undying love for him in every breath, and give us the empire we vampires truly deserve."

"Well…I will give you credit for your bluntness."

"You did ask." Elizabeth smiled dryly.

"My mistake."

"You are a smart woman. There is a sharp intelligence that burns behind those beautiful eyes of yours. I would hate to see them grow glassy and empty. I am sure he feels the same. No, he wants to win you of his own accord, sister."

"He has gone about it in a superbly backward fashion." Maxine shook her head. "Abducting me and destroying this city in hopes I might still love him when all is said and done? It's nonsense."

"Then you know him quite well!" Elizabeth laughed again. The vampiress was wont to do that frequently. Now that it was not harsh and vindictive in quality, Maxine did not mind so much. "You must look at all the world like a game. To him, we are all but pawns on a board. He does not care if he loses this match or any other, for he must simply reset the game and try another. Indeed, sometimes I do think he enjoys losing. You have seen the expanse of his power. He could rule this world like a god if he wished it."

"And why does he not?"

"I was hoping you could tell me."

Maxine went quiet for a moment and let out a long breath. She pondered the problem for a while. All the world was a game to him. A game he could never willingly stop playing. "I think he is curious if the hunters might be able to end him, once and for all. He told me once that he wishes for me to either kill him or obey him. I do not honestly believe he has a preference either way."

"Walter said the same." Elizabeth grunted. "Damn. I hoped he was spouting out of his asshole again. But it seems not. Maxine, I will be blunt—I have no desire to die. If you destroy him, it might end us all."

"Or it might not."

"I do not wish to take that chance."

"I cannot promise anything, Elizabeth." She looked out at the city, and could only imagine the survivors hiding in basements, or being torn out of their houses. "How many are dead?"

"A fourth of the city is now either our food or become like us."

"Twenty thousand…" She blanched. She felt sick. She had to stop walking for a moment and pushed Elizabeth away from her gently so she could move to lean on the side of a building. "And what of the rest?" She was afraid to ask, but she knew she could not hide from what had come to pass. Their fate was her responsibility.

"They are either still cowering in holes or have been taken into our care."

"Your 'care?'"

"If we kill all of you, what will we eat?" Elizabeth smiled sweetly, sympathetically, as if she truly regretted her words. Maxine knew she wasn't being sincere. There was an emptiness to the woman's heart that troubled her.

"How compassionate," Maxine muttered and shook her head. She was developing a headache.

"I am hardly that. But if you are in the mood for sympathy, I think I would like to take you to see a friend of mine." Elizabeth motioned her to come back over to her. "They are not far."

"They?" She furrowed her brow as she allowed the vampiress to take her arm again and lead her down the street. "You said a friend, singular, then referred to them in the plural. Which is it?"

Elizabeth chuckled knowingly. "Both."

Maxine raised an eyebrow at her.

"Oh, you'll see." Elizabeth squeezed her arm in a hug. "You're going to be *so* much fun."

If only Maxine could find the strength to believe that.

BELLA WASN'T QUITE certain how long it had been since she had managed to climb out of bed for longer than twenty minutes. She could blame it on Mordecai and his *impressive* stamina and needs, but she knew she was equally at fault.

She had not once told him no. She had not once pushed him away. When she woke up from slumber to find them tangled together, with him firmly cuddled into her, it made her smile.

"I think perhaps we should come up for air soon," he said through a yawn. "We can go rustle up a proper meal and eat it in the courtyard. I would say we could eat it in the sun, but, well…" He snickered. "The red moon'll have to do."

"I figured that this was my prison."

"This is my room. And you aren't my prisoner. You're my ward until this mess is all settled." He rolled over and stretched languidly. He really was quite feline in his movements. He had a contented, sated, broad smile on his face as he draped himself out as large as he could be.

There is no other reason a creature could be so beautiful and not be by design. But it wasn't only his body she was beginning to enjoy. It was his goofy smile. It was his easy laughter and his playful sense of humor. It was all of him.

But a darkness still hung over her. "I am worried for Alfonzo and Eddie."

"Mmh…Right." He sighed and sat up. He stretched his shoulders again before turning to look at her. There was remorse in his eyes. "About that."

"Oh, no…Please, no, tell me they aren't dead."

"Well, then, there's good news?" Mordecai smiled sheepishly. "They aren't dead, although they probably won't survive this. Master Dracula does not forgive something like what Alfonzo did, and Eddie is probably on his way here to try to 'save' you."

"Alfonzo did nothing to Dracula that I did not also do."

"You didn't punch Miss Parker."

Bella went quiet for a moment. "I told him that was stupid."

Mordecai laughed and flopped over her to kiss her. When he finished, he was smiling. "You're adorable."

"We are talking about the death and murder of my friends."

"You're still adorable."

She shook her head and placed her palms on his chest

Curse of Dracula

to push him away. He went up to his knees willingly, and she climbed out of bed. Her clothes were somewhere—oh, yes, there—and his offer of fresh air and more food than what he could carry in on a plate for them was welcome. It was halfway through dressing before she realized he was sitting on the edge of the bed, watching her with both fascination and something close to worship in his eyes. Her cheeks went warm, and she focused on lacing up her dress. "Am I going to have to choose?"

"Hm? Between what?"

"You and them."

Mordecai stood and approached her. Mid-stride, a long loincloth appeared on him. It was black with blueish purple archaic writing threaded into it—the same that was carved into his horns. She didn't have much time to think about it before he had pulled her into his arms.

He held her tenderly. This wasn't—for once—about pleasure. This was about comfort. He nuzzled her hair, kissed her temple, then rested his head on hers. "Thank you, Bella."

"For...what? What did I say?"

"You implied there was a choice to be made. That you might...even struggle with it, should it come down to your old friends or me. That is a greater gift than I could have ever asked for, my angel."

She blinked. He was right. She hadn't even realized what she had said. She rested her head on his chest and felt his chin atop her hair. He was so warm. He smelled like spices and that comfortable scent of a wood fire. "I don't want to have to choose."

"I know. I know it's cruel. But...life is terrible. I understand you want to save your friends, but there's nothing we can do. They chose these paths for themselves. Alfonzo could have spared this city. He could have saved you too, but he picked his hatred instead. Eddie could turn away now and leave the city unharmed, but he will not relent until he frees you."

"What...?" She looked up at him, fear clutching at her. Fear and shame. If he found her like this—with an incubus—what would he think? "Does he...does he know?"

Hurt washed over his beautiful features. "No. He has not been told with *what* you now spend your time. I'm sure if he was told, he would not believe the words. He would claim that you are too good of a person to fall prey to such a monstrous thing as me." He let go of her and stepped away. He looked so wounded.

"I..." Her heart ached. No. It was more than that. It was as though she had been stabbed. It was as though his pain was her own. She was no empath like Maxine, but the look on his face and the way his shoulders slumped twisted in her stomach. "Mordecai."

He turned away from her, his head down, and he ran his long, sharp, black nails through his hair, scratching at his scalp. It ruffled his already messy blond hair even further. "If he comes for you, you will go to him." It was a statement of certainty. The betrayal in his voice stung.

She didn't want to hurt him.

She tried to force herself to picture how it might all play out. Eddie would come for her, burst into the room, and riddle Mordecai with bullets. The incubus would lie dead at her feet. She would take her friend's hand and let him lead her from the darkness. They would seek out Alfonzo and either save him or be too late.

But then what?

She allowed herself to presume the likely impossible

feat that they would defeat Dracula and save the city. The light would stand victorious.

But then what?

Would she be expected to marry Eddie? To be with him simply because she *should*? Because that was what was *expected*? Perhaps have his children and live "happily" ever after? Could he live with what she had done with the incubus?

Could she live with the memory of him? Of how happy she had been in his arms?

The image of her with Eddie felt cold. It was empty. It was a lie. It was imprisonment, like the promise of spending her life in a cage. A gilded cage, yes, but one constructed around her all the same. Its bars were all the things she "should" be. That she "should" do. All the expectations placed upon her by the world and those who dwelled within it.

And she knew that every day and every night she would be haunted by dreams of him. Of Mordecai. Of the creature who had left such an indelible imprint on her. Not only on her body—that was undeniable—but on her heart and her soul.

"If he comes for me, will you try to stop him?"

"Not if you wish to go." Mordecai shut his vivid purple eyes. He hung his head, accepting his fate. "If you wish to leave this place with him, I will ask him to kill me. I cannot live my life knowing the only soul I have ever loved has chosen to love and fuck another."

She smiled faintly. She knew how to cheer him up. "How, exactly, am I supposed to be with Eddie now that I know what it's like to *fuck* a demon?"

He whirled, his eyes wide in shock. Not only because she had finally said that ugly word he had been goading her into using, but also because of what she said. "Bella?" He was clearly caught in disbelief.

She stepped into him and, reaching up, took his horns in her hands and used them to force his head down to hers. She kissed him. Passionately. Roughly. She shut her eyes and let herself take from *him* for a change. He moaned and wrapped his arms around her to hold her close. When she was done, she rested her head on his chest and closed her eyes. She had no words for him. Not yet. She needed a little more time.

He seemed to understand and only held her, not pressing for more. Well, he wasn't pressing for more. Something against her stomach, meanwhile, was. "We should go get food and fresh air now before I throw you over the table," he grumbled. "Although I'm happy either way. Actually, do you want to pick the table? I could go for the table."

She laughed. "Later."

"Promise?"

She kissed his cheek. "Promise."

15

Maxine had no way to describe what she was looking at besides "magical architecture." There was no other way she could fathom how a thatched hut that looked like it might have come from the bayous of the deep south might have found its way into the frog pond in Boston Common.

A hut with what looked like lightning rods extending from the top. It was not simply a crude structure. In fact, the back half looked like a modern building with all the typical bricks and mortar. It was as though the two had been somehow meshed in ways that made little logical sense.

What manner of creature lived here?

It seemed she was meant to find out. Elizabeth stopped at the end of the winding wood plank pathway that stretched from the shore to the stairs of the strange amalgamation of a building that stood at its center. "Go on, then," the vampiress urged her. "Go speak to some of Dracula's loyal subjects."

"Why have you brought me here?"

"If you only see the corpses of our victims, you might think us to have no redeeming value, hm? That is what the hunters have hoped. But perhaps if you lingered for a moment with some of those who serve him of their own accord, you might find reason to spare him."

Maxine shook her head. The vampiress was only doing this for her own ends. But she saw no harm in going to speak with whomever dwelled within. "I hope they do not mind an uninvited guest."

"Oh, they will not mind you at all, I promise." Elizabeth curtsied to her. "Now if you will excuse me. I do feel a little peckish." And with that, she exploded into bats and swarmed off into the sky.

Maxine flinched as she did. That would never not be alarming. Shaking her head, she looked at the strange twisted building. It was like two buildings had tried to overgrow the other, and neither had won. She could not say she was not more than a little curious. She walked across the planks, testing them with her toe before putting her weight upon them. The pond was not a deep one, but she did not exactly want to wind up spending the rest of the evening soaked to the bone in the unseasonably cold air.

Climbing the stairs to the porch of the merged structure, she reached out to touch the doorjamb. The wood of the bayou structure transitioned smoothly into the carved, clean lines of stone. She could not identify exactly where one began and the other ended.

She shrieked as the door flew open.

"Come in! Come in, come in, sweet one." It was a man's voice who greeted her. Deep and gravelly, but warm. "No need to linger. No need to lurk."

"I was doing neither of those things. I was just..."

"Trying to understand that which you can't hope to reconcile with your eyes alone. Come, sweet thing. Come inside. It's warm in here."

Curse of Dracula

Being warm would be quite a nice change of pace. They hadn't dared burn a fire in the house where they had taken up residence. They had not wished to risk it. But she could smell the fire burning inside the strange building, and the idea of thawing her chill bones by it was too much of a temptation to pass up.

She stepped inside, and her jaw immediately dropped open in surprise.

The room was utter chaos.

It was filled, top to bottom, with *things*. Bowls and pots, spoons, dried herbs, dried flesh—she could even make out a few leathery objects that looked like they might have been skinned heads hung up to dry. Animal parts mixed with more human remains as if they were all the same to whomever mounted them. Some of it was tied into bundles that looked like they were prepared with express purpose. She recognized them—maybe not for their exact mixtures, but for their purposes. Magic.

But mixed with them were vials and glass jars, containing objects pickling in liquid she could not begin to identify. Spools of copper wire mixed with gears and pulleys. Beakers and Bunsen burners were scattered about. For every ounce of black magic that seemed to fill the space, it was matched in equal measure by science.

There was a figure standing by the fire, having retreated into the room to stab at it with a poker to kick up the flames. He was looking at her.

But he was facing away from her.

He was doing both at once.

Maxine froze, gaping. Not understanding what she was seeing. There was a face on the back of the man's head. Indeed, there was a body *facing* her, bent in improper ways like a suit he wore over his back. It was the face of a pale man, with a close-trimmed goatee and glasses. His eyes were closed. Yet the posture of the man was facing the other way, stabbing at the fire.

"Don't be frightened, sweet thing." The other half of the man turned to her, and she drew back reflexively.

There was another face on the other side. Another whole man. At the edges where the two met was black cording, holding together flesh like one might sew a canvas sail.

This one's skin was dark, his smile broad and easy. He was cleanshaven, but his hair hung around his face in thick braids. She recognized his accent now—Creole. She had been to the deep south once or twice in her travels with the Roma. A few escaping slaves had even joined their band. She had always loved their way of speaking.

But the warmth and friendliness of his smile did not distract from what she saw before her. Elizabeth's words suddenly made sense. Why she had spoken of one person but used "they" in reference.

There were two men, stitched together.

"My God…"

"No god here, sweet thing. No god worth listenin' to, at any rate. Mine only jabber, and they'll take little notice of you. Come, come, don't be frightened of the old Witch. Come." He waved her over and gestured to a chair by the fire. There were two. "Tea? Yes? You folks love your tea." He gestured to the back of his head and grinned lopsidedly. "Would you prefer to speak to him first, hm? Is it the color of my skin that gives you pause?"

"No, it is the fact that it appears you are two men cobbled together into one body that I am reacting to, sir. Sirs. Nothing else."

"Forgive me, forgive me. Never can tell with folks. Come, sit. Please. And no, no sirs are here at this moment. He is a sir," he pointed again at the back of his head with a jab of his thumb. "Not I, not I."

Maxine hesitated, and he gestured broadly again at the chair. Not knowing what else to do, she walked to the chair cautiously and sat in it. It was comfortable, and the fire was indeed warm. She did not know what to say. "Elizabeth—"

"Is a vicious cunt."

She laughed at his bluntness. "I would not have gone that far."

"Then you don't know her well yet." The strange creature in front of her was now plucking a pot off the fire from the hook on which it dangled. He walked to a kettle on the table and poured the water into it. He began to scoop some leaves out of a jar and into the hot liquid. "You must be Miss Parker."

"I fear I do not know what to do with this sudden fame."

He snorted. "The cunt dropped you here, why, exactly? The bones did not say."

"You are a soothsayer?"

"I am a witchdoctor." He cackled in a joke she did not understand. He turned to look at her, and smiled again, lopsided and goofy. "Get it?"

"I'm afraid I don't." She smiled back even if she did not understand.

"Witch"—he pointed at himself—"Doctor." He jabbed a thumb at the dormant face on his back. He laughed loudly as a look of understanding must have washed over her. "You are such a sweet thing. Poor girl, caught up in all this mess." He gestured at the room, but she knew he meant the city. "Master Dracula has not been kind to you."

"I think he has tried, for what it's worth."

"Sometimes that's all a person might ask." He cracked his neck, and it crunched loudly. She winced at the sound.

"Mhn. He wishes to come say hello. He says I am mucking up the tea."

He shut his eyes, and she shrank into her chair as he… changed. Every bone in his body seemed to crack and shift as the front of him became the *back* of him. Going from hunched in one direction, to perfectly straight, to suddenly facing the other way. Eyes behind glasses opened and met her with a faint and polite smile. He tugged on his suitcoat and bowed his head to her. "My lady."

"I…forgive me, I do not usually swear in English, but I feel I must in this moment. Holy *shit.*"

The gentleman smiled and stroked his hand over his hair, smoothing back the braids and looking all the world like a courtier of some fine gala if it were not for the simple fact that he had *another man stitched to his back.*

"It is quite all right. I understand. You are handling our unique condition better than most, I must say." He turned back to the teapot and sighed. "The Witch means well. He was simply ruining the tea." Picking up a spoon, he fished out some of the leaves from the hot water. "He does not understand the concept of subtlety. Too many leaves in the water will make it unpalatable. My lady, how do you take it?"

"I couldn't possibly bother you to—"

"Please." The gentleman looked back at her with a gentle and sad smile. "Entertain a lonely Doctor." He placed his hand to his chest.

She stammered for a moment before trying again. "With honey, if you have it. If not, sugar will be more than fine."

"We have plenty of honey." He walked across the mess of a room and opened a pantry. Fishing through jars, he pulled one from a stack of others that looked far less inviting. She hoped it was indeed honey and not some other terrible liquid, but the amber tone gave her hope.

"May I ask you a question?"

"Of course! Do not be shy."

"It is quite personal."

"The best questions are."

She smiled faintly. "How is it that you've come to be this way? I have never seen nor heard of anything quite like…you."

"Ah, yes. Well, you will find many of us with terribly unique afflictions serve Master Dracula. We are limited only by his imagination, I believe. And you can't begin to fathom how troubled a mind he owns."

"I am beginning to suspect."

"I suppose you are." The Doctor stood there, looking down at the tea, waiting for it to steep. "How did we get to be the way we are? I fear neither of us were left whole enough by death to exist apart. He took two souls, broken and destitute, shattered and empty, and…we did the rest. The Witch and I are one because we chose to be. We were not forced into this arrangement. Without the other, the one would die. We were joined by a common plight."

"Which was?"

"Persecution. He for his magic and the color of his skin. I for my science. They really are one and the same, you know —magic and science. One is simply the other without all the hypotheses to back it up." He waved his spoon idly in the air, then placed a strainer over one teacup and began to pour the liquid into it. It steamed in the warm air. He poured the second cup and spooned a glob of the amber substance that she sincerely hoped actually was honey into each glass. Placing a small spoon into each, he walked over to hand her one.

"He did not kill either of you?"

"No. We died in close enough proximity to him that he collected us." He sighed. "His curse extends to far more than him. He spreads into the ground and air around him in wide swaths. Anything within its reach is subject to become part of him. We died—each of us at different times, mind you—and lingered in the ether until we could form together as one."

"I'm afraid I don't quite understand." She looked down into her glass of tea. She stirred it, and it did smell wonderful. And surprisingly normal.

"It's quite all right." He stirred his tea, the silver spoon tinking against the porcelain. "Think of it this way. Dracula is a tree. And from him grow the branches, and the leaves, and the fruit. But a tree does not support only its own life and its own progeny. It provides life to the birds, the squirrels, the ants, the bees, and more. We are drawn to that tree, and without him, we would die."

She sipped the tea. It was honey. *Thank God.* "The metaphor helps greatly. And the tea is lovely. Thank you for your hospitality, Mr..."

"Doctor. Call me Doctor. And he is Witch. That is all." He smiled, a gentle expression she would have expected from any highborn man. But there was true kindness in his eyes. A softness she would not have expected. "I spent my life in the pursuit of science—real science. The kind that might save the world someday. The Church did not agree with my work. They called me a heretic, a demon worshipper, and a monster. They burned me at the stake." He grimaced.

She flinched, feeling the sting of the rope herself. The Doctor was remembering his pain and shared it with her. "I am so sorry."

"You are, aren't you? You can feel it."

"Yes, sir. I can."

"Then I am sorry to have thought of it. It is not your burden."

"All the burdens of others are mine to share. Such is the nature of my own affliction, I fear. And again, I say I am sorry for what you have suffered. It was needless cruelty."

He shrugged a shoulder. "Humanity is its own downfall. No one else is to blame for their plight. Ignorance is their greatest sin."

"And what of him? Of Witch?"

"He died with a rope around his neck. He was dragged behind a horse by a white man who feared his arts, thinking them the same as my science. Men will see demons in any shadow they do not understand."

"That is true. My mother...my mother felt the same."

"There is compassion in your eyes, Miss Parker. Compassion that only comes with real understanding. You were rejected because of what you are, yes?"

She nodded.

"By your own mother." He sighed and shook his head. "You are not the first, and I fear you will not be the last." He cringed, his face scrunching up in a strange expression like a twitch of some kind before it smoothed. "The Witch sends you his condolences. And that your mother was several foul words I will not care to repeat."

She laughed. "Tell him I appreciate the sentiment."

"He likes you very much, Miss Parker. And the Witch is an excellent judge of character. Tell me, why is it that the Lady Elizabeth brought you here?"

"In hopes that I will come to see more facets of Dracula's curse other than the bodies he has left strewn around the city I called home. She hoped I would speak to one of his 'loyal subjects' and come to know another side of him."

The Doctor let out a long sigh. "Yes, yes. Very well. Hold on one moment." He set down his tea, stood, and once more she watched in disgust as his body crunched loudly, joints popping in and out of place as the two of them switched places.

He turned around, and the Witch slumped heavily down into the chair, nearly upending his tea. He had to scramble to catch it and grumbled under his breath. "Always leavin' things in stupid places." He sipped the tea, blanched dramatically, and set it aside. "I don't put that many leaves in there because I don't know what I'm doin', I do it because I like things with real flavor."

Maxine couldn't help but laugh, if a bit nervously.

"It's disgustin' to watch, I know. We're sorry." The Witch smiled at her again lopsidedly.

"It's all right. It isn't your fault, I suppose."

"I suppose some of it ain't. But some of it is." He shrugged. "Could have gone on to the afterlife. Didn't. Stayed with him. With Vlad. Tell me, girl, do you love him?"

"I fear I am not certain. How can one love someone who does such terrible things?"

"And so is the question you must come to answer. You do love him, then—you just do not know how to do it." The Witch sat back in his chair and reached for something on the table behind him. It was a brown glass bottle of something she could only assume was alcohol. He picked it up and swigged from it, setting it down on his lap. Even their clothes were sewn together to match the appropriate man, back-to-back as they were. "He comes to us for advice, from time to time. Other times he comes to play cards. To drink tea. To drink barley wine." He picked up the bottle briefly.

"And what is it you two...three...talk about?"

He cackled at her correction, his eyes glinting in amusement. "He speaks of the world. Of his place in it. Of wanting."

"Of wanting what?"

"Everything that matters." He leaned forward and set his elbows on his knees. "You know what I mean."

"Life or death. He wants one or the other." She sighed. "And it rests with me to give it to him."

"So it seems, sweet thing. So it seems." He leaned back and took a deep gulp from the bottle. "Here's what I will say to you. He is only human."

"He is hardly that. He—"

"Ah, think about it." He lifted a finger, cutting her off. "He has lived more life than any of us. But what has he known in all those years? Life. Death. Suffering. Love. Happiness. Sorrow. Grief. He is the most human of all of us, I would say. He collects those haphazard vampires around him because he wishes to salve the loneliness he feels. They do the same. Even Walter, though he loathes to admit it, needs to feel like he has *family*. A purpose. A place to be. That is what he is to all of us. A home for those who can find no other."

"What of the homes he has robbed of those who now lay dead in the streets, or cowering in the shadows?"

The Witch stroked his hand across his face thoughtfully. "He is human. And humans are so rarely benign, eh? They take and keep, they kill, they fight, they conquer. His creatures—we creatures—must eat. The tree pulls nutrients from the soil, and the weaker things will die. He shadows the ground around him, and no other saplings will grow. He kills to eat. Mortals kill for much worse. And in much higher numbers. Look at the war that split this country."

She shut her eyes and sighed. "I suppose."

"It is the nature of the deaths out there that you find so troublin'. Men do not find themselves often hunted by monsters. But if this were a war—man against man? Have you seen what that looks like?"

"I have witnessed what war can bring."

"Then tell me this, sweet thing. Tell me this looks no different save for that the creatures who are doing the slaughterin' do not wear human faces. Tell me their cruelty is not matched by the generals who left boys lying in ditches to rot. Tell me this is worse at its heart, more rotten in nature, and I will believe you."

She paused for a long time. She sipped her tea. She put it down in the delicate porcelain saucer that looked so out of place in a home like this. Looking into the fire for a moment, she finally smiled. It was faint, it was weak, but it was there.

She could not find the means to argue with him. "He is a warlord."

"And what is more human than that, I ask you?"

She smiled sadly. "Well said, Witchdoctor. Well said."

16

When Maxine left the side of the Witchdoctor, it was many hours later. The Doctor had taken over to offer her food, apologizing for the bad manners of his other half. She had gladly accepted, and with the warmth of the fire and the conversation, she lost track of time. Both men were fascinating to talk to, and the "three" of them chatted until she heard the clock of Park Street Church toll out that it was eleven-thirty in the evening.

"Ah, we should not be keepin' you." Witch pushed up from his chair. "As lovely as it is to have you keep a fool like us company. Tell me, Miss Parker, have I helped you make up your mind, I wonder?"

"You have. But perhaps not in the way you had hoped."

"How so?"

"You have reminded me of who he is and that I should treat him as such." She stood from her chair and walked to the door. "But you are correct. I should be on my way. It has been lovely to speak with you—both of you—and I am happy to have met you."

"And us, you, sweet thing." He reached out a large hand,

and she shook it with a smile. The longer she was in his presence, the less horrifying his double-sided body became. Perhaps that was the case with all of Dracula's creations. They carried their sins on the outside for all to see.

Perhaps it was a more honest way of going about their lives.

She bid him—both of them—farewell and walked from the amalgamation of a building across the wooden planks and back to the grass of the common.

There, she saw Elizabeth leaning on a tree with a faint smile. "I was planning on introducing you to many others, but it seems you and the Witchdoctor became fast friends."

"They accomplished your goal well enough."

"Good. Have you decided not to destroy him?" Elizabeth pushed away from the tree to join her as Maxine walked down the cobblestone path toward Tremont street. She did not know where exactly she was going, perhaps to the fountain by the underground rail station. But she supposed it did not matter. It would be midnight soon enough, and Vlad would come for her.

The thought was both frightening and exciting all at once. It must be par for the course with the Vampire King.

"Well?" Elizabeth prompted at her silence.

"Not quite. But I am reminded quite keenly of how I should approach this particular dilemma."

"I would ask for details, but it seems you are in an enigmatic mood this evening. Very well." Elizabeth shrugged and opened a parasol—why she bothered, Maxine did not know. There was no sun or rain. Only the crimson moon hanging full overhead. For the style of it, she supposed. She was a creature of vanity; that much was clear.

Maxine shook her head. "Forgive me. I am distracted inside my thoughts."

"I do not think I can fault you for that. But tell me this, Miss Parker. Do you love him? Truly?"

She nodded in response. "It remains to be seen how I can allow myself to accept that fact."

"I think you shall do the right thing, either way." Elizabeth smiled.

"Alfonzo urged me to do the same. To seek the righteous path. The issue remains that I am not quite sure I can distinguish what is 'right' and 'wrong' at this point in time."

"And so you have discovered the crux of all our lives. Do you think I wished to spend eternity drinking blood to survive? Do you think I wished to rely on my gifts for manipulation and deceit to seek happiness? No, dear sister. I had dreams of another life once. One with love, and family, and joy. Instead, I find only coldness. The only warmth I enjoy comes by taking it from others. What is righteous in my life, then? Nothing? Should I commit myself to the damp soil as so many of us have done out of desperation to end it all?"

"No. I do not think so."

"Judge him, and you judge us all, sister. Remember that."

Maxine looked up at the fountain at the Park Street station. It had once been a beautiful wrought-iron creation featuring Greek gods and acanthus leaves, pouring water into the pool below. It rose some twenty feet in the air.

Now, like everything else, it had changed. The gods had become demons and angels paying equal violence to the figures of screaming mortals they held in their clutches. It was a warning as much as it was a promise—*this is what awaits all who linger here.*

With a long breath, she sighed and sat on the lip of the fountain. She was not surprised to see it no longer poured water, but blood. She supposed that was to be expected.

"I will leave you with your thoughts, then. He will come for you soon. Goodbye for now, sister." A white gloved hand settled on her shoulder. "I do hope we might become friends."

Maxine smiled back to the vampiress and nodded once in reply. And, with that, Elizabeth once more took to the skies as a swarm of bats.

Just in time for the clock to begin to strike.

Midnight had come.

This sucked.

Eddie knew he was sulking. He didn't care. He was putting holes in monsters and fighting his way, tooth and nail, to the North End to save Bella. Alone. But he also knew he was doing the right thing.

Wasn't he?

Part of him wondered if he shouldn't have listened to Al and helped to kill the vampire. Strength in numbers and all that. But he was too worried about Bella to much care what happened to Dracula.

He loved that girl with all his heart. He would follow her to the ends of the Earth or the end of his life. Whichever came first. But it gnawed at him to split from Al.

"This was your own stupid idea," he mumbled at himself. "Don't blame anybody but yourself for this."

He scratched the back of his neck. His fighting and walking went on for hours, until he heard a child weeping. A little girl was crying, just like his sister so many years ago. He shuddered, swore, and knew this was likely all by design. He walked down an alley and into the side door of a building in search of the source of the sound. A nightmare

Curse of Dracula

played itself inside his head—the sight of his little sister, turned into a hungry vampiric beast.

When he entered the room, it was mirrored before his eyes.

A little girl was hunkering in the shadows of the room. Her arms were thrown over her head, and she was sobbing. That kind of unabashed weeping that only children could do. The color of her skin, a ghastly grayish blue, revealed her to be as he feared. Her sundress was stained in old, aged tones of crimson as her blood was already drying.

If that was all hers.

When the little girl turned to look at him, he saw the red ringing her mouth. Gore dripped from her lips and down her chin.

No, it was not all hers.

"I killed everybody," the girl whined.

The confession made his heart hurt. He pulled out his weapon and thumbed back the hammer, aiming his gun at the child. "I'm sorry. I'm so sorry."

"Please…I'm so hungry. It hurts."

"It won't hurt anymore."

Bam.

One bullet. Straight to the brain. The little girl slumped to the ground. It was not long before she began to burn, like some vampires did when they died. The fire was going to spread and consume the house, if not half the neighborhood. He sighed yet had no need to extinguish the blaze.

He turned and saw four bodies lying in the room next to where he stood. A mother, a father, and two other children. Each devoured as if by a wild beast. The little girl had murdered her entire family in her mindless hunger.

It was right to let them burn.

To let it all burn.

He walked from the house and pulled his hat lower over his eyes as he walked away from the smell of charred flesh and fabric. He wondered if the whole city would catch fire now. He decided he did not much care.

It was all doomed anyway.

Maxine stood from the fountain and brushed herself off. The toll of the bells counted out as she waited for what was coming. She shut her eyes and tried to steel herself. She had not seen Vlad in the waking world since the hunters chose to forsake his offer and trade her for the city. The poor city.

What she would not do to turn back the clock that was doling out the time. What she would not surrender to spare the city the fate it had suffered. What she would not do to ensure that it went no farther.

Perhaps…even destroying the creature she had come to love.

The tolls reached their end. Twelve.

"Hello, Maxine."

A chill ran up her spine. Deep and resonant, it carried easily without trying. She turned to find him standing nearby, dressed in his long black peacoat and a crimson vest. He looked as intimidating as he ever had. The King of Vampires. The Master of the darkness that had taken the city. The dread warlord.

Her dread warlord.

He reached his hand out to her, palm up, pale skin tinted red by the light of the moon. He silently beckoned her to him with sharp-nailed fingers.

And she was helpless to deny him. For many reasons, most of all being that she simply did not wish to. She walked to him and slipped her hand into his. He smiled faintly and drew her close.

He banded an arm around her to pull her flush to his chest. The smell of roses washed over her, and his proximity and touch instantly made her feel as though she were lost in him. Red velvet and black silk. Hunger and passion. Need, and the lust for life and death. It was as though she were lost in the very night sky itself.

And as his form and hers exploded into a sea of bats, she was.

When Maxine once more found her feet on solid ground, it was no longer cobblestone, but marble. The ceiling overhead was vaulted in a classical style that was rare in the city. Glancing around, she blinked. The walls were covered with books. Rows and rows of them. The piece of furniture that seemed to be the outlier was a small table in the center of the room. A white tablecloth was thrown over it, and it was carefully prepared for two.

It was the new library, lauded for being a monument to learning. She had been inside its walls only once before. Now it seemed the vampire had taken it for his own purposes, which apparently included a meal with her.

Her cheeks went warm at the memory of the last dinner they had shared, and how it had ended. With her sprawled out on a tabletop tomb, his teeth in her neck, and her deeply wishing for more.

"My poor thing." Dracula sighed from where he stood next to her. He took a step away from her to shrug out of his long black peacoat, placing it over a hook by the wall. He was still well-dressed in his thinner jacket, and no less intimidating. "I have not been kind to you."

"It is not I to whom you have been cruel." She pointed out at the city through the tall window on one side of the room. "It is Boston and the thousands of its now-dead souls to whom you owe an apology."

He shrugged. "I suppose." He walked up to her, closing the distance between them. "I have not destroyed it." He lifted a hand and gently trailed his knuckles over her cheek. She shivered. "It will be restored to its former qualities once we depart this place."

"It matters not to me that you have decided to treat the city like a melted wax model and rearranged it to your dark designs." She took a step back, unable to handle his nearness. It was as unsettling as it was alluring. "It is not for the buildings I mourn, Count Dracula. What of those who lie dead in the street?"

"Those lives shall remain spent. Humans will spawn and replenish their numbers like weeds, as is their nature."

"I do not know how to forgive you for them. Or your callous dismissal of their meaningless part in this world."

She drew back, but his hand caught her wrist before she could retreat any farther. He pulled her gently back toward him. He lifted her hands and removed her gloves. Carefully, he pressed her palm to his cheek. Crimson eyes closed, and he leaned into her touch. The hardness in his expression softened. "I know, Maxine."

There was sadness in his voice. Regret. She sensed it, along with the rest of his emotions. Beneath the hunger she always felt from him, there were others flickering in the darkness. Determination and resolve. Curiosity. Grief. Then there was something strange. Something truly unexpected.

Hope.

Crimson eyes met hers, although he did not release her hand. "Yes. For the first time...in thousands of years...I have hope. And it is you who have brought it to me."

She could do little more than whisper. "Then let me

Curse of Dracula

fulfill what it is you wish for. But I cannot do it while you hold this city hostage."

"We have discussed why I will not negotiate with you for this city. We will leave, but not until my revenge on the hunters is complete. And not before you can look at me without sadness in your eyes once more." His other hand slipped to the back of her neck, and he pulled her another step closer to him. A moment later, he kissed her forehead. He held it for a moment before stepping away and gesturing to the table, already decorated with trays of food. "Join me. Please. I do not wish you to suffer." He paused at her incredulous look. "This has never been about torment. Not yours and not the innocents who have died, at any rate. Only the hunters should pay for their actions."

He pulled out her seat, and she obediently took her place as he pushed it back in. She waited for him to pour them each a glass of wine and take his own chair. He gestured that she should help herself.

And so, she did. There was no need to deprive herself for the sake of her wavering morals. No one would win in that regard.

He waited until she had taken a bite out of a savory pastry before he sat back in his chair and began to speak. "You spent the day in the presence of one"—he corrected himself—"two of my dearest friends. What do you make of them?"

"They were kind. Wise. They did not deserve the fates that befell them. But I saw what they had drying on the walls around them. They have succumbed to the cruelty that was paid them and have decided to add to it."

"Indeed. As you might find with all who serve me. My army of the damned. Shockingly few of them are vicious purely by nature. Even then, perhaps insanity could be blamed." He shut his eyes, and a weight appeared to settle over him. Something deep and intrinsic he must carry at all hours bared itself in his features. He looked...tired. Weary.

"Then stop this. You have me, do you not? End this rampage and let us leave. Take us to the wilderness as you offered to the hunters."

"Do you not understand the inevitability of what I am? Of what I mean to this world? The lives I have taken here in this city are nothing compared to those I leave in my wake."

"I may have been naïve before, but no longer. But I ask you, then, what would you have me do? Look upon the river of blood you have made of the Charles and inure myself to the suffering of those you have killed to fill it? Would you have me forsake my compassion for them, my desire to see them spared? What part of my soul would you have me kill to do as you ask? Would that I could, Vlad Dracula, I would do so. I would give you a shattered piece of me to keep you company if I could rip myself asunder in such a way."

He flinched at her words. "That is not what I desire." He sighed. "Forgive me. You are defined by your compassion. To rid yourself of it would be to diminish that which I have come to adore. I have asked you to love me in full. To deny you the same rights is beyond even my capacity for callousness."

"Then what would you have me do?"

"Do you love me, Maxine? Even still? And do remember our accord. We shall speak no lies to each other."

She pushed up from the table and paced away, needing space. She put her head in her hands. "You believe that if I am to know you and choose to love you, you may find... what, exactly? Redemption? Purpose? The chance to stave off the inevitable emptiness that—"

Maxine let out a startled noise. Not because of his

sudden movement—she was quite accustomed to the abrupt comings and goings of the creatures around her. It wasn't even the noise she made that had cut off her words. The source of her interruption and her wide-eyed surprise were one and the same.

He was kissing her.

From nowhere, he had appeared and stolen her lips with his, tipping her head back to ease his approach. It took her a moment before the shock wore off and she placed her hands to his chest. She went to push him away but was reluctant to do so and stopped.

He has killed thousands in the span of only a few days. He is a monster. He will continue to destroy the world around you simply to prove a point.

But the loneliness that was eating at his soul, burning away beneath her hands, kept her in his embrace. Not only that it existed, but she could sense how much she eased that pain. Her hesitation was long enough that he draped an arm around her, pulling her tightly to him, never breaking the kiss. He knocked the legs out of her resolve in a single moment.

When he finally broke away from her, she was breathless. Her eyes had shut, and she kept them like that for a long moment before looking up at him. There was a mild, tender look on his hard features. Hardly the gloating she had expected.

"I never figured myself a weak individual," she murmured. "Yet here I am."

He crooked an eyebrow down at her. "Weak, how?"

"I should despise you. I should rail against all that you have done. I should condemn you for the murders you have committed. I should seek to destroy you, as the others wish me to. But..."

"But?"

She shook her head and gently pushed out of his arms. He let her go and did not do anything to stop her as she walked away from him to move back to the table. She was in need of wine. Picking up the glass, she finished the third of it that remained in one go and poured herself another from the bottle that sat on the table. She heard him chuckle, and she smiled despite herself.

"Perhaps it is my gift. My empathic disease." She sighed and took a sip from the glass. "I can hear what echoes in your soul, and I am drawn to it. When I am near you, I cannot escape."

"I know."

"Stop this madness, Vlad. Stop the death and destruction."

"No. Not until the hunters have been punished."

She shut her eyes and hung her head. Then she had an idea. "If the mass death is not what you seek to accomplish, then let the living leave the city. Call a temporary cease of aggression. Give them a day to evacuate. Many foolish souls will stay, enough for you to adequately make your point and to feed your hungry creatures."

"Clever." The word was spoken close to her, and she turned to look up at him. He appeared at her side, and his hand was tracing through her hair. "Very clever indeed." He grinned. "So quickly you learn."

"If you wish me to judge you fairly, then...be fair." She turned to face him, placing her glass down on the table. "Give me something to weigh on the scales across from the tragedy you are clearly able to wreak upon the world around you."

"Am I not enough?" His voice was a playful purr as he leaned down to kiss her again.

Curse of Dracula

She pulled away so she could speak, teasing him. "That remains to be seen."

He grazed his lips her cheek then wandered to her ear. "Very well. You shall have your ceasefire, clever negotiator."

"Your friend reminded me with whom I was dealing—a warlord."

"Hmm...dangerous words. There is little more that I have come to desire than the joy of conquest." His breath was tepid, but warmer than it had been but moments before. She ran her hand to his neck, finding his pulse thumping beneath her touch.

There were only three things that brought a vampire's heart to tempo. Lust for flesh, for violence, or for blood. She would hope he was not in the mood for the second of those, but the other two were likely equally matched. Her heart lodged in her throat.

She should deny him. She should push him away. She should refuse his touch. If she did, she knew he would back away. He was many things, but he was not a brute. He would not pin her down and force her. He sought to make her *want* him. That was his prize upon the battlefield, and he was an ancient and practiced captain.

"In the morning, the sun will rise for one day and one day only. The living will be told to leave this place. If they remain, they are fair quarry. I shall give you this, my darling Maxine Parker. But what shall you give me in return?"

Heat rushed to her face so fast that she wondered if she had burst into flame. "I..."

"Do you not desire me?" He slipped his hand to the back of hers and pressed her touch firmer into his warming skin. "Is this such a loathsome price to pay?"

She did want him. Oh, she very much did. "That is not the issue. You have laid siege to the city of Boston. You have killed thousands. Whether or not I desire you is of no importance."

He pulled his head away from her so she could see his victorious grin. "Oh, but it is." He stepped into her, forcing her to take one backward. She bumped into the backrest of a chair, and she was caged by the enormity of his frame and the wood object. "It is of great importance."

"I—" She struggled to keep her voice a normal pitch. She swore at herself for how childish she was. How weak, how careless. She should be crying at his feet. Instead, she was nearly swooning each time he touched her. He was terrifying. He was exciting. The combination should not be as attractive as it was. "Am I always going to be losing debates with you?"

"Now you are cross with me."

"No, I would simply like to prepare myself for the future, should I live that long."

He laughed again, a real and mirthful sound. He stroked his hand over her hair. "If I have my way, you will live long enough to lose many such debates with me." He crooked a finger under her chin and tilted her head up. His lips ghosted over hers once more. "I can be gentle. Do you fear that I will hurt you?"

Her response came out as little more than a breath. "No. But I am afraid."

"I will not take from you that which you do not wish to give. You desire my body. You asked me not to let you die a virgin, did you not? Let me fulfill that wish."

"You say it as if you do not stand to benefit as well," she murmured, feeling her resolve weakening. He was everywhere around her. His touch, his emotions, his power, they wrapped around her like a cocoon. There was no escaping him.

And that made her want him even more.

"Hardly. I must confess something to you. Something I think you may already know." He took her hand and placed it over his heart, and she felt the beating tempo. His gaze was smoldering, lidded, watching her with an intense hunger and passion. "I have loved many a soul in my long years. But never have I known anything like this. I need you, Maxine…"

17

His words echoed in her mind. She knew he meant that he needed her more than in just a physical sense. She knew he meant it far deeper than that. She had brought him hope—the first he had known in thousands of years.

Oh, how she loved him.

He kissed her. Slow and passionate, it drove all doubts from her mind. He teased her lips, urging her to reply in kind. She was helpless to fight what rose in her like a tide. Her hands were tangled in his vest, and she chased his lips with her own. He slipped his hand to cradle the back of her neck, holding her as he deepened his embrace. Soon it became more demanding—harsh and bruising. With a flick of his tongue against her lower lip, she parted for the invader and let him take her mouth the way she knew he wished to take the rest of her.

She was the spoils of war this night.

And she wanted to be.

Beneath it all was the current inside him, pulling her deeper. When she let her tension ease from her shoulders,

Curse of Dracula

surrendering to her own need, he let out a hungry growl in his throat.

Without warning, she was lifted into his arms. He carried her with an arm under her knees and the other behind her shoulder. She squeaked at the sudden movement and threw her arms around his neck to hold on.

The world folded away on itself, and suddenly they were somewhere else. It was a dizzying transition, and now she knew why he had picked her up. If he hadn't, she would have fallen to the ground.

It was dimly lit, but warm. She did not know where they were, precisely, but she knew the nature of the room well enough to set butterflies loose in her stomach. The enormous silk-covered bed was enough of a hint. A fire in a hearth by one wall chased away the cold and cast amber light dancing across the floor.

Fear gripped her once more, and she locked up in his arms. He chuckled at her reaction and gently placed her on her feet. Taking her hand, he led her to the edge of the bed, and he sat on it. He pulled her to stand between his knees. It was one of the first times she was taller than he was.

The gesture was purposeful. He was trying to be as unintimidating as he was capable of making himself. It *mostly* worked.

He leaned in and kissed her stomach over the black dress she wore. "Beautiful child...don't be afraid." He kissed her a second time, a few inches higher than the last, moving his way north up her body. "If you change your mind, say it."

"I...I don't know as I explicitly agreed to anything."

He placed a kiss to the swell of her breast. Although it was still through her clothes, her body lit up from the simple gesture.

"You needn't say a word." He began to untie the laces of

her dress in the back. "It is all right. I will not hurt you. There may be a brief sting, but that is all."

"It's not that." Not entirely. "My gift..." Her hands went to his shoulders. She needed to hold on to something. She sensed the strength in him, and it soothed her somewhat, even if he was the source of her nervousness. "I do not know what will happen."

"I am not concerned."

"I might destroy you without intending to."

"I do not know of a means by which I would rather die." Slowly, painstakingly, he finished unlacing her dress. Hands, once cold but now warm with his beating heart, drifted carefully up her body. He took his time, each moment drawn out, each gesture with enough warning that she might be able to protest.

Instead, it left her trembling in anticipation of what he might do next.

He slid her dress down her arms and to the floor around her feet. He leaned in to kiss at her collarbone, his breath hot. She watched him, rapt, unable to look away. Unable not to feel as though every touch of his fingers and his lips sent lightning coursing through her.

His tongue ran a slow line over the exposed skin, and she moaned quietly, furtively, ashamed by it. He glanced up at her, seeing her chewing her lip shyly.

"Do not feel shame for this. Not now...not ever."

She shivered. Goosebumps coursed over her body as her silk slip joined her dress on the floor. He leaned in and feathered kisses over her bare skin. In no rush, taking his time, he untied her undergarments. They pooled around her ankles, leaving her fully naked before him.

"So beautiful," he purred. He ran his hands up and along her body, coursing over her.

Curse of Dracula

She was trembling. She was utterly lost in his grasp. She clung to his shoulders as he captured one of her nipples in his mouth, already pert from his attentions, and whimpered as he tongued the sensitive flesh. Suddenly, he bit down hard enough to sting, but not nearly enough to break the skin.

She cried out at the feel of it. Sharp, but not unpleasantly so. Far from it. It sent heat pooling in her, and she gasped at the sensation it left. When he parted from her, he rolled his tongue along the soft flesh once more.

"I will be gentle with you tonight. But that will be… worth exploring." His voice was dark, husky, and thick with obvious desire. He wandered his lips to the other side, lest it feel neglected. His hands never stopped exploring her, caressing her, palming her. He wandered his hands down to her rear, and taking a globe in each hand, squeezed.

She squeaked, feeling his sharp nails dig into her skin. She slapped his shoulder. He laughed quietly. Looking up at her, he grinned wickedly. "What?"

She glared back at him. "I thought you said you would be gentle."

"This *is* me being gentle." He grazed her skin sinfully with his teeth. She shuddered, her anger shattering in the wake of his gesture. "Do not be afraid to touch me if you wish."

"I…I don't know what to do." Shame hit her again. Not because she was standing nude before the Vampire King—that was well enough a problem on its own. No, she felt shame redoubled since she did not know how to bring him pleasure.

"Trust your instincts. Do only what you desire."

She let her hands roam over his shoulders first, feeling the strength beneath the fabric. She then did what she had been wanting to do since she had seen him. She ran her fingers through his dark hair, combing through the silken tendrils, brushing her fingernails along his scalp.

He hummed in appreciation and tilted his head back, his eyes shutting slowly as she repeated the gesture. His hands did not stop roaming her body, but now they pulled her closer. "Yes. Touch me, my little empath."

She ran her hands under the edge of his coat, and she silently urged him to take it off. He obeyed, shrugging out of it, then his vest, tie, and his shirt. She watched and followed his hands with her own as he worked to bare his chest to her. When it was done, she let out a breath.

He was a marvel. A sculpture of a man. Perfect and pale, like he should be in a gallery. A few scars ran over his chest, some large, some small. Some looked to have come from claws, some from weapons. But they didn't detract from his elegance in any way.

She went to touch him, her hands hovering over him. She wasn't sure what to do. Or how to do it. Or that she should. But oh, how she *wanted* to. And how he clearly wanted her to do it.

He bent to kiss at her fingers where they hovered over him. He nipped at her playfully. "Go on."

Finally, she gave in. She let her palms run over his body. And there was plenty of him to explore. He was like stone covered in velvet—the barest softness over the muscles beneath. She let out a shuddering breath. She had never touched anyone like this—never in her life. It was overwhelming, and she needed more.

When her hand ghosted over his abdomen, the muscles rippled as if she had triggered something. He growled, and he pulled her head to his, kissing her deeply. It emboldened her. She slid her hand lower, skin transitioning to the smooth fabric of his pants.

And finally, she worked up the nerve to touch what lay there in between his legs, begging to be freed. She should have the presence of mind to be terrified of his body. At the enormity of it. Certainly, he couldn't mean to make it all fit inside her. But her fear did not stop her from continuing her shy exploration. She had denied herself this basic human act for so very long, and suddenly she was starving for it.

He growled thickly, turning his head to flick his tongue over her lips, asking once more for entry. She granted it, and he invaded her mouth, claiming it. He twitched beneath her hand, and she wondered if he wanted more.

Her answer was given to her when he undid the buckle of his belt and pulled the black leather strap from his pants. He undid his fly and, taking her hand in his, guided it to the entrance. She pulled from his lips, watching him, uncertain and fascinated as she ran her fingers into his trousers to find the object of her curiosity and desire.

He moaned low, leaning back to give her more room, his own hands holding on to her hips. She wrapped her fingers around his length, feeling its throbbing heat. She stroked him, or what she could manage. It was rather frustrating to not be able to explore him fully. With a hand on his shoulder, she gently pushed him back, hoping he understood what she did not quite fathom herself.

It seemed he did. With an amused smile, he obeyed. He let go of her to remove the rest of his clothes, letting out a small, relieved sigh as he was freed of their confines. He lay back on the bed. If she wanted to enjoy him, he would allow it.

By the old gods, he was gorgeous. He might as well be a god

himself, she realized. He was lying there, watching her as she took in his form, and she knew there was no backing away now. Not after seeing him. Not after knowing what she could have.

He was a temptation—and one she had no ability to refuse.

God or devil. Man or monster. It didn't matter. She wanted him.

She leaned over him, propping her weight up on one hand, and kissed his chest. He shuddered beneath her, growling in his throat. His hand drifted up her arm and rested there, not stopping her, but not pressuring her to continue.

He was letting her become comfortable with him. She appreciated it beyond words. She kissed his chest again, trailing along his body, down his abdomen. He was stoic but not immovable. He reacted to her touch, to her kisses, he shuddered or moaned quietly in his throat with each of her explorations.

Then she came to that about which she had been so curious. *Oh, lord.* She let her hand wrap around him, and she caressed him slowly, feeling the heat, and the throbbing heartbeat in him.

He groaned, his hips lifting, stroking himself into her grasp. "Yes, Maxine..."

It was instinct. It was an impulse. She didn't know what she was doing. She knew how men and women enjoyed each other. She spent years in a Roma camp, and she had seen plenty of it by accident. Leaning down, she ran her tongue along his length, tasting him.

He roared, biting back the sound halfway through. She looked up to see his head thrown back, his eyes shut. His fangs were long, caught in a sudden snarl, inspired by the hunger she sensed in him. His sharp-nailed hands grasped

Curse of Dracula

the air by her uselessly. She realized he was fighting his desire to grab hold of her. He must not want to scare or rush her.

She ran her tongue along him again and watched his reaction, fascinated and wishing for more. She was…deeply enjoying this, she realized. She took him into her mouth—what she could, anyway—and he let out a broken-sounding howl of pleasure.

He barely fit inside her mouth at all. It was hard to do much else but to focus on the sensation of him there. She pulled him from her mouth to roll her tongue around him once more before repeating the action. How he moaned when she took him into her—it was a beautiful, amazing sound, and she wanted to hear more of it.

This time, he placed his hands on her. One on her shoulder, the other tangling into her hair atop her head. Gently, not hard enough that she couldn't resist him, he urged her to take more of him into her mouth. She did, and as she reached her limit, he pulled her back. He began to repeat the pattern, showing her the proper rhythm. She stroked what she could not take with her hand.

She had no concept of what she was doing. She was suddenly very eager to learn.

"This is not what I would have expected," he growled huskily. "You are forever a surprise. Ah—" He broke off in a breathy sigh. "You are perfect. Yes, like that. Oh, Maxine…"

Shutting her eyes, she let herself enjoy him and the strange pleasure she derived from feeling him in her mouth. Of his girth, his warmth, the taste of him. She understood why people did this now. It was bliss. It was power. And she, too, hungered for more.

He urged her away from him after a few long moments, scooping her up to pull her onto the bed with him.

Suddenly, she was beneath him, and he was kissing her. Desperately, hungrily—his lips worked over hers as if he would devour her by that means alone.

When he broke off, she was gasping for air. He ran his lips to her ear and nibbled upon the lobe for a moment before speaking. "As much as I hate to pry you away…as I could watch you do that for hours…tonight is about your needs, not mine."

She had no words for him as he kissed his way down the length of her body, his weight on his elbow as he stroked and caressed her with his other hand. When he reached her navel and threatened to go lower, she froze. "Turnabout is fair play, my dear." He kissed her right beneath her abdomen.

"I…"

"You're shy. I understand. There is no shame in this." He settled himself between her legs. Her face went warm as he parted them to lean his head down to her core. She gasped, her back arching off the bed as he ran his tongue up along her.

Her hand flew to his hair to try to pull him away, but he snatched it and buried it under his palm. Her other hand met a similar fate, leaving her helpless as he explored her.

All thoughts fled as her mind went white with pleasure as he delved his tongue into her. She cried out as he moved north to capture the sensitive bud, rolling his tongue over it. He released her hand, knowing she was not going to fight him any longer. His fingers had another goal. She nearly bucked out from under him as one of his digits took the place of his tongue, allowing him to return his attentions to the rest of her. He knew what he was doing. And, oh, he seemed to know her body better than she did.

Pleasure in her built suddenly and unexpectedly. She

whimpered, tossing her head. Needing it to end, yet never wanting it to stop. The sensation sent her pitching headfirst over a cliff into ecstasy. She arched her back again, grasping the sheets beneath her hands, crying out his name.

When she came back to reality, he was kissing her cheek. He was lying between her legs, nestled there, his weight on his elbow by her head. She was gasping for air, and he was patiently waiting for her.

She turned to look at him, meeting his crimson gaze, and saw passion, and desire, and...love. She caressed his chest, letting her hands settle with one on his shoulder and the other on his side.

She knew what was going to happen.

She wasn't an idiot.

But it didn't mean she wasn't afraid. Especially after she had seen—and tasted—the size of him.

He lifted her knee, hooking it over his elbow, and she felt him press against her entrance. She bit her lip, and he tutted. "Don't be afraid." He leaned down to kiss her. Slow and gentle. He parted to let her breathe, and he went back to watching her. "Relax."

She did as best she could.

"Do you wish for me to put you in my thrall until the first moment is over? You would be spared any pain."

She shook her head. "I want to feel it. I want to feel this."

He smiled faintly. "Good." And with that, he pressed forward. She gasped. Pressure built, and she wondered if it would not work. Until suddenly, it did.

She moaned at the feeling of him inside of her, even the barest amount that now had claimed. There was much, much more to come. And she knew the pain of it had not started.

He snarled quietly, not immune to the sensation either.

He pressed his hips forward a little farther, inching his way into her body. It felt impossible. It felt *incredible.*

He paused when he came to a barrier. He leaned down to kiss her. "This will hurt only for a moment."

She nodded, understanding. "I trust you."

Crimson eyes caught hers, and through the haze of his pleasure and his desire, she could see the tenderness that flickered there. Those words had meant a great deal to him. "That is the greatest gift you could give me this night. Your trust."

He pressed forward then, breaching her. She cried out and winced as he did. It stung. She pounded her fist into his shoulder, knowing he would not mind it. He continued to press forward until he filled her. Until he was seemingly everywhere.

It was that sensation that broke her out of her pain—the throbbing fullness. The sensation of him buried so deeply inside her. Of reaching every part of her body. It took her a long few moments before she could even fathom the truth of what had happened. As he promised, the sting faded away until it was nothing, leaving only his presence there.

But she knew there was still more of him. She shuddered at the knowledge. "I would have it all from you, vampire."

He furrowed his brow. "It may hurt."

"Now you wish to spare me a part of you that might bring pain, vampire?" She smiled and lay her head back. "If you would have me in full, then I will ask the same of you."

He growled low in his throat, a pleased, hungry, needy sound. "As you wish." And with that, he pressed his weight against her, forcing her body to take to what remained. He was now sheathed to the hilt, and she moaned as her body surrendered to him.

Curse of Dracula

She saw stars. But not from pain. She was astonished. It did not...feel *bad,* though perhaps it should. It was different from the sting of being taken for the first time. It was an ache. A delicious and terrible, wonderful ache. She wondered if her pleasure would peak from that alone. From the way he filled her. She gasped for air, her heart pounding in her ears. "Oh, Vlad," she whispered.

"Good girl. Now, breathe slowly," he murmured into her ear. "You will adjust."

She took his advice and forced her lungs to slow down their rapid pace. As she did, her lightheadedness began to subside, leaving only that deep, very pleasant ache. There was so *much* of him, stretching her, forcing her body to comply, however willing she was.

He did not move. He lay in her, pulsing with his heartbeat, clearly itching for more, and he waited. He waited for her to be ready. She pulled his head to hers and kissed him slowly. When she parted, she smiled at him gently. "Thank you."

"Then let's begin." He pressed harder, using his weight to deepen the ache inside her.

She did not think it was possible that he might possibly go farther, but once more he proved her wrong. She moaned loudly as he did, arching her back and grabbing at him in surprise. Pleasure lanced through her like lightning. "Oh, God!"

"Am I? Many would beg to differ." He purred against her throat. "But you...oh, Maxine...you feel divine indeed." He growled as he relented from the pressure, pulling back out of her until barely anything remained before he surged forward again. Not quickly, not forcefully, but as unstoppable as the tide.

He was a force of nature. And he was going to love her

like one. He continued the pace, nearly leaving her then filling her. Every few strokes, he would press harder into her until she took him in his entirety. He would hold himself there, making her gasp and whimper in pleasure. It should hurt, being impaled in such a way. She knew it should. But somehow, that was not the right word for what it made her feel.

She was panting, her body wracked with pleasure. By all the gods, she had been deprived of something too wonderful to describe. She lifted her hips to meet his downstroke, and he growled in approval. The next time he pressed hard into her, fitting all of him inside her straining body, she pulled his hips down to hers. She needed the ache he gave her. She wanted more of it.

"Perfect, beautiful child…yes. By the night, yes," he moaned into her shoulder, pressing even harder. "You are too wonderful…this is bliss."

"Vlad," she gasped, breathless. She wasn't sure what she was asking for. All she knew was that he had more to give her, and she wanted it all.

"Patience." He grinned and kissed her. He pulled himself back once more and surged forward, a little harder than before. "I am going to enjoy you. Every inch of you. For as long as I can. But here is a taste of what I can give you when I desire to be merciful." He thrust into her, fast and hard, ramming into her end and sending sparks of pleasure crashing through her, jolting her against the sheets. "Is that what you want?"

"Yes!" She gasped. "Oh—oh Vlad, yes—"

"Soon." He slowed his tempo again, and he chuckled at her frustrated whine.

Then it happened.

It rushed toward her like a tidal wave. It was going to

drown her. She tensed, trying to hold it back. She would not let it consume her. She struggled with it, turning her head to the side and squeezing her eyes shut tight.

"What is wrong?" He leaned closer and tilted her face to his. "What is causing you pain?"

"Nothing—it's fine—I—"

"Do not lie to me." He cradled her cheek in his hand. "Look at me, Maxine."

She obeyed, and she saw in his red eyes what she was trying to hold back. What she was trying to keep from crashing over her—him. All of him. Her control over her empathy was threatening to shatter and snap. She had no idea what would happen when it did, and it scared her.

"Let go," he whispered. "I have you."

"I..."

He pressed into her all the way. She gasped, and she could see the pleasure in his eyes. She knew hers carried the same. "Does it look as though I wish to be separate from you?"

That was enough to break her grasp on the reins. The horses charged away from her, and she was overtaken. He filled her body, and now he filled her mind. She was tangled up in him, and she knew he was the same. She moaned and arched beneath him. "Vlad!"

―――

PERFECT CREATURE. *His* perfect creature.

He could smell the fires of a Roma camp. He could see the household she grew up in. He could feel her there in his mind, every part of her, dancing with him. Tangled in the silk of his web, he was both the spider and the fly.

She twisted beneath him in pleasure, in bliss, and he

could feel it like it was his own. He had not been expecting to know her experience like an echo chamber. He gasped and moaned. and he could not help but quicken his pace. He had wanted to take it slow with her—to make her beg for more. To make her ask him to take her and show her what he had to offer.

And she was so close to begging. She had begun to surrender to the pleasure. She was so quick to adjust and learn. He had savored the moment her body relaxed and opened to him, wishing to take all that he had to give her. And he had so very many things he would like to give her.

All in due time.

Now she clung to him as he took her, feeling the blissful, perfect, volcanic heat around him. She warmed his body, his heart beating fast and loud as her own ecstasy echoed with his. All at once he was in her, and she was around him.

He had expected a terrified child. A trembling virgin he would need to coax and console every step of the way. Instead, he found a shy but *very* eager little creature dwelled in his companion. Unsure of herself, yet so very willing to explore him. It was not shocking that she could intuit what might bring him pleasure. She could hear his emotions, after all. He could see her take joy in the act. He would teach her to be a master in time.

But now, feeling her desire and his own twist together and merge, he could not help himself. He would not hurt her. He would not leave her sore. But he could not keep the same patient tempo as before. He needed her. He had said it before, and he had meant every word.

I need all of her.

And in that moment, they were one.

18

Bella looked up at the crimson moon. It hung in the air over them, forever full, casting its foreboding red light.

She found it strangely beautiful. Tragic in that it represented freedom for some, but death for others. Such was the way of predators. And that was what sat next to her on the planter box, happily eating the food he had taken from the kitchen for them. They had already had their dinner, but Mordecai was voracious in more ways than his sexual appetite. He had stolen a good-sized plate of food to bring with them.

She couldn't deny she was helping herself to some of the grapes.

When his tail wound around her ankle, holding on to her, she couldn't help but smile at him. "What?"

"You were morose. I don't like to see you in such a mood, so I'm going to distract you. Besides. I love it when you smile at me."

She stood from where she was and moved over to him. He released the wrap around her ankle as he watched her, curiosity etched onto his sharp features. She gathered up her skirt to straddle his lap, sitting on his thighs.

"Well. All right, then." He let his hands settle on her hips. His tail was once more wrapped around her leg, this time higher on her calf.

She ran her hand through his hair. It was soft, despite its rough-cut appearance. She loved to rustle it with her fingers, mussing it up even further. He didn't complain—indeed, he purred. Literally purred like some great panther. His violet eyes slid half shut as she watched him become lost in her embrace.

He loved her.

She had no doubt of it.

And now, she knew she loved him too.

Maybe it was too fast. Maybe it was wrong. Maybe she didn't care.

"If Eddie comes here, I will choose to stay with you."

"Bella! Oh, Bella!" He wrapped his arms around her fully and hugged her to him. He leaned his cheek against her chest and let out what she assumed was a happy noise, although it sounded more like a sob, if she were honest. She laughed and held him. His horn dug into her a little, but she did not mind it too much. "I have to ask. I have to. It is okay if you tell me no, but I—"

"I will be your mate, Mordecai." And there it was. She said it. She had taken the leap, and it was as though a weight had been lifted from her shoulders. She would become like he was—she would let her humanity drift away. But demons could love. And she would taste the freedom that he knew, and she would do it with her hand in his.

She was not frightened. She was...excited.

Dampness touched her skin, and she lifted his head

from her. A tear streaked down his cheeks. She dried it away with her thumb and smiled. "Why are you crying?"

"I couldn't honestly tell you." He laughed softly. "I am just…I am happy, and I should not cry when I am happy, but here we are."

"How very human of you."

"Now you're insulting me!" He glared playfully. "A cruel mistress you turn out to be."

She kissed him, and he met her full force. She wrapped her arms behind his neck as they embraced. She parted the kiss. "Let's go," she whispered.

"Mmhh," he groaned. "Say it. Please. Say the words to me."

She smiled down at him. "I love you, Mordecai."

And with that, she was free.

———

Maxine could not remember much of what happened. Flashes of imagery. Of wings against a night sky, of ancient stars, of the endless night that he was. Of the feeling of him with her sending her soaring to the extents of the sky in his arms.

She remembered the bliss.

Pure and utter ecstasy had crashed over her. Both hers…and his.

It had been more than simple physical affection. He had been inside her *soul*. She must have fallen asleep after it ended. She could not remember. Her hand went to her throat to search for a fresh wound that was not there. Someone chuckled beneath her.

"I did not bite you. I am not sure as I could have much managed."

She looked up and realized she was lying in his arms. They were in his bed beneath the sheets. Both still naked, by the feel of it.

He saw her quizzical expression and reached up to stroke her hair away from her face. "I felt the same as you. I think only by benefit of my years did I manage not to pass out. It was close."

"I did not pass out," she tried to argue indignantly, then realized how utterly hopeless it was. She sighed. "I am sorry."

"For what?"

"I did not know what my gift would do to us. It had exactly the effect I was worried about."

He stroked her hair. "I am not complaining. That was exquisite. In all my thousands of years, I have never experienced anything like it. I thought I had joined with another in all the ways that were possible. You have taught me otherwise."

She smiled, her face going warm. "I am sorry I am not more...skilled in the act. To someone like you, I must be quite awful."

"You have talent, believe me. If you are worried about skill, then...what is it they say? Practice makes perfect?"

She slapped his chest. She tried not to laugh and won but did not manage to keep a smile from escaping. "How long was I out?"

"An hour, maybe less." He shut his eyes and held her close, a matching smile on his features. "The sun will rise in a few hours' time, and you will have your ceasefire."

Snuggling into him, she let her head rest back on his chest. His heart had stopped, and his touch was already cold once more. It didn't bother her. "Thank you."

Curse of Dracula

"You realize I will have a rather rabid need to do this again. You will not be rid of me now."

She laughed quietly and curled her hand against his chest. "Perhaps I will find the inspiration to trade you such a thing again in the future."

"Ah, I fear that is not how this works. You're mine now. You are my prisoner of war." He kissed her forehead, and she felt the playful twist to his lips. "You are powerless now to resist me."

She tried not to laugh again, and this time failed. She was exhausted, and the idea of sleep was more than welcome. It came for her quickly, and she drifted off to the sensation of his hand drawing lazy circles over her lower back.

He was a monster. But damn if she didn't want him in spite of it. Damn if this didn't feel like happiness.

Vlad could still feel her thoughts, echoing in the distance of his mind. Weaker now, as her blood in his body became less and less prevalent, but still there. He could hear her internal debate, but he sensed her surrender to the peace he brought her in his arms.

When they had been joined in body and mind, he heard her love for him, echoing the call of his own. They were meant to be together. No matter her turmoil, he knew now that she truly was his. It was only a matter of time before she came to accept it.

Beautiful child. So sympathetic. So bright-eyed and intelligent. Wise and naïve in the same breath. She was so gentle to those who did not deserve it. And it might destroy her. A lesser creature would have long since given up her morals and adopted his depravity instead. It only made him adore her more.

Damn him to the pits. Damn his foolishness. Damn him to Hell that his heart seemed to have never learned its tragic lesson. *All will die before me.*

She would share the same fate. How, he did not know. By his hands, by another, by old age or illness, by insanity if he turned her into a creature like himself, it didn't matter. She would fade away into dust the same as all the rest. It was all just a matter of how soon it would come to pass.

He kissed her atop her head again. She smelled like the fall, crisp leaves and fading summer light, and he adored it. She claimed to dislike death, but he wondered if she were not the end of life itself wearing gorgeous features. Certainly, an angel of death had come to visit in him in her guise, promising him sweet relief from his eternity only to find comfort in his arms instead. It would be wonderfully fitting for him if that were true.

He had called her perfect. He had meant those words as well.

She nuzzled into him, the guileless gesture of a sleeping mind. He pulled her tight and tucked the blankets closer around her. He regretted that he had no body heat of his own, but there was little to be done about it.

Not once had she flinched from his cold touch. Not once had she recoiled from his corpselike flesh. He stroked her hair, careful not to wake her, and he shut his eyes.

How long he might hold his angel in his arms, he did not know. But he would cherish it for as long as it lasted. Even if it was by his hands that it would eventually be destroyed.

The humans would have their day of ceasefire. They

would be allowed to flee his city. And ...she would witness the downfall of Alfonzo Van Helsing.

If she could still love him after what he planned for that wretch, she could love him through the end of days.

And if she could not, he would embrace her wrath as much as he would embrace her forgiveness. Either would be a mercy. Sadly, he had business to attend before the sun rose. He slipped from her arms and tucked another blanket around her. He commanded the fire to burn brighter and heard it roar obediently. He would return before she woke.

He laid a kiss on her temple. "Sleep, Maxine...you have earned it."

She murmured and hugged the pillow closer to her, no doubt dreaming it was him. It made him smile. She did not deserve to endure what he would put before her.

But then again...who did?

———

EDDIE WAS sick of this shit.

He really was.

He shoved the corpse of the monster off him where it had pinned him to the ground with its literal dead weight. "Stupid, ugly bastard," he grumbled at it as he managed to finally roll it off. It smelled like, well, shit.

Some of the monsters would burst into flame when they were killed. This one, not so much. This one fell atop him like some sack of ugly, stinky potatoes. Once he had finally freed himself, he stood and brushed off as much of the muck as he could.

Fifty-four monsters, twenty-eight ghouls, three lesser vampires, and one that might have been a bit older and more impressive. That was what he had killed so far during his trek toward the North End. He had nothing better to do but count. Count, walk, fight, count some more, walk some more, and so on.

Oh, and talk to himself.

"I told him we shouldn't split up. Should've gone with Al. Maybe I could've done something to stop all this." He sighed as he started walking again toward the center of the city, reloading his revolver. He was happy he had plenty of ammunition. He preferred his rifle, but it was crap up close.

"Or maybe I'd be dead. Fuck, Al, I hope you're not dead." He grunted and sighed, shaking his head. "This is stupid. I should leave and go home."

"Then why don't you?"

Eddie whirled to the source of the voice—his gun instantly pointed at the creature who had spoken. A tall man in a long black peacoat, his long black hair that shone in the crimson light of the perpetually red moon. The creature was imposing —a monolith that seemed to seethe with pure darkness. On seeing him, Eddie could only think of one thing to say. *"Fuck."*

Dracula.

"Fuck!"

The vampire smirked at his second outburst. Holding his arms out wide at his sides, he invited Eddie to take a shot.

He knew he didn't stand a chance. He released the hammer and lowered the weapon. "If you wanted me dead, you'd have attacked already. You had the jump on me. You're here to talk. Am I right?"

"Very good, boy." The vampire tilted his head slightly, watching him studiously. "Do you not wish to kill me?"

"No, I do. I'm just not stupid enough to try."

"You are smarter than you look."

"Thanks. I think." Eddie grunted and kept his gun in his hand, even if he didn't aim it at the monster.

"What is it you wish for, then, boy? If not to try to kill me?"

"I want to free Bella. I want to take her and go."

"Noble, but futile. I'm afraid to say that Bella does not wish to be freed."

"What?"

Dracula sighed and tucked his hands behind his back. "She is mated to an incubus."

"What have you done to her?" Eddie pulled his gun out again and pointed it at the vampire, his hand shaking. "You're lying!"

"She is likely already beginning to change. She is a demon now. She will become a succubus before long. And she did it out of love for the creature who has taken her. If you find her now, she will choose to stay. But I do not think you have dignity enough to let her have such autonomy, do you?"

"You perverted *freak!*" He was trembling. Even if he thought he stood a chance against the vampire, his hands were shaking too hard now to try. "You're lying…you have to be lying."

"I fear I am not." There was an odd look of sympathy on the vampire's face. As if he…truly regretted what he had come to communicate. "The girl does not love you, Edward. Let her go. Spare yourself this pain."

"I can't…I can't give up on her."

"She has given up on you."

"No. No. I don't buy that. I don't believe Bella wants to be with—with—" he stammered, broke off, coughed, and refused to say it. *There's no way she'd pick an incubus over me.*

"It's bullshit. She's not like that." His eyes stung, and he bit back tears.

"Mmhm. And you know her so perfectly, do you?"

"We've traveled together for years. I've been in the trenches with her. We've fought side-by-side. Yeah. I'd say I do."

"Not well enough, it seems. Zadok masqueraded as her for two days and two nights, and you did not notice the charade."

"Shut up!"

The vampire sighed. "You are young. Your heart has been misplaced in the girl. She does not care for you. By her own admission to the incubus, she never held you in any more regard than a trusted friend. She is gone to you, and Alfonzo's life is as good as over. Spare yourself the pain. Spare yourself the torment. Leave this city. This morning, the sun will rise. For the duration of its journey across the skies, the survivors here will be free to leave. And in a few days' time, I will be gone from this place, and so will my creatures. There is no war left here for you to wage."

"See, you make sense. But that's the problem. The devil always makes sense."

"Then perhaps you should listen."

Eddie grunted and shoved his gun into its holster. If the vampire wanted to kill him, they both knew he could. It was stupid pretending he stood a chance. He'd only be wasting bullets. "I can't give up. I can't. Not on them."

Dracula bowed his head. "I acknowledge your commitment. It is a difficult thing to stand against a fight you cannot win, yet to hold up your sword and face the oncoming horde with your fate ascertained. It is for that reason I will let you live. You may wander my city as you wish and destroy my creatures until one might succeed in ending you."

"Why? Why let me live?"

Crimson eyes glinted in the light, flashing like those of a wolf in the shadows. "Every now and then, a doomed soldier can turn the tide of battle. I think I am curious to see if that is who you are. Imagine my world, Mr. Jenkin, if you can. I can never die. Knowing such, do you not think I have not, from time to time, allowed myself to lose a fight to a worthy opponent?"

"You have higher stakes this time. Maxine."

"True. Very true. And should you threaten her life, you will be a smear upon the cobblestones."

"She's a nice girl. A good person." Eddie shook his head. "I won't kill her because she loves you. That would make me worse than you are."

"Oddly enough, I appreciate the sentiment. And for that, I will correct Zadok's lie that he used to split you and your mentor apart. Bella is not in the North End, but dwells within my fortress with her new 'husband.'"

Eddie blanched. He barely managed to keep himself from being sick all over his shoes. "Why? Why do that to her?"

"Nothing has befallen her that she has not embraced with open arms. That, and I fear she has a hand to play in my plans." He paused. "At any point, should you turn back, your exit from this city will be unimpeded. I encourage you to leave. I hope you do. I have no desire to kill you."

"Appreciated and noted. I won't come after Maxine. She loves you. And it's plain to see you feel the same. I won't get in the middle of that. But I'm going to do everything I can to save my friends."

"Appreciated and noted." Dracula bowed. "Until we meet again."

And in an explosion of black bats that swarmed up into the sky, he was gone.

Eddie exhaled in a rush as he scratched the back of his neck. He turned to walk deeper into the city. *Yeah. This is fuckin' shit.*

19

Bella lay in their bed and pressed her hand to her abdomen. The deed was done. She was panting, covered in sweat. And it had been glorious.

Mordecai was over her, kissing every inch of her. She basked in it. She was his mate now. She was pregnant with their child. She was a demon. She could feel it. Not just the life she knew would sprout inside her, but of the change that was slowly washing through her from the inside out. It was blooming in her like a flower, spreading out inside. Warmth was filling her.

She had wondered if it was going to hurt. If it would feel like poison. Instead, she writhed beneath him, seeking contact with his body. Any contact. She needed him to *touch* her. Mordecai was happy to oblige.

"The change will happen slowly. It will come over you piece by piece, then lay dormant for a time. You won't fully be like me until you feed on your first victim. When you take them into you, you will be complete." He was kissing her bare skin slowly, wandering feathered touches over her.

"Won't you be jealous?"

"Never." He grinned. "I cannot wait to see you take your first victim. I will be there to help you. You will be glorious. You will be a thing of pure beauty. No one will be able to resist you."

"Will I have horns and a tail?" She hadn't thought about it. She hadn't cared. She wasn't sure she would mind. Mordecai certainly put his tail to good use.

"No...you will have wings, my angel." He kissed her stomach then wandered lower, kissing her abdomen over where their new life would grow. "And your transformation will feed our baby." He crawled back up her form until he was over her. "I love you."

Wings. She was going to have *wings!* She smiled. It sounded incredible. She couldn't wait. "I love you, demon." She reached up to kiss him, and he eagerly matched her.

———

Maxine awoke to the feeling of someone kissing her.

It was a sensation she knew she would never forget. She blinked her eyes open and found Vlad lying next to her, propped on one elbow with his other hand holding up his weight on the other side of her, caging her in. The length of his body against hers was chill but not unwelcome.

Anything but unwelcome.

She smiled against his lips and raised her hand to place her fingertips against his cheek. He hummed and withdrew just far enough that they could watch each other. "Good morning."

"I would have preferred to let you sleep, but I have business to attend to. I did not want to let you awaken alone. The sun rises soon, and, despite that, much is about to be set in motion."

Curse of Dracula

"What is it that you scheme, vampire?"

"Let us speak of it after breakfast." He kissed her forehead. She shot him a glance at his dismissal, and he smiled. "Do you not wish to enjoy a hot bath and warm food?"

That did sound wonderful, she had to admit.

He nuzzled her, his lips tracing over her throat. "Unless you prefer to linger."

She nudged him in the chest. "You are terrible."

"Was this ever a question?" He supported his weight on his elbow to run his fingers through her hair. "Come. Before I give in to my temptation and spend the rest of the day here with you, teaching you all the pleasures of the flesh."

Her cheeks bloomed in warmth at his threat, and she refused to let her mind wander down the road of what that could entail. He kissed her one last time and climbed from the bed, dressed in his silk shirt and trousers. She couldn't help but watch him. He moved gracefully for a man his size. She was staring, and he caught her doing just that.

"Wicked creature." He grinned playfully. "I will make a sinner of you yet."

She realized her shyness over climbing out from under the sheets naked was utterly childish. He had seen her in such a state. He had done things to her. Yet she knew she was blushing when she slipped out from under the covers. "I have never claimed to not be a sinner."

"Perhaps. Tell me, Maxine, have you ever killed a man?"

"You know I have."

"I ask if you have ever stopped a heart, not killed by your more spectacular means." He walked to a dresser nearby and pulled from it a black silk robe. He handed it to her, and she was happy to put it on. Namely, because his gaze on her was becoming heated, and she knew if he threw her back to the bed, she would not tell him no.

"No, I haven't. I came close once. I was in Rome. A man attempted to rob me and to rape me. I tore out his soul before he could. I had a knife, and I was very near to stabbing him before it became a moot point." The robe was comically oversized for her, and they both laughed at how silly she looked wearing something sized for him. She did her best to roll up the sleeves and tie the band around the waist. She continued to talk. "I would consider him dead because of me, even though it was not by my own hands that he ceased to breathe. He still died from atrophy and starvation because of what I did."

"He is dead because he is a criminal. What you did was not wrong." He stroked her hair gently, his fingers then trailing over her jawline. She shut her eyes at the sensation. "What I do and what you have done to protect yourself are very different things. You are no sinner."

"I have lain with a demon, have I not?"

"You show him mercy and love." He traced a finger over her cheek. "Those are not sins."

"I have enjoyed it. I think that is the difference." When she opened her eyes to smile up at him, he was standing there formally clothed in a vest, tie, and coat. She blinked. "How…?"

He grinned. "I am capable of many wonders. That was nothing."

Magic. He could transport himself without effort. He could turn into bats. He was thousands of years old. But she was amazed at his ability to apparate clothing from thin air. She shook her head, feeling like a fool.

"Nothing of the sort."

Yes, right. That. The mind-reading. He drew her into his arms and pulled her flush against his chest. The world once more folded around them, and she clung to him to keep from toppling over when they reappeared. "That is quite an awful and unsettling sensation."

"You will adjust to it in time."

The early morning sun was streaming in through a window. She squinted at the sudden change in light. He had made good on his promises, and she smiled. "Thank you."

"I am a creature of my word," he responded and leaned down to kiss her forehead. "And what I received in return is a far, far more valuable gift than sparing the lives of innocents I care nothing for—your trust."

Trust. She pulled him closer and kissed him. He valued her trust, and not his conquest of her. For that, she could not have been more grateful. He broke away after a moment and pulled her into his arms.

Someday, she would remember he could hear her thoughts.

Today was not that day.

"It was not conquest. You do not belong to me like the spoils of a campaign. I am an ancient and fearsome tyrant. I know the difference." He tilted her head up to look at him, and she tried to avoid meeting his gaze. "Look at me."

She finally gave in. "You have said frequently that I am yours. What is that, if not the battle cry of the invading force?"

He smirked as she used his own words against him. "You are mine, Maxine. Make no mistake. But you asked me once what I would give you in return for all that I demand of you. I gave you my heart, and you have given me yours. You gave me your body last night, and I gave you mine in return. Did I not repay you adequately? If not, I am happy to make amends." He purred as he lowered his lips to her ear, nipping at the lobe.

She slapped at his chest and took a step away. "Terrible."

He laughed and bowed. "Hello. I am pleased to meet you."

She shook her head and turned away, mostly to hide her smile. "Tell me, if I were to refuse you—what would you do?"

Hands settled on her shoulders. "I would not force you, if that is your concern."

"Would you kill me? If I wanted to lie with another instead—"

He growled. One arm banded around her, yanking her against his chest. The other hand slipped between the folds of the silk robe to press against her bare lower back, his fingers splayed wide. "I would demand to know what they could give you that I cannot."

She gasped but found herself slinging an arm behind his neck as he caressed her, his hand wandering over her body. "What if I—"

"No. None shall have you but me. None shall taste you but my lips or the grave. I am a jealous and covetous thing, my darling Maxine. Do not tempt my wrath. Are you curious for another?"

"I am testing the edges of the chains you have me wear."

"You wear no chains. Yet." He growled into her shoulder, pulling the robe away to kiss her there. "Someday, you will. And you will beg me for more."

She shuddered and shut her eyes. He was all-consuming, and she hungered for it. If he would have her now, she would happily agree.

But he sighed heavily and released her, stepping away. "We do not have time for this, I fear. I have much to do. Come, I have brought you here to bathe."

She blinked at his sudden absence, disappointed. She looked to him, and he was walking to a large metal tub that looked as though it had been recently installed. There was no need for such things in a public library, after all.

Copper tubes ran up from the floor to spigots that poured over the edge. Following him, she reached out to touch the pipes. He gently nudged her hand away. "One of them is quite hot. Do not scald yourself." He turned the valves, and she watched as water poured into the tub. Placing her hand under it, she discovered he was right—hot running water.

"How?"

"I have had such marvels in my possession for a long time. What I do is not magic, Miss Parker. It is science not yet understood by the modern mortal. Although I believe this particular amenity is starting to enter usage."

She sat on the edge of the tub and swirled her hand in the water. She had not enjoyed a hot bath in a long time. She was eager for it. When the level was high enough, he turned off the spigots and walked to the door. "There is clothing on the table for you here. I will be outside. Breakfast will be ready soon."

She was mildly surprised—and a little disappointed—that he did not stay.

He grinned wickedly. "It would defeat the purpose of your bath if I did." He left the room then, shutting the door behind him.

Terrible.

"I know." He called from the other side. "You needn't continue to remind me."

She laughed.

———

The bath and the food had been wonderful. She felt more put together than she had since the whole ordeal began. The clothing he had given her was lovely. He had even provided her more comfortable shoes and a proper coat.

He was oddly thoughtful.

Now they stood on a balcony overlooking the city. It had not existed before, but neither did most of the building she had walked through to arrive here. It was twisting together with a memory of his past, or a dream of his present. Otherwise, she doubted the library would have copper-fed bathtubs or luxurious bedrooms.

"I am afraid I must leave you here for the day. I will return once the sun has set. My work will be finished by then." He lifted her hand to his lips and kissed the back of her knuckles. Then he turned her hand over and placed a second kiss at the sensitive spot in the center of her palm. It made her shiver. "Then my night will belong to you."

"I will ask you again, what do you scheme, vampire?" She stepped closer. "What has become of the hunters?"

He smirked. "I scheme much."

"Begin at the top, then."

"Well, for starters, Bella is now a succubus." He grinned.

"What?" she exclaimed, wide-eyed in shock. "How?"

He arched an eyebrow then hummed. "Ah, yes. For a moment I thought you were asking me to describe the process in detail. Then I remembered how uneducated you likely are as to the ways of demons. She has become such a thing willingly, I assure you." He raised a hand to trace his sharp-nailed fingers through her hair, and she shivered again at the sensation of them against her scalp. "You are not the only one to give your heart to the shadows. Incubi and succubae turn those they mate with. She has pledged herself to Mordecai."

"It's hard to believe."

"I would prove it to you, but she is busy at the moment." There was a dark gleam in his eyes at his words, and it made her nervous.

"What have you done?"

He smiled thinly. "You shall see soon enough. It shall be the final test you will need to endure."

"Why must you seek to break my love for you? Why must you pile the stones upon it and see at what point it might shatter?"

"Because I have suffered the loss of too many fragile gifts, my love. I would rather watch it break of my own accord than…to live in the lie of willing ignorance. I cannot do it again, no matter how tempting it might be to pretend, even for a time, to be less than what I am."

She wound her hand into his and laced her fingers through his stronger ones. She leaned her head against his chest and shut her eyes. "You wish to torture Alfonzo. You wish for me to see the depths of your depravity to one man and see if I can love you regardless."

"Yes."

She sighed heavily. "I worry about what you plot for him. I can only begin to imagine the reaches of your imagination."

"Would you like to sample my creativity?" He leaned down and placed a kiss against her cheek, wandering to her ear, his voice becoming a low and gravelly rumble. "I can be quite ingenious indeed."

"Come to me once the sun has set, and we shall see." She lifted her head to his ear and nipped the lobe.

He growled. "Dangerous game, tempting a predator such as I." He straightened, and there was a heat in his eyes that made her stomach twist. "And if I were a weaker, younger vampire, I would fall for your secret ploy."

"What ploy? You are the one who plays games, not I."

"Mm. I do not believe you. You wish to distract me from my tasks this day. I fear that I cannot allow you to sway me." He kissed her forehead. "I will see you when the sun drops beneath the horizon. You are free to wander my home, for it is yours now as well. But if you feel the need to wander the city, I insist you take an escort."

She sighed. She had no desire to set foot in the city and see more of the devastation she had caused, even indirectly. "You have spoken of Bella and Alfonzo. What of Eddie?"

"I spoke to him last night while you slept. I wish for him to leave this place alive. I have no desire to harm him. If he refuses to leave, as he has, then he will meet his death. Such is my compassion, and such is my cruelty." Vlad stepped away from her. "Enjoy your day, my dear Miss Parker."

He bowed even as he exploded into a swarm of black bats and flew up into the sky and away.

Shaking her head, she shut her eyes and leaned against the bannister of the balcony and fought the urge to cry. All she could do was pray for Alfonzo, but she knew it would do no good. A far more tangible god was now seeking him with only wrath in his heart.

20

To say that Eddie was shocked when the sun came up was to put it mildly. Still, he knew the monsters hadn't retreated. Not permanently. Whatever was happening, he had the sinking sensation that it was only temporary. "Miss Parker, I don't know what you did..." Then Eddie snickered to himself as he realized exactly what Miss Parker probably gave the vampire in exchange. "But I'm thankful."

He sighed. His humor crumpled like a flower in a hailstorm. His thoughts returned to Bella. Poor Bella. Cringing, he bit back the tears that threatened to fall. What the vampire had told him couldn't be true...could it?

His hopes of making progress in the sunlight were dashed when he realized there were many people who were taking the opportunity to flee the city. They needed help gathering their things onto carts or horses or tying things into better stacks to carry with them. He wished he could do more.

But no matter how many people he helped, he was plagued by regret. He should have noticed that Bella was missing! He should have seen through that vampire's disguise. Was he to blame for this? Even in part?

Yeah. Yeah, he probably was.

Maybe he should have gone with Al to stop Dracula. But he couldn't stand the thought of abandoning Bella. Only to then learn that the damn fuckin' vampire illusionist had lied! *Of course he lied, you gullible piece of cow shit. What else was he going to do? Pave the street and put up road signs? Come on...He knew how to play us, that's all.*

But maybe, just maybe, a few more people might make it out of the city alive. A few more innocents might survive this chaos and bloodshed. So, he did all that he could, whenever he could, for whomever he could.

If he wasn't in this to save lives, then this whole thing lost its meaning. Then it became about hate...and revenge. He shook his head. He looked up to Al like a father. But to see him so bullheadedly attached to destroying Dracula above everything else was wrong. And if there was one thing Eddie had learned over his years—it was to trust his instincts.

And his instincts told him this was all going to end very badly for everybody.

He could be sure Al was doing a hell of a lot better than he was.

He hoped.

―――

MAXINE COULD NOT EXACTLY SAY she approved of the renovations Vlad had made to the public library. It was a magnificent building when she had visited it before, and now it was as the rest of the city had become—a twisted nightmare of its former self. Not to mention, it was quite easily ten times

Curse of Dracula

the size of the original, much of it connecting in nonsensical ways.

Magic.

She shook her head. It was still much to absorb, even for her. She stopped to look up at a huge portrait. It took up nearly the whole wall, and it towered over her. It was, of course, of Vlad. But it was a face she had only seen in her dreams—a man with long white hair and a cold, cruel, impassive expression. She reached out to place her bare hand on the oil painting and sensed a little of the creature who had painted it. They had four arms. She pulled her hand away and shuddered. She did not want to linger in the memories of a creature that was not human. There was no telling what that might do to her.

Vlad had not given her gloves to wear. She wondered why. *Perhaps he wishes you to live free of that constraint? Or perhaps he wishes it to serve as a warning to others. Once more, the answer is likely both.* She shook her head and tucked her hands into the pockets of the coat she had been given. It was warm, comfortable, and fit her wonderfully.

Her fingers touched something unexpected. Something hard and rectangular. Blinking, she pulled it out of her pocket and looked down at it. A small paper box tied with a red ribbon. *What on Earth?* She pulled the ribbon off and opened it, not knowing what to expect inside. An eye, maybe. A finger.

She laughed. Hard. Leaning her back up against the wall, she smiled down into the box and couldn't help but feel...she wasn't quite sure what the word was. Perhaps it was love.

It was a small box of chocolates. Six of them, arranged in a row. By the looks of things, they were expensive. Vlad Tepes Dracula—warlord and tyrant, demigod and Vampire

King, the creature who had plagued humanity and sent a third of the city of Boston to its death—had given her *chocolates.*

What an utterly confusing mess her life had become.

Plucking one of the treats from the box, she looked down at it. She didn't remember the last time she had eaten chocolate. She had certainly never been gifted any. Even her clients, when they did give her gifts, preferred to give her things they thought were far more "thematically appropriate." Crystals, books on the occult, tarot decks, incense, things of that nature. Never anything like this.

She ate the confection with a smile. It was as good as she would have expected. Perhaps better. Dracula had left her to wander the halls of his home with its twisted architecture and depictions of torture. He had left her to see to the downfall of the hunter Alfonzo Van Helsing who had come to stop him. Not merely his death, but his utter destruction.

And he had given her a box of chocolates.

"You are a complicated creature, Vlad Dracula."

Alfonzo wiped a bit of sweat and blood off his brow before it dripped into his eyes. He didn't know if it was his blood or that of the creature whose ribcage he had just cleaved with his sword. It didn't much matter. He was close now. The library was near the center of the city, and he was only a block or two away. He could see it. Adrenaline drove him forward. It would all soon be over.

The sun had risen unexpectedly. He had to stop to look at it in surprise when the sky began to glow brighter. He knew it was not because the vampire had been defeated.

Curse of Dracula

Why Dracula had chosen to do it was a mystery to him. Nor did it make much difference.

It hadn't stopped the creatures from attacking him. It seemed that some of them did not care for the glowing orb in the sky. But perhaps it gave the innocent civilians the chance to escape. He could hope, but he couldn't stop. He couldn't help those who struggled in the streets as they evacuated their cursed and ruined city.

The vampire needed to die. Once he was lifeless in the dirt it would not matter how many escaped—all the rest would be spared. If he could cut the poison off before it spread, the rest would fall, and no demons would linger in the shadows to plague those who ventured too close.

He had prayed Maxine would do what was right and rip out the vampire's soul. For a moment when the sun had risen, he had thought perhaps that was what had come to pass. But as a creature crawled from the shadows of a home to lash at him, he knew it had been a pointless and futile hope.

Finally, through all the pain, the muck and the mire, he made it to the courtyard between the library and a large, gothic reproduction church. It, like all the rest, had become perverted and warped by the curse of the vampire. Not even a house of God seemed to be spared from the depravity that followed the creature wherever he went.

Statues that he was certain once depicted saints and angels now showed anything but—sinners, demons, and monsters that tore into the flesh of stone victims whose faces were caught in silent screams. Their eyes rolled to the heavens as if to beg for forgiveness from the God who had abandoned them to their fate.

Alfonzo tightened his grip on his sword.

It was an abomination. All of it. But to see the perversion

of a house of worship—a house of mercy—sent rage coursing through his veins. He could not let it stand. He would burn it to the ground, and hopefully take as many of the monsters inside down with it as he could.

Glancing at the library, which now resembled more of a fortress or a castle than its original structure, he gritted his teeth. He would use the church as a warning to the creatures that dwelled within the library proper. Setting the structure ablaze might also serve as a distraction and draw several of them out into the open.

Storming up the stairs, he kicked open the large wooden doors and prepared himself for a fight.

He had not expected the room to be empty. No one was there. Stepping carefully into the structure, he kept himself braced for a fight. For this to simply be a trap. But there was nothing but empty pews and shadows, rays of light shining in from the stained-glass windows and streaming into the building.

Perhaps they had all retreated into the darkness of the basement to avoid the sunlight.

It was only after a few seconds that he noticed the sound of someone crying. Turning toward the source of the sound, he paused. At the head of the sanctuary stood the altar. It once likely featured a statue or depiction of Jesus and provided hope and guidance to many. Now it was an enormous brass sculpture depicted a twisting mass of naked bodies, all enjoying the sins of the flesh in profane and twisted ways. It was revolting.

There on the altar was a young woman, wearing a dress made of thin white lace. It was sheer, all but showing her naked body beneath it, leaving little to the imagination. She was blonde, her hair flowing loose around her in delicate waves. She was gagged and bound, her arms tied over her head, her feet lashed to the base.

She was weeping, muffled against the fabric tied around her head.

Alfonzo's heart leapt into his throat as he raced forward. He was moving out of instinct before the thought even fully formed in his mind. He knew the woman.

"Bella!"

Hopeful blue eyes turned to him, wide and tearful, and she thrashed in her restraints. Alfonzo sheathed his sword and pulled out a dagger and quickly cut her restraints then helped pull the cloth gag from out of her mouth.

"Oh, oh Alfonzo! Oh, I'm so happy to see you!" Bella sat up and swung her legs over the side of the altar, and before Alfonzo could do much else but stand there in shock, she had thrown her arms around his neck and hugged him close.

He was suddenly standing between her knees, her dress riding up dangerously high—not that it was much of a dress at all. She was clinging to him as though he were the only thing that existed in the world. Alfonzo hugged her back, wrapping his arms around her, and pulled her tight.

Even through his leather coat, he could feel the pillows of her breasts against him. He bit back what unexpectedly surged in him. Lust. He fought it like he always did. He had watched the girl grow up from a child into a woman. He had watched her bloom into such beauty.

It was wrong.

It was a sin.

But God above, if he hadn't always wanted her. Her fierce intelligence. Her indomitable spirit. Watching her learn to fight had been one of the proudest moments of his life. More than once, he had watched her in awe.

And desire.

He hugged her tightly. *No. She is like a daughter to me. I raised her. I took her from the orphanage. I am over twice her age.*

Her hand wandered from his shoulder up through his hair, stroking slow circles at the base of his neck, her nails lightly scraping at the skin. He tensed—it was that, or he would shiver at her touch. She smelled like flowers.

He forced himself to focus. "Are you all right? Dear God above, Bella. I was so worried…"

She nodded then nuzzled into his neck. Christ above, she smelled so good. Like warm summer days and the promise of happy memories. "They didn't hurt me. I was so scared…I was so very scared, Alfonzo. Please, hold me tighter."

He was helpless but to obey. She felt so small against him. So young. So *perfect*.

When the fingers of her other hand traced over the collar of his shirt along his neck, he couldn't help but shudder. "Bella…?"

"I'm just so relieved. I'm so happy to be safe in your arms."

Safe.

"Eddie, he—he went to find you."

"I'm glad it was you who found me." She tilted her head up, her warm breath washing over his jaw. "I've always been so much safer with you. He's a nice boy. He means well. But he doesn't have the experience I want. The strength."

Without realizing it, he stepped closer to the lip of the altar. Closer between her legs. She was so warm. She smelled so goddamn *good*. And the way she nestled in his arms, nearly naked, it felt like all the dreams he had wished would have left him alone. "Bella…I…"

When her lips grazed his cheek, something in him broke

loose. Something in his mind...gave way. He felt drunk. Slightly detached. But like with alcohol, his reservations seemed to be what left him. It only left a growing heat that seemed to coil low in his body.

"I've seen you watching me. When I train...when I sleep. I've seen the looks you gave me, over all those years," she whispered.

Her breath was like Heaven against him. He wanted to feel those soft lips. He wanted to taste them. "This is wrong," he murmured.

"I never wanted Eddie. I never wanted the boy." Her legs hooked around his waist, and she shifted her body against his, pressing the bare heat of her core against his own eager need. "I wanted the man."

"I—"

"Shush..." She ran her fingers slowly through his hair, looping behind his ear and tracing over his jaw. She tilted his head to hers, then...then she kissed him.

All his restraint crumbled at the feeling of those lips against his. It was what he had always dreamed of. What he had always imagined. And now they were his. She tasted so sweet, so perfect. It was wonderful. It was bliss. There was nothing wrong about this. He had loved her, raised her, trained her—this was right.

He kissed her back, harder than she had begun the embrace, his hands slipping over her body. She was lithe, but soft in all the right places. It had been so long since he had known the embrace of a woman—and this was *Bella*.

Her hands were at his belt, undoing it, letting his weapons thunk to the ground, abandoned and forgotten. They were not her goal. Not his either. He had other needs. He undid his pants, freeing the painful urgency that had grown swollen and tight in desperation.

When her hand grazed over his hard and eager member, he moaned. "Please..."

"You've wanted me for so long. I've wanted you too, Alfonzo." She breathed against him, her hand grasping him, stroking him, and he almost buckled from the pleasure of that simple, tentative gesture.

He watched, dumbstruck, as she lay back on the altar, spreading her legs wider for him, her fingers twisting in the lace fabric of her dress and pulling it slowly up to her waist. He could make out the hard peaks of her breasts through the lace as she breathed, her chest heaving with her own desire.

Heavy-lidded eyes gazed up at him, the blue shades turned darker with need. She was so beautiful...so perfect. So ready for him. He stepped into her, and leaned down to kiss her, her tongue rushing into his mouth to twist with his.

Her legs wound around his waist, pulling him to her. When he broke the kiss, he was breathless. He watched her writhe beneath him in abandon. She was undoing his shirt, her hands finding his bare skin and running over him like he was her lifeline. "Please, Alfonzo...Please, I need you. I've wanted you for so long..."

It was when she chewed on her lower lip, furtive, as if she was unsure of herself, that his remaining control shattered. She looked so innocent. He grasped himself, pressed against her wet heat, and slid himself inside her. He growled in ecstasy.

Her cry of pleasure echoed through the sanctuary of the church.

21

Bella gasped and moaned as she rode the man beneath her. It was so *good*. She rubbed her hands over her breasts as she lifted her hips and drove them down against him in slow, deep movements. Alfonzo Van Helsing lay naked and lost in bliss, his head thrown back, mouth open, as he filled her.

She knew she should feel guilty. The man had saved her from an orphanage. He had raised her. Trained her to fight.

But Mordecai's words echoed in his head. She had not hypnotized him—she had only compelled him to do that which he had already desired. He had wanted her. And she had only given him the small push, the *very* small push, it required.

There was some odd, strange poetry to the whole thing. He had been the one to lead her into this life. And he would be the one to lead her out of it. It was his fault Boston had fallen to Dracula. He could have traded a willing Maxine for all their lives. Of course, then she might not have found Mordecai...but no. They had already met. He would have found her anyway. She was sure of it.

Mordecai had already told her that Zadok had offered

her freedom in exchange for their departure. Alfonzo had said no. His revenge had consumed him. And now...*she* was consuming him. He had trained her how to hunt vampires, and now he was training her how to be a succubus.

She would have felt bad if this were not such a perfect and beautiful moment. If he did not look so stunning beneath her, his body beaded in sweat, his muscles tensing and relaxing in waves. She was bringing him more pleasure than he had ever known.

He wanted this. He wanted her. And he could have as much of her as he wanted, until he broke down and couldn't take any more. Wouldn't this be a better way to die? In the arms of the woman he desired instead of on the end of one of Dracula's pikes? This wasn't a violent death. It was a loving one. He would drift away into darkness, held in her tender embrace as she brought him to ecstasy over, and over, and over.

They had been going for hours, and he was drifting in and out of consciousness now. He was barely awake long enough to cry her name, grasp at her body, and release himself deep inside her.

Each time he did, something inside her surged. It was not merely pleasure—it was a hunger being fed. She was *consuming* him, little by little, and it was better than anything she had ever experienced in her life.

Except perhaps Mordecai. Oh, Alfonzo was fine—firm and big enough to reach some of the right places—but nobody filled her like her beloved. Her mate. The father of her child. No one was better than he was. Nobody made her feel like Mordecai. But Alfonzo—her former mentor, her former friend—held a special place in her heart. He was the family she was leaving behind.

And he was giving her the family of her future.

With him, life bloomed inside her. It was not his seed that would take root in her body. It was his very lifeforce. Alfonzo would be the match that started the fire inside her. "Yes, Alfonzo—yes—oh, yes!" With each weakening eruption inside of her, new life was fed. Her baby. Mordecai's baby. And a little bit of it would belong to the man beneath her.

Alfonzo moaned in bliss, lifting his hips, burying himself deeper. "Bella..." He was breathless, gasping, and lost.

A pair of hands helped guide her, showing her how to roll herself against him on the downstroke as she rode Alfonzo toward his death.

Hands that did not belong to Alfonzo.

"That's it, my angel. That's it. Just like that."

She learned the pattern, and she watched as Alfonzo twisted beneath her, the movement sparking new ecstasy inside them both.

Leaning back into Mordecai's chest, she turned her head to kiss him. He met her embrace eagerly. She moaned against his lips. He eased his lips away from her to kiss her shoulder. "Do you feel him? Do you feel him feeding you? Giving to you?"

"Yes..." She shut her eyes. "I want more."

"Don't kill him. Take little pieces. We need him alive, don't forget. Master Dracula will be very upset if you eat the rest of his life."

She whined like a child. "But I *want* to."

He dug his teeth into her flesh. "Good girl. I know you do. I already have another man ready for you. One you can kill. A new one, fresh and afraid. One you can fuck until his heart stops beating."

That did sound wonderful.

She purred happily—the noise coming from her throat wasn't human. She probably should be scared by that. She should be horrified at what she was doing. She pressed her palm against her abdomen, feeling the life inside. But that was not all she felt. Suddenly, something began to itch on her back. Then the itch began to burn. "Mordecai?" she whimpered nervously.

"Ssh... It's all right." He leaned away from her a little. "Let it happen. Don't worry. It'll only sting for a moment." He held on to her waist, continuing to guide the motion of her hips. "Take him one last time. Ride him to one more climax. Become who you were meant to be."

"Yes—oh, yes—" She leaned down to kiss Alfonzo, waking him from his stupor. His eyes were glassy, and it was as though he were drugged. But he responded to her, his hands drifting to her hips, pulling her weakly down to him, humping up into her. Even through his daze, he remained hard and hot inside her, throbbing.

"Please, Alfonzo—please—I need you," she urged. "Love me, Alfonzo—love me!" She rolled her hips as Mordecai had shown her. She let her breasts press against Alfonzo's chest. She kissed him like she kissed her mate. She let her tongue tangle with his.

He twitched inside her, his body spasming beneath her. He cried out in bliss as he painted her body with his very life. Something on her back burned, but it wasn't pain.

It was freedom.

She spread herself wide, and she looked up in awe as she saw feathery wings to each side of her. They were white, the feathers tipped in tones of light sky blue. They were beautiful. And they were hers. She gasped, and the shock stilled her movements. She pulled Alfonzo free of her body, used and forgotten, and reached up to trace her hand over what she could feel like new limbs.

They were hers.

She had *wings!* The feathers were soft like down under her fingers. New and strange. But wonderful.

"Oh...Bella."

Something in Mordecai's voice sounded wrong. She turned, and he was kneeling there, straddling her victim's legs with her. He was weeping. Tears streamed down his cheeks, unchecked.

She stood to face him, feeling her feathers brush against the furniture nearby. She pulled her wings in—oh, how strange it was to have new limbs—and reached for him. "My love, what's wrong?"

Mordecai stood only to kneel again at her feet, looking up at her with nothing but love and adoration in his eyes. She stroked her hands over his cheeks, gently wiping away the tears.

"Nothing is wrong." He took her calves in his hands and pulled her closer, leaning in to kiss her abdomen. His tail wound around her legs. He tilted his head to rest his cheek against her there. "I am just so happy...now you really are my angel."

———

Maxine found a balcony to stand on somewhere around sundown. She wished to watch the sun set for the last time in likely a very long time. Who knew when Dracula would release it from his grasp once more? Who knew if she would be alive to see it when he did?

She looked down at the street beneath her. The very city itself had been turned into a battlefield. Fences were torn asunder, trees knocked over, doors and windows punched in. Bodies littered the roads, shredded and half-eaten. She tried to ignore it all, but it was hard to do so.

She had slept with the man who had done this. She had given him her body and had reveled in the pleasure—in the happiness—they had shared. She was a traitor to the living. She should rail against him for causing the agony washing over her. But, damn her to the pits, she still didn't want him to die.

She simply wanted him to stop.

Around and around her mind reeled, unable to find purchase on one side of the argument or the other. All that she knew was that her sanity and her moral value were deeply in conflict. When she was around the vampire, she willingly fell into his hands. Apart from him, she had wondered if his influence would fade. If his proximity was truly to blame for all she felt for him—a product of her empathic gift.

But now, she *missed* him. She wished he had spent the day with her. Last night she had given him her body, but he had already owned her heart. And she had been given his in return.

No one had ever loved her the way he did. She had been cared for well enough by the Roma—but never like *that*. Even to them, she was always an outsider. Never one of them. Never truly family.

Family.

What an odd concept. She had always thrown it away as something she would never have. Never belong to. But it seemed that was precisely who Dracula collected—those who found no companionship elsewhere. Zadok. Elizabeth. Witchdoctor. Even Walter, she knew, must serve his master out of a familial sense of friendship and love.

Curse of Dracula

She was loved. She pulled out the small box of chocolates Vlad had hidden inside her coat. She had eaten two and had resisted the urge to eat the rest over the course of the day. It was so rare she was given things, she wished to savor them.

It did funny things to her to think about it. She felt butterflies. It made her smile, even as she dwelled on the wreckage of the city.

I deserve to go to Hell for this, don't I?

The odds that I would ever be allowed into Heaven were rather slim. She sighed. *And now they are certainly dashed. He is the King of the Dead, even as he is the lord of vampires. I cannot escape what I am, even as he cannot escape himself. I cannot ask him to be that which he is not.*

I love him. This is no trick of his nearness. It is truth.

But this suffering—this death and torment—it had to stop. It was too much for her to forgive. Even for someone she adored.

What could she do? Destroy his soul? The thought hurt her like a physical wound. She leaned against the railing and let out a wavering breath.

"Miss Parker. Good evening."

She turned and saw the cold redheaded vampire standing by the door. She smiled faintly at him and motioned him to come closer. "Hello, Walter. Good evening to you as well."

He squinted a little at the rays of the fading sun but came out anyway. She gasped. "Oh! I'm so sorry. I didn't even think—"

"It's quite all right. I would not have come out here if I were in any danger. Being so closely tied to Master Dracula's blood allows me the benefit to walk in the sun if I choose. I find it simply too bright to enjoy, although the warmth is nice."

She turned back out to look at the city. "Do you miss it? Being alive?"

"Sometimes. It was certainly simpler. My days as a mortal were not the most pleasant, though, so I cannot say I miss the events, per se." He stood beside her, a hand folded across his lower back, the other resting on the railing. He looked out over the city. "I have seen worse than this, I fear."

"I suppose that is meant to be a comfort."

"No. Not particularly."

She laughed at his strange dry commentary. She looked up at him and could see nothing on his features but stoicism. That icy nothingness that reminded her so much of a carving and less of a sentient creature. But her gift allowed her to feel something more. There was a sorrow there—the memory of old grief. Of regret.

"I think you are not as cruel as you look, Walter. You do not wish for this fate to have fallen the city either."

He smiled lightly. "No. I do not enjoy death."

"What would you have him do?"

"Leave here and go to the mountains as he has offered before. Away from all the prying eyes. I do not like the level of visibility this forces upon us. The world may well rally to breach our defenses. We can stand against them for a while, but for how long, I do not know."

"It is not the human lives spent that troubles you?"

"I am afraid not. While I do not relish the blood, it does not trouble me."

That was fair. He was a vampire, after all. She looked back out at the city. "Would you tell me how you came to be as you are, Walter?"

He was silent for a long moment, and she worried

Curse of Dracula

perhaps she had offended him. Just before she was about to apologize for her question, he began. "I am nearly a thousand years old. I hail from northern England. I was the mayor of a small village there. Perhaps there were a hundred of us? Two hundred at our peak? We had no armies. We had no defenses. We had nothing to offer. But it did not stop him from coming. It did not stop him from setting upon us like a plague."

His hand on the railing tightened. "One by one, night after night, people began to die. It continued like an illness, spreading, until more and more of my people—the ones I had been chosen to protect—were preying on the survivors. What manner of terrible sickness raises its victims from the grave? It was not until I took a torch and threatened to burn everything down if he did not show himself that he came from the shadows. I stood there and knew I was helpless. If he wished me dead, he would have it. If he wished us all to be his slaves, that would be within his right."

Crimson eyes slipped shut, as if he were picturing that night in his mind. "He asked me if I wished to serve. I told him I would kneel at his feet if he spared the rest of my people his terrible fate. It was my duty to protect them, and I would proudly lay down my life to do so. He agreed. With one gesture of his hand, all the vampires he had made seized and burst into flame. He freed them from the curse... and burned the city to the ground. All of my people around me. He proved my threat had been nothing but childishness. I had also not been clever enough in my definition of the word 'spare,' it seemed. He freed them from his curse, and the humans from their lives. He made me as he. I stayed true to my word and have served him ever since."

"I...I'm so sorry."

"I am not." He opened his eyes again and looked out at

the city. "I have come to understand that what he did was indeed mercy. It is I who have suffered, not those villagers."

"Then why do you not choose to die?"

"I made a vow to serve him. I will do so until he releases me. I am a man of my word. And he..." He paused, as if he had spoken too much. He sighed and continued. "He is in need of counsel. Left to his own devices, his wrath is far worse. He cannot be changed—his temperament is not capable of being mended. Some wounds never heal, and some blood shall never dry. But he can be tempered."

"Is that advice or a warning, Walter?" She smiled. He was such a dour and curmudgeonly thing. "I shall take it to heart either way, I suppose." She pulled the box of chocolates from her pocket and, lifting the lid, offered him one.

Looking down at her quizzically, he blinked. Carefully, as if he were afraid the box might bite him, he reached in and took one of the chocolates. He looked down at it in his hand as if he was utterly perplexed. "Thank you, Miss Parker."

"You're very welcome."

He ate the chocolate, and she took another as well, and they stood there in silence for a long moment.

"Tell me something, Walter," she began, unable to contain her curiosity. "Do you care for him? Do you love him?"

"Certainly not in the way you do."

She laughed, not certain if that was intended as a joke. But she took it as one, regardless. "I suppose one must need specify when the likes of Zadok wander your ranks."

"I am terribly sorry you were forced to spend two days in his company. The man is a cretin."

"Yes, perhaps. But there is tragedy there that has made him what he is. Same as you. Same as all the rest. Same even as Dracula himself. Very few wake up in the morning and decide they are to be the villain of their own life stories. What cruelty we pay to others we have learned to dismiss. Save perhaps in the case of mental illness or in the deranged. But he is neither of those things."

"You are a wise creature."

"I have witnessed much of human life despite my few years." She shrugged. "It is not by choice."

"To answer your question—yes. I have come not only to respect him, but to call him my friend. He is the closest thing to family I fear I have ever had. I loathe the idea of a world without him. But perhaps he deserves his rest. Perhaps this suffering should come to an end once and for all."

"Are you suggesting that I should destroy him?"

"No. I am merely saying I would understand it if you did. And I would not find it as loathsome a concept as perhaps the others have done in their bids to you."

"Ah. You know of Elizabeth's and Zadok's treaties to such an effect?"

"It is hard not to know of their comings and goings, or indeed of quite literally anything that passes across their infantile minds. They speak loudly of it at all times. Pity me, if you will, Miss Parker. I have had to spend centuries with them."

She laughed again, smiling up at the dour vampire. The one who seemed somehow even older than Dracula himself. Vlad had a shocking amount of life to him—*no pun intended*—in spite of his thousands of years. Walter looked and acted like the grave. "And you have my sympathy, Walter. Although it is an easy thing to come by."

It was his turn to smile. "And you will have no shortage of those hungry for it. I fear you may become exhausted by the needs of monsters wishing for a tender hand and a gentle word."

She sighed. "There are worse fates than to pay kindness to those in need of it."

A hand settled on her shoulder, and she nearly jumped in surprise. She was not expecting the vampire to touch her. Luckily, it was over her coat, and she did not find herself careening through his memories. "I do hope you choose to forgive him. I hope you can come to love him for who he is. But I have come to put little value on such things as hope." He paused. "Dracula will come for you soon. I should leave you be."

"It has been nice to speak to you, Walter."

"And you, Miss Parker." He lifted his pocket watch, flicked it open, then shut it once more. "I also have business to attend. I have been placed in charge of hunting down those who were too foolish to flee. The ceasefire is over."

She cringed and hung her head. It was not a surprise. It stung, regardless.

He turned to walk away. "Ah. You should know that Alfonzo Van Helsing is now our prisoner. His torment has already begun. You will come to witness his downfall. And if you still love our Master when he breathes his last...perhaps I will learn to hope again."

And with that, he was gone.

What hope could be had in a world of such darkness?

The idea of paying such creatures any mercy at all should turn her stomach. They did not deserve such things. That was the crux of her dilemma at its heart. It was not whether she loved Vlad enough to forgive him.

It was the possibility that some souls no longer deserved mercy.

22

Eddie was covered in muck. It was a putrid combination of blood, dirt, and debris. Some of the blood was his—most of it wasn't. That was a win, he supposed.

The sun had set. He wasn't anywhere near Copley. A whole day passed since he and Al had split up. He had gotten hung up helping people, then stream after stream of bastard monsters kept coming out of nowhere to try to kill him.

He kept trying to tell the monsters he had somewhere to be and somebody to save, but, *shockingly,* they didn't listen. He had killed seventy-two monsters, thirty-nine ghouls, eight lesser vampires, and three vampires who had really given him a run for his money. "And a partridge in a pear tree," Eddie sang to himself sarcastically.

This was getting old. The joke had worn thin. He wanted to go home.

"Hello, handsome."

Eddie stopped with a sigh and pulled out his guns. "What? What now?" He turned to look at the woman who had spoken. She had long, chestnut hair pulled back into curls in an intentionally sloppy bun at the back of her head. Christ, she was probably the most beautiful woman he'd ever seen. Her lips were painted deep red.

But her eyes were an unnatural green.

He raised his guns and pointed them at her.

"Is that how you greet a lady?" She raised her hands in a show of harmlessness.

"You ain't no lady, vampire." Eddie narrowed his eyes. "And don't give me any of that 'boo-hoo, I'm an unarmed woman' bullshit."

The woman grinned wide and lowered her hands. "My name is Elizabeth. I am an elder vampire. I am nothing like the creatures you have fought so far. I have served at the left hand of Master Dracula for more than three hundred years. I will be your death, tasty boy. Come, embrace me, and I will make your exit from this world one of bliss and ecstasy."

"Going to have to pass. Thanks for the offer." Seemed he was going to get that pear tree for his list in the form of an elder vampire. Or he'd die. One way or another. He clicked back the hammers of his guns and opened fire.

———

Alfonzo flinched, jarred from his unconscious state by someone shaking him roughly. His head bounced off the stone floor, doing little to help clear the sensation that he was lost in a turbulent sea. "Wake up, scum."

He didn't know the voice. He didn't know that it much mattered. The room was dark, lit only by a few paltry candles scattered about. The room smelled of rot and death. It might have been him. It was hard to say.

Everything was numb. He could have been missing limbs, and he would not have known. Like the morning

Curse of Dracula

after a drunken binge, he was left with only the pounding ache in his head and the regret over what he had done. Even if he could only vaguely remember it.

Images of Bella flashed before him. Of her naked body beneath him, parting for him, begging for him. Now he could see it for what it was. In the coldness of his clear thoughts, he understood. Succubus. Either one had taken her form, or...she had become a demon herself.

No. It had been her. He would have seen through a lie. *Like you saw through the vampire who was in your midst for two days and you were too bullheaded to notice?*

And he had fallen prey to her like a fool. He remembered her over him, and being buried deep in her fire. Shame made his stomach twist in disgust, and he wanted to be sick.

He was a failure. Not only in killing Dracula—but as a friend, a mentor, and as a man. He had betrayed Bella the moment he didn't notice she was gone. He betrayed her when he fell victim to his own temptation and sin.

The only thing left was to let God judge him. "Let me die."

"Oh, you will. Just not yet." The man—or monster, it was hard to tell—stood from where he was crouched. Alfonzo wondered if that would be the last of it. He let his cheek fall against the grit and grime of the dirty stone floor. If it was the last thing he felt, he would be grateful. He was a wretch. He could not even greet his death with honor. He had not fallen by the blade, dying in combat against his enemy.

He had fallen victim to lust.

Lust for a girl he had sworn to protect. The haze of desire that had driven him to madness did not keep the images from flashing through his mind. The memories of what he had done, all the pleasure he had experienced, and how eager he had been to defile her.

He could not pretend his desire had been a lie. But he *never* would have acted on it without intervention. Without the poison of a succubus sinking into his mind. He was weak. The city was now doomed for nothing.

I will burn in Hell for what I have done. And I will deserve it. God, forgive me. God, please, take pity on me.

The man picked up his ankle. Alfonzo grunted. "Let me die—"

The other voice only laughed. "Pathetic."

Then he began to move. The man was dragging him out of the room. The edges of the rough-hewn stone dug into his back and exposed flesh. He was still naked. Bits of rock scraped at him, opened wounds, and stung him. His head bounced painfully on the first step of a stone stairwell. Then a second. Then a third.

Alfonzo hollered and prayed for death. But darkness took him instead.

———

MAXINE SENSED Vlad's presence a second before he appeared, standing at her back. Hands settled on her shoulders, heavy and sure. He moved to fold his arms around her waist in an embrace, lacing his fingers with hers as he held her.

He was cold. But the smell of roses and the feel of the strength in him lured her into resting her head against him and simply basking in his presence. There was the night sky in the touch of his hands. But it came with more than that. It was accompanied by the flash of white teeth in the darkness. The bloodlust. It was a keen reminder that she was surrounded by the suffering of others.

"Walter told me that Alfonzo has fallen."

Vlad's voice was a deep rumble. "He has."

"Did you face him in battle?"

"No. The coward was felled by his own hubris and lust. He thought himself untouchable by sin. Bella was his undoing—not I."

He sounded a little too amused by the idea for her comfort. "Vlad...you didn't."

"She has accepted her nature as a succubus. She has fallen in love with Mordecai and made her choice. She has opened her arms and embraced her fate. I did not have to do much convincing when I asked her to be the trap for his downfall."

"I have a hard time believing you made a request of her. You mean to say that she did not resist the order she was given." She glanced up at him and found his lips curled in a slight smirk. "You do not typically ask for anything."

"That is very fair."

"And I do not appreciate the insinuation that I am somehow being stubborn in this ordeal by not doing as Bella has done." She looked back out at the city. "Why did she agree to do it? To destroy the man she once called family?"

"I think she has come to resent the demands placed on her by the mortal world. And I believe she appreciated some of the poetic justice in that the man who made her a vampire hunter would be the one to complete her transformation. He was given the chance to save her, and he turned it down. I think she felt betrayed."

"It is shockingly callous. That does not sound like the woman I met."

"She does not see it as so. She does not view what has been done to her as a tragedy, but a revelation." He gently kissed the top of her head. "I wonder if you would not feel the same should you accept my immortal kiss. Or would you loathe me for what I had done, turning you into a monster and a predator?"

"I cannot imagine what would become of my empathic gift were I to do such a thing." Maxine shuddered. "I fear what would happen to my sanity."

"It is for that reason alone that I have not already turned you, I admit."

"Was my opinion not to feature into the arrangement?" She laughed.

"As you so aptly pointed out, I am not one who much asks for anything." He turned her around in his arms. In one step and with the grasp of his hands on her hips, she was suddenly seated on the balcony railing. Squeaking in fear, she clung to the front of his coat tightly. It drew a genuine and soft laugh from him. "Do you think I would let you fall?"

"I—"

"This is simply easier on my neck." He was smiling at her fondly. There was such a warmth in those crimson eyes that it soothed her fear of falling. Sitting on the railing did give her over half a foot of height. And as he stepped in between her knees to wrap an arm behind her back, she understood why he had sought to even them.

The fingers of his other hand drifted up over her knee and began to ride her dress up to her thighs. She squeaked again and tried to stop his progress. "We're outdoors."

"And?"

"Someone will see!"

"No. No one is near." He stepped into her and pulled her

Curse of Dracula

hips against his. She gasped at the feeling of him there, already eager. Already wanting. He captured her gasp with a kiss that was feverish and needy. Bloodlust. His heart was beating with it, his lips warm against her. His violence against the hunter had turned into a different form of need.

He cradled her head in his hand as he devoured her lips. It was bruising. It demanded she give him control, and she was more than happy to relinquish it. She surrendered to him and the invasion of the warlord who was bent on conquering her.

Victory rang through him like the toll of the bell. His enemy had fallen. There was a violence in his yearning for her. He may not have come from the battlefield of the slain, but the celebration was still there.

When he finally broke from her, she was gasping for air. She clung to him, feeling lightheaded. It was as though her body had been set ablaze. Fire pooled in her. He watched her, heavy-lidded crimson eyes dark with the promise of something sinful. He had been a gentleman to her last night. She knew she would likely not receive the same care tonight.

Or right now, if the feeling of him pressed against her core, his pants and her undergarments the only thing separating them. The thought of him taking her like this on the railing of the balcony made her cheeks grow hot.

A slow smile bloomed over him. He traced his thumb over her cheek, clearly relishing her blush. "Such a shy little creature you are. I wonder if that will change."

"You assume I have not made the decision to destroy your soul."

"Have you?"

She paused. "No. I have not made my choice yet."

"Hm. Well. In the absence of my imminent demise, I

think I would like to invite you to dinner. That is...before I lose what is left of my restraint and bend you over this railing and rut you here and now."

Her face exploded in heat once more. "You are a passionate thing tonight."

"I am taking pride in my successes. I return to my encampment of war as a victorious soldier. I find the need to celebrate. I enjoy what triumphs I can garner." He stepped back, adjusted her dress back down to her ankles, and helped her from the railing. "I also enjoy making you blush."

"You are quite skilled in that regard." She smoothed the folds of her dress.

"Come." He held his hand out. "Unless you wish to take me up on my offer."

She placed her hand into his. "I think it best if I eat. I would not like to faint at an inappropriate time."

"Hm. It might not stop me if you did." He grinned wickedly and pulled her into him. With that, the world exploded into the weightless sensation of flying through the sky as a multitude of bats. It still made her ill, even if it did not frighten her anymore.

At least not terribly.

When she came back to herself, she was standing on the roof of the library. She gasped. The view was gorgeous, even if she did feel somewhat precarious standing on the copper sheets, even if this portion was perfectly flat.

A table was set up near them, using the beautiful view of Boston, cast in red light as it was, as the backdrop. Draped in a white cloth, a candelabra was burning in the center of it. The food was already set out and two glasses of red wine already poured.

It looked so wonderfully cliché that she had to laugh.

Curse of Dracula

"What is funny?"

"You have outdone yourself." She shook her head. "All we need now is some soft violin music and we would have the perfect date."

"It can be arranged."

"I am joking, you great oaf." She turned to him and batted him playfully on the arm. "I am not going to make some pack of vampires sit up here and play in a chamber ensemble for our amusement."

"For shame." His smile revealed how much he seemed to enjoy their candor. "I suppose I shall have to tell them their evening is freed up. Now, whatever shall we do without the accompaniment? And here I had been looking forward to a dance. I suppose we must make do, regardless." He offered her his hand, and she was struck by the image of it. It was not the first time he had done such a thing, and she doubted it would be the last. She hoped not. She slipped her hand into his, and he brought her into the position for a waltz.

It seemed he was remembering how they met. He danced with her to a silent tune, careful to avoid the ledges of the roof.

Their first dance had been exhilarating, terrifying, and wonderful. She had so much enjoyed their debate, even if she had been an utter fool for not seeing his inhumanity hidden behind the façade of a living man.

Now, here they were. Together. She had been hunted by a monster, and now she willingly danced with him atop the library of a city he had ruined. "We have come a long way, Count." For better or worse.

"So we have, Miss Parker. So we have."

The dance ended when he drew her close to him and pressed his lips to hers. Cold but wonderfully inviting. She chased his lips as he pulled away, and she stole one more embrace from him before he finally drew back with a dusky growl. He laced his fingers through her hair, combing the strands with his sharp nails. His fingers wandered along her jawline, and he tilted her head back and let his thumb rest against the hollow beneath her lip. He watched her as if he would burn the image into his mind. Perhaps he was trying to do simply that.

"What is it?" she asked.

"I thought I would mourn the day you no longer feared me. But I find myself with the need to celebrate the occasion instead."

"You will always scare me, Vampire King. You needn't worry." She took his hands. They were so different. Ashen and pale, not olive. Cold, not warm. The nails were long and pointed, dangerous and sharp. She lowered her head to kiss his palms one at a time. "I think I have come to accept that I enjoy the fear."

"Good." He lifted his hands from hers to trail a sharp nail through her hair again, tucking a loose strand behind her ear. The feeling brought a shiver out of her, and a wicked grin ghosted across him. "Come. Dinner is growing cold."

She followed him to the table and sat as he pulled out a chair for her. Steak—her favorite—prepared flawlessly. Yes, it would be a shame to let it go to waste. They ate in silence for a long time as she turned over her thoughts in her mind. She tried to keep them quiet. She did not wish to overturn the applecart and send it all rolling over the road.

But he seemed to sense her unease. "What is it?"

"Nothing."

"You are a poor liar."

She smiled faintly and sipped her wine. "Nothing is wrong."

An arch of an eyebrow challenged her words. "The city lies in ruin around you. One of your brief companions has become a succubus, the other is my prisoner to be tortured horrifically, and the third remains doomed. After all you have witnessed, I challenge your assertion that nothing is wrong."

"I will amend, then. Nothing *new* is wrong."

"Fair."

They ate in companionable silence. It did not feel strange—it felt right. She sighed, sitting back, looking down at the glass of red wine she held and watching the red moon shine off the surface.

"There you are again. What is wrong?" he pressed.

"It would be so easy for me to forget. In your presence, it is so simple to ignore all that you have done…all that you are. I can see why others would be lulled into the quiet moments you might gift them. Moments where you are not the demon, but the man."

"And such is the challenge I have placed in front of you. Tomorrow, I will take you to see what will become of Alfonzo. I will show you his fate. If, when it is done, you can look in my eyes and tell me that you accept your love for me, then I will be satisfied, and I will release this city."

She stood from the table and reached for his hand. When he gave it to her, she tugged gently, urging him to follow her. He did, wordlessly standing and letting her lead them across the roof to the far side where she could see the bay. The harbor was beautiful, even if it was a little hard to see from where they were due the slowly growing buildings.

Everything glinted in the crimson light.

He walked up behind her and wound his arms around her, holding her to his chest. She once more leaned back against him and let out a wavering breath. She rested her hands atop his where they clasped around her waist.

All may come and go, but she now knew the one thing she wished to remain her constant. "I thought I would never come to think of anywhere as home again. I thought after I left Virginia, I would never want one. The life of the Roma was attractive to me at the time. Never staying in one place—making the hearth wherever you were. It was about those who lived around you, not the walls you structured there in an attempt to make it permanent. When they sent me away, I was convinced I would never have a family. Never have a home. Then I came here. I never thought much of this city. It was simply a place to conduct business. But after all the cities I've seen, after all the places to which I've traveled, this one always was my favorite."

He let her speak uninterrupted, his arms tightening around her slightly.

"Life had become routine the past few years. I had income. I had a reputation. My life has ever been normal—not by any stretch of the imagination. But it was beginning to feel comfortable."

"Then I arrived."

"Then you arrived. My life has always seemed to have one purpose—to collect the suffering of others. To feel the pain of all those around me, and to sympathize with all that I witnessed. I should not have been surprised when the very King of Dread and Suffering himself came to call."

She turned in his arms to face him and laid her hands on his chest. "The King of Vampires came and demanded everything from me—my body, my heart, my soul, and my mind. You have successfully earned the first three. Could I give you the fourth in this moment—could you even rip it

Curse of Dracula

from me—there is little else I would wish for more. But I do not know how. I am sorry for my turmoil."

"If that is all I receive before I meet the grave, I will die happy, Maxine. Know that I will be content with either path you choose. But tonight belongs to us." To her surprise, he sank to his knees in front of her. "Maxine Parker, I give you my body, my heart, and my mind. I give you my soul—what little remains of the wretched thing." He lifted a hand to cradle her cheek in his palm. "I offer you all that I am in return for what I demand from you. All my horror, all my death, and all the love in my blackened heart. My existence is in your hands. I lay myself at your feet, my angel of death. My angel of mercy."

Tears stung her eyes. She leaned down and kissed him. She spoke to him of her love in silence, in her touch, in her embrace, and in her soul. If she had to destroy him to save the lives of others, she knew she would throw herself from a cliff shortly after. She did not wish to live without him.

Moisture touched her fingers. When she looked down at him, she expected that her own tears had broken loose. But crimson stained her thumbs. He was the one crying. He smiled up at her, a sad and somewhat embarrassed expression. He stood and swiped his sleeve across his face before she could stroke away the tears. "Forgive me. I can hear your thoughts, do not forget. They are quiet now, for that I have not drunk from you in some time. But that...that was hard to miss."

"If I commit you to the grave, I—"

"No. Do not say it." He stood and gathered her into his arms, pressing her close to him. "I wallow in grief enough. I do not wish to do it more than necessary." He caught her face in his hands and held her. His crimson gaze was intense. It bored through her and pinned her to the spot. "Say that you love me."

She would have laughed if not for his intensity. Instead she was only left to whisper. "Vlad Tepes Dracula—I love you."

She squeaked in surprise as she was suddenly lifted off the ground—and to a considerable height, no less. Damn his height! He had picked her up off her feet, and for the second time that day she was twirled about in a circle. She squealed in laughter and clung desperately to him. "Put me down at once, you fiend!"

"Fiend?" He growled playfully. "A fiend, am I?" One of his hands caressed half of her rear before squeezing it tightly. "I will show you a fiend." His gaze shadowed with dark promise and hunger. "Remember my words to you. Kill me or obey me. And as you have not decided to kill me yet, then you are forced to do the other."

"Wait—"

23

His little empath had wanted it all. And Vlad had eagerly given it to her. He had twisted together their bodies. He had drunk her blood. And she had mingled their souls. She was so careful with him; he could feel it. Tender and delicate as if afraid to break him.

If she did, he would greet the void, and she would take a piece of himself into her. But if he died in such a way, he would go quite happily.

Vlad had never known such contentment. And if he had...he could not remember it. She lay in his arms, the poor, well-worn, well-loved creature. She was fast asleep in his coffin. There was no part of her that he had not reached. No part of her that he had not defiled. He had ridden her like a man possessed.

He had been possessed by her. She had been the demon in his mind driving him to continue, to show her everything he wanted to do to her. Sadly, she had only begun to imagine the depravity he enjoyed.

One thing at a time.

They would have plenty of evenings for him to teach her

the darker side of love, should she choose to embrace him permanently. For now, he held her in her peaceful sleep. Her thoughts were quiet. She dreamed of pleasant things. Of love.

Tomorrow, he would force her to witness what would become of Van Helsing. Tomorrow, he would force her to decide whether to kill him or to accept his embrace. Tonight had been about love; tomorrow would be about death.

He was a cruel master.

Perhaps, she might even come to love that part of his soul. He smiled and held her close and dreamed of what might become of them if she accepted him. He would let Maxine stay mortal for a few years more. He would let her become fully inured to his ways before he turned her. He did not look forward to the day she became as cold as he. He did not relish the idea of her taking pleasure in the pain of others.

It was so very much against her nature.

But it was inevitable. All his kind became deaf to the pain of those they fed from. It would break his heart to see her change. But if it would mean he could hold her for a hundred years? Two? Ten? Then he would do it. It was a sacrifice he had paid before, and for her he would happily pay it again. She was *his*. She belonged to *him*. And in turn, he had given her all that he was.

I love you, Maxine.

And for as long as I walk this Earth, I will never, ever let you go.

———

EDDIE LOOKED DOWN at the body of the vampiress he had fought. She had claimed to be an elder vampire, and she

Curse of Dracula

was right in warning him that she was stronger than anything he had faced before.

"Fuck." He coughed. He was bruised everywhere. But that wasn't the biggest problem.

He looked down at his left hand. He was missing a finger. He had already bandaged it up as tightly as he could after he had picked himself up off the ground. He had lost a finger, but in the end, Elizabeth was dead, and he had won. He fired off one more round of holy ammunition into her corpse and watched her begin to ignite and burn away into dust.

His hand stung like a bitch. He looked down at the strip of cloth that was already turning red, but slowly. He had seared it shut with the hot muzzle of his gun when it had happened in the fight. He figured he wasn't going to bleed to death. It had hurt. A lot. But he was going to be okay.

Whatever. It didn't matter. It was only a finger. He had nine more, right?

Who knew what Alfonzo had already lost by now, if he was even still alive? Or Bella? He wasn't going to whine about the finger he didn't need to shoot. *Poor Bella...*He couldn't believe she had become a succubus willingly. He couldn't. It had to be a lie. He was going to get to the bottom of it. He was going to save her.

Or...or kill her.

No. There must be a cure. He shoved the thought out of his head. He wouldn't let himself even consider having to bury a bullet in her head. Even if it was the right thing to do.

He still found the need to kick the dusty fanged skull of the vampiress as he walked away. It crumbled to ash and fell to pieces as it rolled away.

Stupid vampires. Stupid demons. Stupid Dracula.
Stupid Boston.

Eddie wanted to go home.

———

Maxine woke up slowly. She was so utterly comfortable; she didn't want to move. She curled into what was lying beneath her. It was cold, smooth, hard yet soft, like stone covered in velvet. When she nuzzled into it, enjoying the sensation of its chill surface against her warm cheek, it chuckled.

Right.

Yes.

That.

She yawned and stretched, feeling a hard surface close to her back. She did not need to open her eyes and see the pitch darkness she suspected surrounded her. She knew where they were. Half-awake, she had less of a filter than perhaps she should. "Why do you sleep in a coffin, Vlad?"

"Hm?"

"You do not burn in the sunlight. So why sleep in a coffin at all? Certainly, someone of your considerable height would enjoy more room to stretch out."

"You have asked me this once before."

"And you gave me a half-answer. You claimed it was the light that troubled you. I think you are more than capable of purchasing shutters. So why?"

He was silent.

Fearing she had committed a misstep without realizing it, she placed her palm to his bare chest. "I am sorry. I did not mean to offend."

His hand laced over hers, and he let out a slow breath. "You have done no such thing. I merely am deciding upon how to phrase my response."

His arm was slung across her lower back. The strength and the power that burned in him, even if it did not beat in his heart, was soothing.

"I am a dead soul trapped in an immortal body. While I may never be at peace, I am dead all the same. One must have both halves to be truly alive. To be as I am, neither one nor the other, I am as good as a corpse. I sleep in a coffin to remind myself of what I truly am. I have spent eons attempting to pretend that I am a man. I have dressed as them, lived amongst them, and hidden my ghastly nature. It is a lie. I do this to remind myself of what I am and that it cannot be forgotten or forgiven."

"You do not wish for forgiveness? I thought..."

"I do not want forgiveness from you, Maxine. I ask to be loved as I am. I shall never ask to be absolved. Such a thing is impossible and would never come to pass." The hand that rested over hers moved to wander through her hair, combing the strands through his sharp-nailed fingers.

Tragic creature.

"Save your pity for someone who deserves it."

She swore under her breath and sighed. "I do hate that you can hear my thoughts."

"Turnabout is fair play."

"As you've said. I—" Her stomach growled, interrupting their conversation. They both laughed at the sound.

"You missed breakfast. I should not be surprised. You mortal creatures and your love of food."

Suddenly, she realized she had been remiss in her manners. "Oh! The chocolates. Thank you for them."

"Hm? Ah. Yes. I thought you might enjoy them."

She smiled and placed a kiss against his bare chest. "No one has ever gifted me chocolates."

"Truly? Is it not what mortal gentlemen are expected to provide? Flowers, dinner, and sweets?"

"And when do you suppose I have been courted by a mortal gentleman?"

He paused. "Touché." He shifted, and she heard the creak of the coffin lid as he swung it up on its hinge. With it came the introduction of light into their small space. She was in her shift, and he was shirtless. A thick blanket was pulled up over them, and it was shockingly warm despite his lack of body heat. She pushed herself up to sit in the space between his hip and the wall of the coffin.

She traced her hand over his chest thoughtfully.

"What is it?"

"It is still a marvel to me that you exist. Vampires. Monsters." She shook her head. "Demons. I never figured them to be real. Even with all I have seen, I know I have not begun to witness it all. I know there are horrors that live inside this nightmare of yours that you have yet to show me."

He caught her fingers and lifted them to his lips. He sat up as he kissed them. "Are you afraid?"

"No...I only hope I am that which you wish me to be. But I do not know yet that I am."

He smiled and gently urged her back down to him. She met his lips eagerly with her own. She had come to desire his touch. More than that, it had begun to bring her comfort and solace.

Her stomach growled again.

He pulled back from her. "Yes, yes. Let us feed the great beast before it consumes us all." He climbed gracefully from the coffin and helped her step out of it.

Looking around the room curiously, she was shocked to see that she recognized some of it. Most notably, her wardrobe stood against one wall. And there, on a small table, was a music box. She walked up to it quickly, snatching it into her hands. She opened the lid. Sure enough…it was hers. The one her father had made before he had died and before she was born. "You…saved it."

"I had Walter gather your things from your house the night I unleashed Hell upon this city." Dracula replied nonchalantly. As if it were a trivial thing. "I thought perhaps you would wish it salvaged."

"Very much so. I would lecture you that collecting my personal items and arranging them in your bedchambers is presumptuous at best, but I find myself incredibly grateful that you saw fit to save this. My cards?"

"Your tarot deck is in your wardrobe."

She would have been sad to part with them. "Then I suppose I find myself doubly grateful and only once annoyed. So I shall say thank you, Vlad Dracula, for your kindness in rescuing my things."

"You should say nothing at all, for while you are twice grateful, it is I who upended your life in the first place. Therefore, we are in balance."

She smiled. "I suppose, yes."

When she looked at him, he was dressed, finishing the knot of his cravat. "I will fetch Walter and inform him that you are in need of breakfast. I shall return shortly." And with that, he seemed to vanish into his own shadow and slip underneath the door.

Strange man.

Stranger creature.

Yet she smiled at the thought of him. He was kind and cruel. Temperate and ruled by rage. Tender and violent. He was neither half, nor was he truly both. He was one thing to be certain—complicated.

She would happily tell him that she accepted him for what he was this instant and have him whisk them all away from here. Except for one small thing that remained, one small matter that had to be resolved.

Alfonzo Van Helsing.

———

Alfonzo did not know when his screaming ceased to sound like him. When the noises he made were no longer recognizable as his own voice. They merged with the pain until they were one and the same. It wasn't a sound anymore—it was a sensation. It was pure agony. Pure suffering.

A tight strap around his thigh was keeping him from bleeding out.

But it did not stop the feeling of teeth tearing at his flesh. He had been turned into a meal for a ghoul. It slathered over him, sticking its tongue deep into the folds of his muscles and sinew, seeking the flood of blood that it was denied by the tourniquet.

He had been propped up against the wall. His arms were chained over his head. They wanted him to watch.

He had passed out a few times, only to be slapped awake with a wet cloth and forced to drink water. He wanted to retch it back up, and a few times he did. But they would not let shock and horror be what killed him.

Not yet.

They wanted it to last.

The demon that laughed over him was skilled in his trade of torture.

And still the ghoul ate.

It was down to the bone of his calf, gnawing and tearing, stretching at his flesh like a raw chicken bone. It brought back memories of sitting in a tavern, biting into the leg of a turkey and happily eating his dinner.

And to this thing, that was all he was.

Food.

MAXINE WAS NOT QUITE certain if food had ever tasted as good as it did that morning. Sausage, roasted potatoes, scrambled eggs, and a side of fruit that she could not honestly say if she had ever eaten before. It was called a "kiwi," she was told. She was starving, and she did her best to keep from devouring the food like a wild animal.

Vlad did not seem to mind her voraciousness. Indeed, he looked quite pleased. It was a good ten minutes into the meal before she managed to slow down and sit back in her chair, drinking her coffee and tearing off small portions of a roll. Spending years with the Roma had ruined her table etiquette. But, once more, if the vampire was bothered by it, he said nothing.

They sat in companionable silence. Him, drinking tea, watching her with a scrutinizing, but tender expression. And her, trying to not let it bring warmth to her cheeks. "My poor table manners cannot be that amusing to watch."

"I am simply enjoying your presence."

"Mmhm." She shook her head. "You are so utterly melodramatic."

"I do not deny that charge." He grinned, and she caught a glimpse of his fangs. They were more retracted than they had been the previous night. She wondered if it might serve as an indication of his own hunger. "I am merely taking great pride in the fact that you fear me no longer."

She shrugged, not arguing the truth. He would always

frighten her. How could someone of his magnitude ever be truly benign? But she did not spend every waking moment quaking in fear, that much was true. "I have begun to believe you might not tear out my throat at any moment."

"A good step in any relationship."

"One that is generally supposed to come *before* physical encounters."

"Ah. So that's where I've been making my mistakes all these years." He snapped his fingers. "For shame. I am lucky that you seem to prefer it the other way around, then, aren't I?"

"You're terrible." Her face went warm, and she tried to hide it behind sipping her coffee. It was a poor attempt, she knew.

"I think you enjoy that as well."

She laughed, and he was grinning at her. She picked up a roll and tossed it at him, hoping to hit him in the head. He caught it easily and, still grinning, tore off a piece of the roll and ate it.

Walter stepped into the room then paused by the entryway, seeing them both caught in what must look like a personal moment. "Forgive me, Master. I come with news."

"Speak."

"Elizabeth has fallen to the hunter Edward."

Vlad sighed heavily and shut his eyes, rubbing his temple. "The boy has talent. That is troublesome. I should not have underestimated him. And neither should she."

Maxine sat back in her chair. She was sorry for the passing of the vampiress and knew she should not be. Elizabeth was a monster, a predator, and had likely done terrible things. But she had also spoken of wishing to become friendly with her. Although she had not fully trusted the woman, she had enjoyed their conversation.

Any death is a tragedy. But...I do not blame Eddie. This is a war. And Dracula is winning.

"Thank you for the news. It is unfortunate, but it is not unexpected. Come, Walter." Dracula gestured for him to enter the rest of the way. "Join us."

"How can you so easily dismiss her death?" Maxine looked up to Vlad curiously. It was not accusatory—she was genuinely surprised.

"How many of my creatures do you think I have lost? How many do you believe I have witnessed die, or have had to euthanize by my own hand due to their madness or loss of control?" His voice was dark, like the void echoed in his words. "Take that number...and whatever you believe it may be, double it. Then double it again, and again, and again until you lose count. I am old, Miss Parker. Do not forget that. She is merely one drop in the ocean of blood that I have left in my wake."

The room was silent.

Vlad gestured for Walter to sit. His mood shifted, and he smiled at his second-in-command. "Now, come. Miss Parker was merely detailing to me how I pursue her in a backward fashion. I was merely retorting that it seemed to work quite well in my favor, so it could not be so faulty. She resorted to violence." He held up the roll with a smirk in her direction.

"Many have thrown far worse and heavier objects at you, my Lord," Walter pointed out with a thin smile. The tall, pale, stoic creature seemed to be happy to see them as they were, even as he was the bearer of bad news. She could sense a quiet kind of hope in his heart. She also felt no grief over the loss of Elizabeth in him. Perhaps even relief. Curious.

"Will you join us, Walter?" She gestured to one of the

empty chairs at the table. It was meant to seat six. "Please, sit by me."

Walter glanced to Dracula, who nodded once. The younger vampire paused for a moment, as if unsure of what to do, before pulling out a chair and taking a seat.

"Tea or coffee?" she asked.

"Ah. Well." Walter went silent and did not answer, glancing back to Dracula nervously. It seemed he would refuse to answer her.

"Very well, I assume tea." She reached for the pot and an empty cup and saucer. "What will you take with it?"

"You do not need to do this, Miss Parker…"

"No, but it is the polite thing to do. Especially since I believe you are the one who fetched, if not prepared, all this food." She looked up to Vlad with a coy smile. "He orders you about like you are his butler. The least I can do is make you a cup of tea."

"I serve him willingly."

"I know. But you do not serve me."

Walter sat there, looking at her as though he had died in that moment. Nothing about him moved. Nothing twitched. Vampires could be so very still. Living creatures moved at all times, even unconsciously. They breathed and shifted in their chairs. But Walter simply froze as though he were a sculpture of a man instead.

He was dumbfounded. She laughed and reached out to pat the back of his hand where it rested on the table. She was grateful Vlad had let her don her gloves that morning. "How do you take your tea, Walter?"

"One sugar." He glanced at Dracula, who was watching the scene unfold with uncharacteristic silence. He gave no indication of how he expected Walter to act. Left on his own, he looked back to her. "Thank you."

"You lot really do not know what to do with yourselves when you are shown kindness, do you?" she observed as she handed him his tea after mixing in the sugar cube.

"No. I am afraid we do not. It is not something afforded to us often."

"Perhaps if you did not demolish entire cities from time to time, that might not be the case." She smirked over the table at Vlad.

"I will take your suggestion under consideration," the Vampire King replied wryly. Thankfully, he did not seem angry with her. He was watching her in fascination instead, as though something about what she was doing struck him as noteworthy.

She wasn't quite sure why.

Walter quietly thanked her for the tea again and sipped it. "Master, I also came to inform you that…" He paused and glanced to her. He was marking his words. "The work with the older hunter has begun to show progress."

"Good." Dracula's expression darkened. "I will inspect him personally this afternoon."

Maxine sighed. "You are committed to torturing him?"

"It has already begun."

"Out of petty revenge? Or because you enjoy it?"

He sneered. "Both."

She winced and shut her eyes. She had been expecting that answer, but it had still stung. For the same reasons he slept in a coffin, she wanted to remind herself of it. "I wish to see."

"Not yet, Maxine."

"Why not?"

He growled. "I wish to ensure that my work is…presentable."

"No, you wish for me to linger at your table. You wish to

draw out this moment as long as you can. I sympathize. But I will not allow it. A man—a city as a whole—suffers at your command. I will witness it. You will take me to see him now."

He raised a dark eyebrow. "And you think I take orders from you?"

"You are not my King, nor my Master. I am not one of your servants. Not now, not ever. You may assert to me that I belong to you all you wish, but I refuse this notion that I am subordinate."

"If I wished you to be my slave, I would already have it." He narrowed his eyes at her angrily. "I have never asserted that I wish to break you beneath my boot. Do not tempt me to change my mind."

"Good. You wish me to witness your horrors? Take me to see him now. I would see the whole of it. Not only your finished work."

"You will beg me to stop. You will plead for his release. I will be forced to tell you no." Dracula stood from the table, smoothing out his coat, and walked to a window to turn his back to her and gaze out at the darkened city below. "Are you prepared for this eventuality?"

"Are you?"

His hands tightened into fists, and she watched as he clearly forced himself to relax. He lowered his shoulders and clasped his hands at his back in lieu of clenching them. "You are unkind, Miss Parker. It is the ultimate hypocrisy that I feel myself wronged by you. I had hoped to spare you the act in progress. I had hoped to soften the knowledge that we do not simply embrace the violence that is our nature... we relish it."

"You wish for me to judge you wholly? Then why are you now too shy to lay down all your cards? Or do you already know how today will end, and you are simply ashamed?"

He turned to look at her, and all the warmth and tenderness she had seen in his gaze had been whisked away as though it had never been there. Finally, perhaps she had gone too far. She stood from the table.

Walter was the last to do so, and he took a step back from them. "I will go and inform the Chainmaster that they will have company shortly." He turned and left the room quickly—a little faster than he had walked in. She was sorry for the poor bastard.

Vlad walked up to her, and she forced herself to hold her ground. She refused to cower, even with the look he was giving her. He closed the distance between them. Without a moment's notice, he gathered the hair at the base of her neck into his hand and yanked back on it, wrenching her head up to him.

Her gasp of pain was captured by his devouring lips. The embrace was searing, bruising, and all-consuming. Her hands flew to his lapels and clutched at them like a drowning man might a raft and held on for dear life as all that he was rolled over her like a storm.

An inhuman growl bore through him, low and deadly, resonating from him and into her. When he broke off the kiss, she was breathless and holding on to him to keep from collapsing to the floor. His hand in her hair did not relent. He craned his head farther to whisper into her ear, cold breath pooling against her skin.

"I have peeled the skin from a man and laughed as he wept for mercy. I have impaled a woman upon a pike and left her there for her family to find and smiled as I did. I relish the pain of others. I wallow in their misery and take joy in their agony. What you will see in my treatment of Van

Helsing is *nothing* compared to that which I have wrought. It is all this I demand that you love—it is all this you should welcome into your heart with open arms, lest we both take the grave instead."

And with that, the world folded away from them.

24

When they reappeared, he threw her away from him. She staggered and fell, hitting the ground hard on her hands. She winced at the pain but made no noise.

"Master and Mistress, hello!" A voice came from near her. Neither male nor female. She looked up, and her eyes went wide. Neither was it human or vampire.

The creature was something else entirely. A demon, perhaps? She had never seen one. It had rough greenish skin, a blunted but delicate-featured face, and a dozen long, thin, terrible horns that bent in graceful arcs away from its face. It blinked like a lizard, and its eyes were a bright and vicious yellow.

The creature was also fully naked, save for chains that draped along its inhuman form. Its legs were canted like those of a beast, and a long tail swished around behind them. It smiled down at her, toothy and dangerous. The glint in its features said that it would like to hurt her—very, *very* much.

"Forgive me for the state of my workbench. I did not know I would have company. Especially not her." A taloned hand reached down to help her stand. She scrambled to her feet on her own. The creature shrugged, placed a hand in front of its waist, and bowed. "I am the Chainmaster. At your service, my Lady."

"I am not your lady..."

"You are his toy, then? Even better."

"Enough." Dracula broke into the conversation. "I have been told you make progress with your newest project."

"Yes, indeed! Come, come. Let me show you." The creature walked away from them. It was only then that she could examine her surroundings—a chamber made entirely of roughly hewn stone, like a cavern that had been chipped away until it was mostly rectangular. Candles burned in sconces along nooks carved into the walls.

This was not the public library. Perhaps it was beneath the city—or perhaps it didn't matter anymore. Dracula's will was imposing itself upon the very fabric of the world around him. It was futile to try to make logical sense of where she was.

Vlad gestured for her to follow the creature. She wished she had not asked to come here, but it was too late. She needed to see what was happening to the ill-fated vampire hunter. She needed to witness the malice that her vampire enjoyed.

And so, she followed.

As they walked, she realized she was in...a prison. The walls were lined with doors with small barred windows. From inside them she heard the whimpering cries. But it was not the sound that made her pull up to a full stop.

It was what poured from their cages.

Fear. Pain. Agony. Death. Hands reaching up from a pit, begging for mercy. For clemency. For forgiveness. *Please...*

please help me. Please free me. Save me. I never did anything to deserve this!

She put her head in her hands. Their emotions threatened to drown her. She couldn't breathe.

Hands settled on her shoulders, and it was as though an ice-cold knife cut through the rest of the voices, silencing them and sending them scattering to the shadows from which they came.

She shuddered at the sudden silence but did not lower her hands from her face.

"Are you able to proceed?" His voice was as cold as a frozen winter. Unreadable and taciturn.

"I need a moment." She lowered her hands and forced herself to pull in a long breath and let it out. "I was not expecting so many." She could keep them at bay, but she had been caught off guard.

Draw a line in the sand. She shut her eyes and tried to visualize it. She was a rock in a river, and they were the water around her. She was not them. She was not their emotions. She was her own mind, her own self, her own soul. Slowly, the feeling of drowning abated. After a pause, she nodded, and he removed his hands from her shoulders.

She felt the press of the emotions around her once more, but she could now keep them under control. Her raft was no long sinking into the seas. Without glancing at him, she kept walking. The creature—the Chainmaster—had stopped at a room some fifty feet ahead of them.

When she approached, they took a step back and gestured for her to go in first. The door was open. From it came the smell of blood and rot. Once, during her time with the Roma, they had come across a horse lying nearly dead in the road that had been there for a day, perhaps more. She had not ever forgotten the smell.

That was what this was.

Something else brought back the memory with a fierce and unexpected slap. The horse had not been left to die in peace. Wild dogs had surrounded it, coyotes ripping at the flesh. Living meat fed the living hunters. The sound of the animals ripping at the whimpering, dying thing had lingered in her nightmares.

And from that room she could hear an animal eating. Like a dog chewing on a slab of tough steak. She knew it contained no such thing. With a wavering breath, she steeled herself. Whatever she was about to see would be a sight she knew she would replace that memory of the horse in her mind with something far more gruesome.

Swallowing down the bile that threatened to rise, she stepped into the room without a second look at either of the monsters beside her.

The room was as dimly lit as the hallway, but her vision had begun to adjust to the light. And she sincerely wished it hadn't. There, lying in the middle of the floor, was a man she vaguely recognized as Alfonzo Van Helsing.

Or what was left of him.

He was unrestrained—and there was no need to shackle him down. For he was missing one of his legs. His left leg was a carefully stitched stump above the knee.

A ghoul was attempting to ensure that he lost the other.

A tight tourniquet was cinched at his thigh, preventing him from bleeding to death. She had heard of many men from the war who fainted at the sight of an amputation. They were grizzly things to behold. But she wondered if a single soldier would not have preferred that to what she now saw. The creature that was hunched over Alfonzo's leg was tearing off strips of muscle and meat like a wolf from a lamb. Its jaw dripped and oozed bright, fresh blood.

Curse of Dracula

"He has already begged me to let him die," the Chainmaster boasted, leaning up against the wall. "He lasted longer than I thought he would. Hunters always make the best toys."

Maxine wasn't sure who they were addressing. She assumed Dracula, but it did not much matter.

"And has he accepted my offer yet?"

"No. But he will. It's only a matter of time before he begs for that too."

"What offer?" she asked, her voice sounding faraway and detached.

"I have offered to have him turned into a vampire to end his suffering. I want to see him plead through broken tears to become the very thing he sought to destroy. Only then, once he has debased himself and his holy mission, will I kill him. I place him upon a spike and let him greet the dawn."

Maxine didn't look at him when he spoke. She didn't want to see the expression on his face. The iciness she could handle—but that was not what was in his voice. She did not wish to see his pleasure.

Stepping forward, she looked down at the ghoul tearing into the flesh of the vampire hunter. Alfonzo had never been terribly kind to her. That was not to say that he deserved anything remotely like what he now suffered. "Send the ghoul away until we are gone."

"Does the sight bother you?" the Chainmaster purred. "I love the innocent ones…"

"I wish to try to speak with Alfonzo, and it will be hard to do so while he is being eaten." She glared over at the Chainmaster and Vlad. She was not horrified—but angry. They would listen to her. She would make them. "Tell it to leave. *Now.*"

The Chainmaster grinned wide and swished their tail around behind itself. It looked up to Vlad. "Master?"

"Do as she says."

"Mmm...innocent and assertive. I like her." The Chainmaster clicked their tongue. The ghoul whined like a dog, but obeyed instantly, stopping in its grotesque work. It slunk out of the room liked a whipped animal.

"Thank you."

"Innocent, assertive, *and* polite." The monster cackled. "Can I play with her, Master?"

"No."

It sighed. "Had to ask."

Maxine shook her head and moved to kneel at Alfonzo's side. She cared not that the blood and muck would stain the knees of her dress. She reached out and ran her gloved fingers along his cheek, stained as they were with tears, gore, and dirt. "Alfonzo?"

His eyes were open, but they were staring at the ceiling, not seeing the world around him. He was in shock. Or his mind was breaking down. Likely, the answer was both. She called his name quietly again, and he blinked. Slowly, painstakingly, he turned his head to her.

For a long time, he gazed at her without seeing. Without recognizing. Then, finally, his brow creased in confusion. "Maxine...?"

"Hello, Mr. Van Helsing," she greeted the poor tortured man. She stroked his hair gently, trying to provide him any kind of comfort. "I am so very sorry."

"I failed." His voice cracked, and she saw tears start to form in his eyes. "Bella. She...she's a demon, and I—I couldn't—"

"I know."

"I wasn't strong enough..."

Curse of Dracula

"It's okay." She tried to console him. She knew it was too little, too late.

"In my hubris, I...I doomed us all." He reached up a hand to take hers, and she squeezed it tightly. "Forgive me."

Maxine smiled faintly. "It is all right."

"So many lives...Bella."

"I know. I am sorry."

"Hubris was not your only downfall, hunter. It was hatred. It was lust. A succubus cannot trigger desire that does not lie latent within their prey. They may only compel you to succumb to it. You wanted her. Your veritable daughter, and you wanted her. For shame." Vlad's voice filled the rancid air like a roll of thunder. At the sound of his voice, Alfonzo whimpered and tried to shrink away. But he could barely move. Maxine shushed him, but she knew it did no good to quell his terror. "You ignored the plights of the innocent souls you claim you were meant to protect. Nothing swayed you. And now, you pay your price."

"He is not the only one guilty of hate." She glared over at the vampire.

Vlad only smiled coldly in response.

Looking back down at Alfonzo, she kept stroking a hand over his hair. "I wish I could help you."

"I know." He coughed, and she saw flecks of blood on his lips. He had chewed through his lip, and by the sound of it, part of his tongue as well. "I will die soon."

No. I don't think you shall. And that is the problem.

"I...I'm afraid to die," he whispered then chuckled. "After all this, I am afraid to die."

"You needn't be so. Death is a mercy. It will not hurt you, not like what you know now." She tried to put on her best gentle smile. "It is a kindness to those in need. A freedom from the pain and the disease of this world. Men may fear its touch, but it is with loving arms that it comes. To be denied death is a terrible thing." She resisted the urge to glare at Vlad again. "It breeds only madness."

Alfonzo nodded weakly and shut his eyes. "Thank you, Maxine. I wish I had been better."

She lifted his hand to her lips and kissed his knuckles. "You tried to do what was right. That is more than most can say. I have seen evil in this world, hunter. It is not the same as weakness."

He smiled wistfully before his expression faded. He had fallen unconscious. It was probably for the best. She folded his hand across his chest and stood. She did not bother to inspect the stain on her dress. She walked from the room without a glance at either the Chainmaster or Dracula.

She spared a single look for the ghoul hovering in the shadows near the door, eager to get back to its meal. After pulling in a long breath, she held it and slowly released it. She forced all that she felt back behind a wall of simple rational thought, even though all she wished to do was scream.

This cannot continue.

Swallowing the rock in her throat, she turned from the door and walked back the direction from which they had come. She needed air. And while she did not know if that direction contained a way out, it was away from Alfonzo and the monsters that preyed on him.

Without warning, Vlad appeared in front of her. She walked into him with a grunt like he was a brick wall. He felt enough like one. She took a step back and rubbed her nose, glaring up at him. "That was unnecessary."

"Where is it you think you are going?"

"Away. Out."

"You have no indication of where you are."

"I rather think that no longer matters. I need air."

Crimson eyes narrowed at her. He took her by the upper arm, and the world folded away once more. When they reappeared, she felt fresh air on her face. She recognized where he had brought her—or what it had once been. It was the courtyard in the center of the public library. It had been a beautiful garden, once. Now it was a twisted and perverted version of its former self.

Statuary of weeping angels were surrounded by blood red roses. Vines threatened to overtake columns, as though they were a cancer infecting a body. Tangled and unruly, she wondered if the bushes around here had somehow become unfriendly creatures, as well. It was a safe assumption to make.

Tugging her arm out of his grasp, she walked away to sit on a bench several paces away. She was fairly certain—if only fairly—that the bench would not try to eat her. She shut her eyes and hung her head. "He is defeated. Let him die."

"No. I will have him tortured until he begs to accept the blood of a vampire to heal him. I will starve him, beat him, feed him to my creatures until he shatters. Once he is of my kind, I will let him greet the sun he worships one last time. That is, if I am feeling merciful."

"And if you do not?"

"I will shackle him into an iron coffin and drop him to the bottom of the ocean. There, his mind will molder and decay into madness for the rest of time."

She put her head in her hands, rubbing her face, before running her fingers into her hair and fisting them. She rested her elbows on her knees and wished she could close out the world by shutting her eyes.

Hands grasped her wrists and pulled them away from

her. She did not hear him approach, but suddenly he was on his knees before her. It was so startling to see him there that it broke through her instant desire to slap him.

He took her hands between his and placed them in her lap. Wordlessly, he bent his head and rested his cheek where he still held her hands in his grasp. He did not ask for forgiveness. He did not feel remorse over his actions. He would not release Van Helsing, nor would he give him a quick death. She knew better than to ask for any of those things. She would not pay either of them the indignity.

But the question remained what she would do in the wake of all these truths. Ones she had known, yes, but it was another matter entirely to see them firsthand. Could she love a creature capable of such things? Could she accept him, even with his barbarous ways?

This morning, she had been leaning toward yes.

But now... "Who else dwells within your dungeon?"

"Countless souls. It runs deeper into the ground than you can imagine."

She winced.

He turned his head and placed a kiss against her hands, followed by another, then another. Her heart began to beat a little faster, and she tried to push away the sensations he was dragging out in her. She had witnessed a man being eaten and tortured at the direction of the very same creature that was now working his way up to her wrist. It should not warm her cheeks the way it was. "Vlad, please..."

He growled, but he did not stop. When she tried to pull her hands out of his grasp, he allowed it, if only after a moment. He stood, and before she could say a word, he lay her down onto her back sideways on the bench with a press of his hand against her shoulder.

"Wait—"

Curse of Dracula

He was over her then, caging her in, his hand pressing against the stone surface close to her head. He kissed her to silence her and left no room for argument. His tongue claimed her mouth as he turned his head to deepen the embrace.

"This is who I am, Maxine. This is who I will always be. Make your choice." His words echoed in her mind.

His touch was warm. His heart was beating beneath her palm where she had unconsciously placed it against his neck. He moved to split her legs as he straddled the bench, placing her thighs on top of his as he gathered her stained skirt up to her waist.

The blood of a tortured man stains my clothes. She tried to push Vlad away. She succeeded in freeing her lips from his when she turned away from him. "This isn't right."

"I am the Vampire King. I am Vlad Tepes Dracula. I have destroyed cities. I have taken a continent's worth of lives in my thousands of years. Stop fooling yourself, Maxine— none of this has never been, nor shall ever be, *right*." He began to unlace her dress. "Do not speak to me of morals. Destroy me if you must. But if you cannot, then I will have you here and now."

"Why?" She gasped as he pressed himself against her core. She felt his desire against her. "Why now?"

Slowly, he ground himself into her, letting out a low snarl in his throat as he did. "Seeing you there, in that place? Demanding the ghoul leave the room—comforting that pathetic wretch—with the strength to watch the horror and walk away without even a flinch...I do not know as I have ever wanted a woman more in my thousands of years than I do in this moment. You did not even shed a tear."

"Crying would have belittled him." She managed to get out the words, although it was challenging. He had begun to rut against her through their clothing, teasing them both with what he wanted to do. "It would have cheapened his loss to add my pain to his."

"Wise girl…beautiful girl." He hovered his lips over her cheek. His hand had finished unlacing the front of her dress and had now spread the panels wide to seek out her bare skin. She hadn't worn a corset since the lace-up dress provided her enough support.

Now she did not know if she was relieved or regretful that there was nothing in the way of his hand as it cupped her breast and began to squeeze and stroke the tender flesh. She gasped and bit her lip as he focused on the sensitive bud that had already begun to grow pert from his attentions. He took it between his fingers and pinched.

She gasped and arched up into his hand, shocked at what the stinging sensation did to her. It seemed to run like lightning through her, waking everything that had been dormant. It pooled traitorously in her core. A place already under attack from the rest of him. She was under siege. Surrounded by the superior army, she did not know how long she could pretend to hold out before her walls caved to his desire.

He lowered his head to capture her other nipple in his mouth, and she whimpered as he bit down on it. Not hard enough to break the skin, not hard enough to draw blood, but hard enough that she writhed beneath him. Her body was seeking more of the beautiful, terrible friction with his.

Damn her to the pits of Hell—she wanted this.

But it all had to end.

The cruelty had to stop. No matter how much she loved him. But if she had to tear him to pieces—an act that she knew would kill her as well, either from exertion or grief—she would do it in his arms.

He had told her to kill him or obey him. That was not what he was asking her. It never had been. It had only been a farce, and now she could see what he was really asking her for, deep beneath the surface. She had turned her gaze from the truth of it for that she was selfish. But now she could see it plain.

Love me enough to destroy me.

And she loved him more than she knew how to express. She would follow him into the abyss. She would take them there together.

Tears stung her eyes, and she bit back a sob.

Lifting his head, he sought her lips. It was a tender kiss, filled with the answering echo of the love that beat in him. When he broke the embrace, he kissed away her tears. She knew he could hear her thoughts. She knew he understood what was to happen this night. There was no need to speak the words.

He hovered over her for a moment, his hot breath washing against her. She gazed into those crimson eyes and saw her eternity. She saw his joy. When she pulled his soul from his chest, a part of him would dwell within her for the rest of her life. She hoped the enormity of the act would kill her.

She wanted to live with him. And if she could not...then she would die with him.

Lifting her head, she kissed him, hard and passionate. She needed to feel him. All of him. She needed him to take her—to show her all that he could give her. She wanted one more time in his arms that might comfort them both. She wanted the world to be simple once more. She wanted to be his victim. Not the other way around.

He growled against her and lifted his head to find her ear. He tongued it slowly, nipping at the lobe, making her gasp and squirm again beneath him. "Mind your thoughts, Maxine." His other hand released her breast to wander down her body, opening the rest of the dress, before beginning to unlace her undergarments. "You wish me to take you? Do you want to feel what it is to be my prey?"

She nodded weakly.

"Then...far be it from me to deny such a wish."

25

EDDIE NUDGED open the door of the church and looked inside. It had once been a beautiful gothic structure, he was sure. But now it was...wrong. The statues of grinning demons and lascivious creatures ravaging screaming mortals didn't help.

He had reached the public library, but this place had called to him. Something about it drew him inside. Something told him...she was here.

Stepping into the large sanctuary, he quickly scanned the perimeter of the room. He was alone. Alone...except for one person, standing at the end of the center aisle. She stood at the altar, her back to the grotesque and perverted statue that hung over her head.

Eddie's steps hitched and froze. As did his heart. As did everything else.

"Bella...?" He had to ask. Because for a moment, he wasn't sure. The girl he had known had always been beautiful—but now she was *radiant.* Now she was like one of those paintings in a gallery. She was perfect. Her blonde hair hung down around her shoulders, free from its usual ties, and did little to help her sheer white lace dress in hiding the naked flesh underneath.

His body stiffened and tightened instinctually. He shook his head. *Succubus. It's a trick.*

It isn't a trick. I got like this looking at her on a Tuesday morning over breakfast.

He sighed. "It's true, isn't it? What you've become?"

"It is, Eddie. I'm sorry." She smiled sadly, looking honestly regretful. "I'm sorry I never felt the same for you as you did about me."

"Is that why you...why you did this?" He gestured at her and had to turn sideways to keep from looking at her. To keep from feeling the pull that made him want to test all the legends he had ever heard about lust demons.

"It wasn't about you. It was about me for once."

He cringed. There was such an accusation in her words that it felt like he had been stabbed. He scratched at his chest, as if he might find an actual dagger buried there. "That's fair. That's fair. I deserve that. I was wrong to think I...I'm sorry if I ever acted entitled. I never meant to. I just thought that—since we were friends—that—"

"I know...and it broke my heart that I didn't feel the same."

"Do you love him? Or her? This...this thing that made you?"

"His name is Mordecai. And yes." She paused. "I love him. I love him very much. And he is going to be the father of my child."

"What?" Eddie couldn't help but turn to her then, and he watched as she spread a hand over her stomach, petting it, although it was still flat and showed no signs of life. "You...you what?"

"It's how we're made, boy." A voice came from behind

Curse of Dracula

him. Eddie whirled and reflexively lifted his gun to point it at the man—demon—who had appeared. Blond hair that seemed human enough draped over one of his eyes in a sloppy, rakish trim, but the horns twisting up from within it and the purple-gray cast of his skin suggested otherwise. He was leaning against the wall casually, as if he were utterly unthreatened, a long tail swishing beside him. Silver glittered at the end of it—as it did from his lip and his ears. "To become one of us, you create one of us. I was born of a succubus and a man who was born a mortal." He shrugged a shoulder. Purple eyes drifted from Eddie's face down to his gun and back. "Are you going to shoot me?"

"Really considering it, yeah."

"Why?" The demon Mordecai tilted his head a little. "Because you're jealous? Or because I'm evil?"

"Why can't it be both?"

Mordecai laughed, showing his sharp upper and lower canines. He pushed away from the wall and stretched. "He's a funny one, angel. You never told me he was witty."

Eddie glanced over to Bella and felt his heart lodge in his throat as she took a step down the aisle, white sheer lace dress flowing behind her and…white wings blooming from her back. They shimmered into existence, and he realized the illusion was to hide them, not to have them. The feathers were tipped in the fairest sky blue, like her eyes, and she was…so beautiful.

"You want her," Mordecai whispered. Eddie jolted, not having realized the demon had come so close. Mordecai wrapped a clawed hand around his gun and slowly lowered it. "You could have her. You'll die. But you could bury yourself in that wet heat you've dreamed about for so long. Kiss her, love her, take her. Feed her life with your own and die happy."

Eddie moaned low in his throat. He was so tempted. His eyes traced back to Bella, his manhood throbbing in need. Calling out. *Yes! Yes, it's worth it. You're going to die anyway. Better to die like this, with her, inside her.*

Mordecai's lips were close to his ear, hot breath washing over his skin. It sent a thrill through him that was perverse, wicked and…wonderful. The image of kissing the incubus flashed through his mind, and he wondered what the ring on his lower lip would feel like. "You could have us both if you wanted. You won't live through it—but you'll die inside her. Just like Alfonzo would have if the Master had not stopped her."

"No!" Eddie reeled back, staggering away from the embrace of the incubus. He nearly dropped his gun. He clenched it tightly with both hands but didn't raise it. "No. Stop it. Stop. I don't—I don't want this."

"Your *stiff sinew* says otherwise." Mordecai pointed at the bulge Eddie knew he was sporting. "It's not a big one, but I'm still tempted all the same. Bella wouldn't let me have a single lick of the other one. She covets her kills already." He grinned.

"You…He didn't. Alfonzo didn't…"

"He did." Bella was there now, standing a few feet away, angelic wings a mockery of what he knew she really was. Or perhaps, just perhaps, all that he knew of what demons and angels were meant to be was all a lie. Maybe there was no line between them after all. "Alfonzo fucked me, Eddie. He did it because he's always wanted to. We can't make people do anything they don't already want. He saved me, then put himself inside of me, and gave life to our child. He would have happily died in me, but the Master had other plans for him."

"You killed Elizabeth." Mordecai growled. "I liked her.

Curse of Dracula

She was fun. I don't like it when my toys are taken away." The demon stepped toward him threateningly, but Bella put a hand on his arm, and Eddie watched as the incubus instantly caved, the tension melting from his posture as he turned to his...to Bella.

The way they looked as they embraced—demon and angel—brought tears to Eddie's eyes. Tears of anger. This wasn't how it was supposed to be! It was wrong! What they were saying—it was wrong. Eddie pulled his other revolver from his holster and raised them both, one pointed at each. "I should kill you both. I should kill you!" He hated how his voice cracked. How it sounded so overwrought and broken. He knew he was crying, and he didn't care.

Mordecai moved to stand in front of Bella, shielding her with his body. Blazing purple eyes met his. And Eddie saw only desperation. Sadness.

And love.

Demons couldn't *love*.

Couldn't they?

"Kill us both, then, if you think you can. There is no 'saving' her. No 'cure' or psalm or prayer that can reverse what has been done. You will have to destroy all *three* of us, if you seek to kill the one." Mordecai's voice lowered and he bared his teeth. "I will protect my family to the death."

That word struck him to his soul. Family.

He was meant to be her family. Not this creature. But that wasn't how life turned out. It wasn't fair. It wasn't right. But it didn't matter what was *right* or *wrong*. It only came down to one thing—love. And she didn't love him. She loved the incubus.

Eddie released the hammers of his revolvers and slowly lowered them. "Bella?"

The young woman with the angel wings peeked out

from behind her lover. Her husband. Her maker. Her mate. Whatever he was. Blue eyes met his, wavering and tearful. She was silent.

"I love you, Bella," Eddie choked out. "And—and I wish you all the happiness in the world."

He turned from them both, not caring if the demon ripped his head off in the process. He holstered his guns and walked toward the exit of the church.

"Goodbye, Eddie. I'll always remember you."

Sometimes that was all a man could ask. He pulled up the collar of his coat.

Shouldering his heartbreak, he knew he would cry and drink for years over what he had lost. Assuming he lived for years, of course. Which wasn't by any means a guarantee. But right now? Right now, he knew exactly who to blame for all this mess. Exactly who he was going to make suffer.

Right now, he had a Vampire King to kill.

Or he'd die trying.

Eddie was fine either way.

―――

"You wish me to take you? Do you want to feel what it is to be my prey?"

She nodded weakly.

"Then...far be it from me to deny such a wish."

The cold marble against Maxine's back was a stark contrast to the heat coming from the creature over her. She wound her fingers into his clothing and found no words to argue.

Her choice had been made. But she wanted to feel the warlord once more. She wanted to be the lamb in the field,

Curse of Dracula

and have the wolf sink his fangs into her flesh. She wanted to surrender to the man and monster she loved.

When the world disappeared around her, she shut her eyes and embraced it. When the world upended suddenly after that, she wasn't certain for a moment what had happened, until she was lying on a soft, silk-covered surface.

He knelt over her. She watched as he stripped her of the remainder of her clothing until she was naked before him. He shed his own clothing and draped himself over her. An arm on either side of her, caging her in, all she could see was him.

Leaning down, he kissed her—he conquered her. It was bruising and possessive, violent and needy. He would be the creature she had come to love. She did not wish him to be gentle. She needed to feel that beautiful ache that he could bring to her.

When he broke the kiss, she tilted her head away. Not in rejection—but to bare her throat to him. "Please," she whispered, her hands resting on his sides.

With that wonderfully low, inhuman growl, he lowered himself and trailed his tongue up the tendon of her neck, sensual and hot. She gasped as he wasted no time in digging his teeth into her tender flesh.

She could make no other noise as pleasure crashed over her like a wave. Not only pleasure—but *him*. All consuming, all encompassing, she let it overtake her. She would die like this in his arms, and he would soon die in hers.

And she could think of no better way to embrace the void.

---

*Oh, Maxine...*She might feel like the conquered. But she could not fathom how he was the one broken and subjugated. He would worship her for as long as he was allowed before she broke him beneath her will.

He would bring her to every height he knew how to reach. As he sank his fangs into her throat, she moaned and pressed her naked breasts against his chest. He hooked her knee over his arm and took her, sheathing himself in her volcanic depths, gentle and careful. He knew he was too much to take all at once without her body adjusting to him first.

Her pleasure peaked instantly, and she writhed in abandon beneath him. The power of their embrace that spanned blood and body would threaten her consciousness, but he would keep her on the edge until he was done with her.

Then together, they would die. He was overjoyed. His wonderful empath had surprised him once more. She could no more accept his cruelty than she could deny her love for him. And so she had chosen not to kill him or to obey him —but to do both.

Beautiful, wonderful, brilliant thing. He wondered if God had finally forgiven him and sent him an angel of mercy. He could think of no other explanation.

He worked his body inside hers to the shared tempo of their hearts. He was in no rush to show her what he could truly do to her. She would beg him for more and weep for mercy when all was said and done, and only then would he let their lives end.

With each thump of her heart, he pressed himself deep into her, filling her to her limits and maybe a bit beyond. The ache did not seem to bother her. It seemed to do anything but. How she arched when he let his weight settle against her. The gasping cries that left her lips were a symphony.

When her empathic gift washed over them, he welcomed it with open arms. He invited her to twist with his own mind, to tangle together in all ways. He sensed her love for him, and he answered it proudly with his own.

And now, even their souls were one.

He did not think she had lied to him, but to feel her love now, burning away beside his own dark flame, he rejoiced. He would have wept in joy if he were not already quite occupied. He drank slowly from her, feeling her lifeblood seep into him, chasing away the cold.

You are mine, Maxine Parker. You are mine...and I am yours.

When she peaked again around him and beneath him, crying out and grasping him like a raft in the tumbling sea, he nearly joined her. Their ecstasy was echoing back and forth between them like the fire of a lighthouse prism. It took all his restraint to keep himself under control. She challenged him in ways he could not have ever predicted.

And he adored every second of it.

And seconds was all they had left, after all.

He might as well make them count.

OH, how Maxine's body sang for him. Every nerve on fire, it was like bliss. Her mind was already tangled with his, their emotions blurring into one, their pleasure shared between them, echoing and reflecting, indistinguishable. Never once had she believed anything could feel like this.

She should have been in agony with how he was loving her like the inhuman creature that he was. Perhaps she should have been a weeping thing, begging for mercy as he unleashed himself on her. It might have been his pleasure, his ecstasy, that drove such things out of her mind. Or perhaps it was her own bliss that was the source of her enjoyment.

It didn't matter.

Nothing mattered anymore. Not her turmoil. Not his cruelty. It was them. Together. The dark threads of his mind wove through hers, like wings spreading wide in the open night sky. He was inside her in a far more profound way than she could have ever imagined.

Maxine could barely grasp what was happening. All she knew was him, and pleasure, and him, and bliss. He had released her throat, but the throbbing ecstasy of it had not abated. It was as though it was merely a snowball sent rolling downhill now that it had been started. And his deep, forceful, powerful strokes inside her body were all the momentum it needed to keep going.

She heard his thoughts inside her, echoing about. *You are mine, Maxine Parker. You are mine...and I am yours.*

She was above him now, rocking her body in a slow tempo. How long they had gone on, Maxine could not say. She was too bound up in him to have any sense of time. It did not matter. Nothing mattered.

Just her. Just him. Just *them.*

She pressed her palm against her abdomen, hard enough that she could feel him sliding inside her. She wanted to commit that memory to her soul. She wanted him never to leave her.

But her decision was made.

The city lay in ruin. Thousands of lives were dead by violence.

The image of Alfonzo's tortured body lying in a puddle of his own blood and ruin flashed through her mind. But it

Curse of Dracula

was not only that image she saw. It was those of all the souls in their cells that cried out to her. In that moment she had seen it all. All the death…all the pain…all the misery.

It had to end.

He had to end.

Crimson eyes met hers, lidded and dark with passion. But she saw in him what she had come to accept. A gentle touch stilled her movements, and he pulled her down to him. He kissed her, slow and gentle, filled with all the love in his heart that he had for her.

When she broke away, he smiled faintly and whispered, "It is time."

She nodded, tears forming in her eyes as she kissed him back. In that moment, she reached deep into his soul. She thrust herself deep into the center of his very being.

He gasped, and suddenly she was on her back. But he was not trying to escape. No. He drove himself deeper inside her, leaning his weight against her hips. She wrapped her legs around his waist and met his force, if not his strength.

She dug deeper into his soul. Into the center of that unknowable mass she had sensed each time she had touched him. There, at its center…was a poison. Tearing his soul free would leave some of it within her. This curse. But she would happily pay the price for her actions.

It would likely destroy her.

Good.

He broke her kiss but did not sever their link. "Maxine… I love you."

Her reach rested at the center of the poison. At the beating vein of corruption that drove him. It was as though she held veins in her hand, if each were made from delicate spun glass. It was so fragile there at its core. She could break it. "I…I love you. I'm sorry," she whispered.

He smiled against her lips. "I'm not." He kissed her.

She shattered him.

It was as though something rent in half.

Something that was never meant to come apart.

She could not say exactly what it was.

26

Alfonzo screamed. Hoarse and almost soundless, but he tried. It was a sound that was familiar now. He thought he could no longer feel the pain of what they were doing to him, but he was very wrong.

The tourniquets had done a good job at dulling the pain of the creatures eating his limbs. But now three of the four were gone. His right hand was gone. His arm that ended in the stump of a wrist was all he had left, stitched shut effectively but painfully.

A ghoul was lying flat on the ground, tonguing the stitches, sucking blood from the wound without fully opening it. He was being defiled. Just as he defiled Bella. More than anything they had done to him so far, now he was being taken apart from the inside.

He wanted to die.

He wanted it to end.

But death was no longer the way it ended for him. This would continue. It would go on for weeks or longer if the mad Vampire King had his way.

His scream broke off in a hopeless, empty sob. "I give up," he whispered. "I give up. Make it stop."

The Chainmaster—Alfonzo's new Master—dragged the ghoul away from him with the yank of a leash. "Good boy. Good." He soothed the ghoul, not Alfonzo. He sent the creature out of the room. "We have one more thing to do before I fetch Master Dracula and give him the wonderful news."

The demon left the room and returned with a silver tray. On it…was a roasted hand. The Chainmaster placed it on the ground beside him, dug deep into his shoulder, and wrenched Alfonzo over so his face hovered over it.

"Eat."

And he did.

THERE WAS A TEMPLE. A temple in the sand. It was built from stones carefully cut and stacked atop each other, covered in white limestone and polished to a perfect shine.

The structure would last for a thousand years and maybe more. Maxine stood there in the center of the enormous room, columns of painted plaster and limestone reaching up overhead. It reminded her of somewhere she had seen before. A throne room designed to inspire horror and dread.

She was in another vision.

This place was designed to make its visitors feel as small and as meaningless and trivial as Vlad's throne room. It was meant to compel its guests to kneel in worship. Although this one was built in dedication to a very different god than the vampire she had known.

Perhaps this was the last dream she would have before she died. She gazed up at a statue of a bird-headed deity. A large, flat disk of polished copper sat atop the head of the falcon. She knew his name. She was not raised among the Roma and did not read the tarot without knowing from where they drew their history.

Ra. The sun god of Egypt in times long past. No one remained to worship him. No one remained who lit candles to him. And if they did, they were few in number. But it was not the *now* in which she stood. This was not her dream.

This was his.

She had torn Vlad's soul from his body, and something had ripped in two. And now she was in his mind. But where was she? *When* was she?

Fires burned in the distance, and she could smell the desert air. It was night, and the sky was lit up with a hundred thousand stars she did not recognize. Structures in the distance were peppered with large obelisks that reached up into the darkness with their polished faces.

"I had forgotten this place."

She turned to find who had spoken and drew back a step at what she saw. It was not a voice she recognized. It was not a face she knew. But the man she saw gazing up at her, from features that were bronzed and foreign, was familiar all the same. It was not his face. It was his eyes. They were brown, not crimson.

Not yet.

He was bald, kneeling on the ground, his hands bound behind him in crude rope. It looked as though he had been beaten. He was mortal. He was...he was alive.

"Vlad?"

"In a fashion, perhaps." He smirked. "I had forgotten all of this." His eyes drifted shut. "I had chosen to. This is where it all began. This was the start of my curse."

"I...what is happening?"

"I cannot say. You were inside me. I felt you shatter a vessel. My soul was the container for the plague that consumed me. Now that the vessel broken, I...do not know what has transpired. Perhaps we are trapped here for the rest of time. How grand."

Two men stood beside him, one on either side. They carried spears tipped in polished metal. They gazed up at the altar, stern and waiting. Vlad—or whatever his name was in this time, since she had a feeling it wasn't Vlad—was a prisoner. "What did you do to deserve this?"

"I loved a princess. She loved me. I despoiled her. And this was my punishment for my love. I was advisor to Pharaoh...the right hand to a living God. It was seen as a deep betrayal."

The sound of a cymbal or a bell echoed in the space. She nearly jumped out of her own skin, she was so startled. It seemed the memory wished to play on. She watched, agog, as several men walked into the room. One was carrying a large bowl with a thick, viscous liquid that she recognized. Blood.

Another was carrying a falcon. Tied and bound, it struggled frantically for freedom. For its life. Falcons were sacred to these people. She could only stand and watch in horror at the memory. There was nothing she could do to change it.

"They killed my love."

She did not turn to look at Vlad where he knelt, so captivated was she by the actions of the priests. They placed the bowl of blood in front of the statue of Ra. While one held up the falcon, the other one said several words she could not understand, before the first submerged the head of the bird in the liquid.

The falcon thrashed, struggled, and eventually...went still. The priest pulled the dead bird from the substance, his own hands and wrists coated in the crimson liquid, and left the room.

It was sacrilege.

Or the worst kind of curse.

The action left the head priest, gold bangles and jewelry swaying as he moved, to carry the bowl to the waiting prisoner.

The man on his knees glared up at the priest in utter defiance. She knew his eyes would turn crimson the moment the deed was done. The man would become the Vampire King she loved so dearly. He yanked on the ropes, but there was no freeing himself. Without looking at her, Vlad spoke to her, his voice quiet even as he struggled against the restraints and the soldiers.

"They drowned the sun within my love and bade me drink of her."

The two guards moved to grab his head and hold it still. They meant to drown him in the blood as they did the falcon. And when he rose from that death, he would be a monster.

"Wait."

The action stopped. It froze. She did not know how. She did not know why. But it obeyed her command. She wavered. *I should destroy him. I need to destroy him. He wishes for death. To be free of this curse. Of this pain that has haunted him since this moment.*

She walked up to him and took his head in her hands. Leaning down, she kissed him. The shape of his lips was foreign to her. But the creature who burned within was not. He kissed her back. It was a gesture of love.

It was a gesture that meant goodbye.

Something in her heart shattered at the notion of losing

him. Tears streaked down her face. When she broke away, she shook her head. "I can't do it. I can't."

"You must. What I am cannot be changed. What I have become is immutable. The torture you have seen me wreak on mortals is doomed to continue. I am what I am. It is as unfaltering as the vision you see here before you. As written in the stones of time."

Leaning her forehead against his, she shut her eyes. "I love you."

"And I you, Maxine Parker. More than anyone else I have ever known. Do it. Please. Let me die."

She placed her hand over his heart. "It may kill me, and if it does not, I cannot—I cannot live without you. I do not know how I can face it." The idea of eating the end of a pistol or drinking poison was preferable to the ache his absence would leave within her.

"You will not be alone. A piece of me will live on within you. I will never leave you. You are mine, Maxine Parker... and I will never let you go."

She opened her eyes and straightened. Looking at the scene around her, she willed it away. The blood in the bowl of the priest overflowed, pouring from the basin like a fountain.

She watched in fascination as the blood spread, seemingly intent on devouring the room. Each object it touched dissolved and added to the liquid until she was standing on a sea of crimson that stretched on in all directions. There was no one and nothing there. The priest, the temple, the bowl, the guards—it was all gone. Nothing but her...and him...and the blood.

He was as she knew him with his ghastly pale skin and long dark hair. He looked defeated, kneeling in the liquid. The fallen warlord. The conquered king.

"I hope this kills me. I truly do. If am to die, I wish to do it in your arms." She tipped his head up to kiss him once more. He pulled her closer to him.

She kissed him.

She reached into him. She felt the soul burning at his core. Alongside it was the corruption and the poison that lingered there. The ancient curse that beat its black heart through him. It fought her. It did not wish to die. Its roots were deep. There would be no pulling it free from the soul it had infected. They were one and the same. He had been rewritten at his very core.

She destroyed it. She destroyed *him*.

Or...she tried.

The enormity of him tore at her like a rabid tiger. She screamed in pain as the curse fought back. It did not want its host to die. It saw her as the threat she was and tried to tear her to pieces. It was too much—too strong for her.

It slithered into her like a vile ink.

But he was there. Around her. Within her. Holding her. Waves of blood consumed them both. But it did not matter. His arms were around her. That was all she needed.

This was love.

———

"You will go no farther."

Eddie looked up at the tall, lanky, red-haired vampire who stood at the top of the library stairs. He sighed heavily and hung his head. "Really? Another one of you motherfuckers? Look. I'm here to kill Dracula. Go save yourself."

"No."

"And who're you supposed to be?" Eddie cracked his

shoulder. "I'm having a seriously shit day, and I don't want to waste time with you if you're only some lackey."

"I am Master Dracula's second-in-command."

"Oh, good. That's a step up." Eddie pulled his guns from his holsters and cracked his neck to the left then the right, readying himself for a fight. "Better or worse than that green-eyed vampire lady?"

"I am by far her superior." The vampire let out a thoughtful hum. "Was."

"Sorry about that."

"Don't be. She was a traitor and a manipulative wench. I did not care for her." Walter motioned his hand, and a long silver rapier appeared in his grasp, summoned from thin air. "Turn back, hunter. Your mentor is lost. Your comrade is one of us. You have nothing to gain here."

"I can stop this." Eddie waved a gun at the city and the crimson moon overhead. "I can free this place. I can stop him from doing it again anytime soon."

"You do not come for revenge?"

"No. Turns out that's not a great way to go. Al came here for revenge. Is he…is he still alive?"

"Yes. For the moment. Although he may not wish he was. He has begged the Chainmaster for death many times over. He has lost three of his limbs, eaten by ghouls…and is about to be forced to dine on the very limb he used to punch Miss Parker in the head." The vampire remained stoic through his entire casual and impassive explanation of the torture. "Do you still claim this is not about revenge?"

"I mean, I'm not going to pretend it won't feel good to make you sick shits suffer. But no."

"That is fair." The vampire twirled his sword and folded it at his back. But Eddie knew it was not a vulnerable pose. "I am Walter Northway."

"I'm Eddie Jenkin."

The vampire smirked. Eddie thought he did, anyway. Might have been a trick of the shadows. "Well met. Let us begin."

―――

"Maxine? Maxine!"

Someone shook her. She gasped and thrashed, feeling silk sheets underneath her. Around her. She struggled against whoever was touching her. Hands on her shoulders were touching her bare skin. Flashes of a gutter, of young boys laughing, of a carriage abandoning him on the street.

Zadok.

She looked up into his concerned face. She was naked. But she could not find the will to care. She looked at him in confusion and reached up to trace her fingers over his cheek. She gasped and pulled her hand back from him the moment she saw it.

Her skin! What was wrong with it?

She looked down at her hands. They were pale. A ghastly gray.

She was so *cold*.

"By God, Maxine..." Zadok tilted her head up to look at him again. He searched her eyes as if he did not understand what he was seeing. "What has he done?"

Vlad! She turned and found him lying beside her. He was on his back, the sheets tangled around his waist. He was looking up at the ceiling. But his red eyes were glassy and empty.

Vacant.

Regret flooded her. She had lived and she was alone. She threw herself atop him, trying to wake him. She shook him, placed her hand on his cheek, and called to him. She remembered the pain. Of something fighting back. But she must have won in the end. He was gone.

Tears fell from her cheeks and landed on his chest.

They were crimson.

She leaned down to kiss him, but his lips were unresponsive.

"He will not wake. I thought you were both dead." Zadok tugged gently on her arm. She was weeping, but she allowed him to pull her from the bed, even though her limbs felt useless and like jelly. He slung a robe around her and pulled her into his arms. "My dove, tell me what's happened. What has he done?"

"He has done nothing. This is my fault." She curled into his chest but could not tear her eyes away from Vlad. There was too much to describe. She pushed away from Zadok and glanced around the room. There, by one wall, was a mirror. She walked to it and carefully stepped up to it to examine herself.

Crimson eyes looked back at her, set into features that were far paler than any she had ever worn. She recognized herself, but barely. She opened her mouth and ran her fingers along her teeth, finding her canines longer and sharper than they should have been.

"You are a vampire," Zadok breathed. "Did he turn you?"

"No. I...I destroyed him."

"You what?" Zadok shook his head. "I don't—"

"I take a piece of those I kill. And a piece of his curse was enough to do this, it seems." *I have freed you from your eternity. I have taken this burden from you.* She looked back at Vlad. Walking to the side of the bed, she pulled the sheets up over him and sat at his side. She stroked through his hair,

Curse of Dracula

smoothing it out, and gently shut his eyes. She leaned down to kiss him.

She let her soul touch the cold body beneath her lips and tried to find him. Tried to find…anything.

But nothing called back to her.

This deathless world is mine now.

"This is all—I don't know how I am to react to this." Zadok leaned on the wall and threaded his fingers into his hair. He began rambling, speaking so quickly in French and English that they blurred together, and she struggled to understand him. "You have become him! My Master lies dead, his Lady is now my Mistress, and there is a hunter at our doors attempting to kill Walter and—"

"What did you say?" She looked up at the Frenchman. "What about Walter?"

Zadok shook his head as though she had caught on to the wrong part. "You have become him, Vlad is—the Master is dead—he can't die. He cannot!" He slid to the floor. He sat there with his legs out in front of him, looking like a man who was told his wife had just died in childbirth.

He has lost his family. He has lost the only man he believed could never leave him.

"Zadok. I need you to focus. What did you say about Walter?"

"The boy. Eddie. He—" He stammered uselessly. "You are my Mistress." He pulled in a breath, held it, then let out his words as a rush. "I can feel it, same way I could with him." The poor vampire was shaking.

She looked down at Vlad, at the form that could be a corpse for all intents and purposes. And perhaps he was. There was no telling what she had done or what had transpired. There were only the facts left to examine. She reached out and stroked his hair, wishing for all the world that he would open his eyes.

I killed him. This is my fault. I do not get to mourn for what I've done.

"You are the Vampire Queen now, Maxine."

She laughed sadly. The title sounded ridiculous. "Never say that again."

"But you are."

She leaned her head down onto Vlad's unmoving chest. She felt so small. So weak. So tired. So alone. She wanted him to hold her. To tell her it was going to be all right. She knew it would not happen. "I can't be. I don't know how."

"I'm afraid you don't have a choice. I don't know how any of this shit has come to pass. I don't know what you did!" Zadok buried his head in his hands and rambled in French so quickly that she couldn't understand him. With a hiss of air through his nose, he sprang to his feet. "Enough. Enough. I can mourn for him over a bottle of wine later. We need to go help Walter. I came in here to get you both out of bed, and instead I suppose you will have to do. You *are* our Mistress, and you *will* save that asshole. Do you hear me? I will not lose more of my family this day!"

"I hear you, cretin." Pushing from the bed, she wiped at the tears streaming down her cheeks. As eager as she was to lie on that bed and never move again, she would not let Walter die because of her mistakes. Zadok was right—she had a duty to them. She had taken Dracula away from them. She looked down at the crimson staining her hands. "That is irritating."

"You have much to learn," Zadok grumbled. "That is the least of it. Come, get dressed, and do it quickly, unless you want to greet the hunter in a bathrobe."

Nodding numbly, she went about the motions. There

Curse of Dracula

was something simple and comforting about getting dressed. It was normal. It was not the end of the world. She even let Zadok tug her corset laces tight. Quite admirably, he kept his hands to himself. His grief was likely to blame.

I have killed the Vampire King and taken his throne.

One last time before she left, Maxine sat on the edge of the bed. She kissed Vlad's lips once more. She tried desperately to find some inkling of a soul within him and found nothing.

I can only pray you have found peace, my love.

He had wished to shed his burden. And she had taken it instead. She was not certain how she would ever be suited for such a role...but she did not have a choice. It was hers to bear until the end of time. But she had understood his need for resolution. He might not have found peace in her love, but he had found peace in the death she had given him.

And now death was never to come for her. The deal they had made was that they would both die. But he left to travel where she could never follow him. She had pushed him through that door, and it had slammed in her face. Hell did not wait for her—only a Hell of her own making now here on Earth.

How many thousands of years had it taken Vlad to become as he was? Cold, cruel, and devoid of compassion?

How many would it take for her to suffer the same fate?

Worry over your own immortality another time. Walter or Eddie is about to die. Save them first, then lose yourself to panic and grief if you must.

She wore black. It was only fitting. She was in mourning, and she would be so for the rest of time. She had taken Vlad's curse, but he had taken her heart. She pulled on her black gloves and nodded to Zadok. He pushed open a large window by the wall, revealing the night sky and the city beyond.

"Time to learn how to fly, Maxine." Zadok took her hand. "Be free. Will yourself to the skies. Dream of freedom, and it will be yours."

She nodded and shut her eyes. She remembered what it was like to fly in Dracula's embrace. It was there, like a muscle she had not known she had owned. She reached for it, touched it, and her body dissolved into a thousand smaller ones. The world dropped away from her. And through it all, she sensed Zadok there at her side, tangled up in her.

Like she had been with Vlad.

Soaring into the sky above, she basked in the beauty of the stars. Of the night. Of the crimson moon. This was her moon now too—she was no longer the prey. She was now the predator.

She could revel in it another time.

Gunfire was ringing out in the stone streets, and she could hear metal clashing on metal. There was a fight raging, and she needed to stop it.

There would be no more suffering this night.

She decreed it.

27

Walter was *furious*.

While it was not uncommon that he was angry, very rarely did it ever creep outward. How many times had he suffered the advances of that insipid woman Elizabeth—thank goodness she was dead—and managed to keep from bashing her head into the plaster walls?

No. He was not a man of outbursts.

But this boy was *frustrating*.

He was only one child! But he was faster and far more intuitive than Walter had anticipated. Each movement of his blade was met with a bullet, nearly shooting the rapier out of his hand, or blocked with the side of a muzzle. The boy was also an exceptionally good shot. He seemed to have an intuitive sense of where Walter planned to appear.

Walter had to unleash his shadows. He did not like to fight with trickery. He did not like to use anything more than his own body to battle. But now the darkness began to leak in from the edges of the steps of the library, lashing out at the young hunter.

Edward would die.

Walter would not lose.

Finally, after far too long, he managed to knock the weapons from the boy's hands after one of his shadows wrapped around Edward's legs and yanked him clean off his feet. "Eddie," as he preferred to be called, slammed painfully into the stones and groaned, holding his face. Walter kicked him over onto his back and held the point of his sword over the boy's throat.

"Do it," Eddie grunted. "Just do it."

"Do you wish to pray to your god first?"

"Nah. I'm good. He knows I'm coming." Eddie grinned lopsidedly.

Walter smiled back at him. "Well met, Edward Jenkin. Well met, indeed." He raised his sword and moved to drive it down through the boy's throat. He would make his death quick.

"No!"

Walter hesitated. He turned to look at whomever had shouted and froze. He blinked in confusion. "Miss Parker?" It was her. But...changed. Zadok was standing at her side and shot him a wide-eyed, panicked, and confounded expression as his only method of explanation.

Her eyes shone crimson like his—like Vlad's. Her skin was pale. She was perfect, removed from all the slight failures of the mortal body that were swept away with the gift of vampirism. She was like them now; he could sense it.

But he could sense something more. Something he had only sensed in one other. Something that called to him like...she was the wellspring of a great and terrible curse that had touched them all. "H...how?" He approached her slowly in disbelief. He reached to touch her face, and she let it happen.

She was cold to the touch.

Curse of Dracula

Something strange brushed up against him. Not physically, but spiritually. It was entirely too personal for his liking. He pulled back his hand abruptly. "I see you retain your empathic gifts."

"So it seems."

"Where is Master Dracula?"

"He is...he is inside. I do not know if he will ever rise again."

Walter bowed his head. His Master was dead and gone. "What have you done, Miss Parker?" He swallowed something akin to bile and took a step back. "You destroyed him."

"I..." She cringed as if he had slapped her. "Yes. And a piece of his soul became mine. Such is the reason I now have been poisoned by his curse."

"And he is bereft of anything at all? He is dead?"

"I do not know. I believe so." She was pleading with him, her crimson eyes looking for any compassion he might be able to spare. "Please, forgive me."

He had the urge to strike her. To kill her for what she had done. She betrayed their Master—the man she claimed to love—and—his fury sputtered and failed. "Did he know what you planned to do?"

She nodded.

Walter ran a hand over his face, groaning loudly. "He embraced his death."

"Yes."

He sighed. "Very well."

"Can I get up yet?"

Maxine laughed, and Walter looked up to see her approaching the young hunter still lying on the ground. It was he who had spoken. She reached out to help him up, and he grasped her by the hand as she hefted him easily to his feet.

"Whoa!" he yelped at her sudden strength.

"Sorry. I fear I do not yet know what I am." Maxine smiled sheepishly at him. "Are you all right, Eddie?"

"No, I'm shit, actually. Lost a finger to a bitch of a vampire, lost my friend to a bitch of an incubus, was about to lose my life to that big bitch over there"—Eddie gestured at Walter, who struggled not to reup his desire to smack him—"lost my mentor to the biggest bitch of them all, and now you're...fuck, Maxine. What did you do?"

"I've been asked that question three times now, and three times I will say I fear I do not yet fully know." Maxine looked down at her hands in confusion. "But there is one thing to be certain—this fight ends here, and it ends now." She turned to Walter. "I do not ask you to serve me, Mr. Northway, or you, Mr. Lafitte. I do not ask it from anyone. But I intend to protect Eddie should you decide to continue this fight."

Zadok and Walter looked at each other for a long moment. It was the Frenchman who spoke first, unsurprisingly. "I...know why you did it. And if he wanted to die as you say, then I shall respect my Master's wishes. I will need more time to accept what has been done."

"As do we all," Maxine murmured.

"I'm not excited to find out what our new master vampire might do with powers untempered and untrained by time," Zadok said with a mild shrug. "Nor do I wish particular ill on the boy. He killed Elizabeth. I think I owe him a favor."

"That is one of the few times I think you have spoken logic." Walter allowed his sword to vanish from his hand. He watched Miss Parker for a moment and remembered her kindness toward him. Her kindness toward all the creatures she met. "I will not serve you, Miss Parker. But I will seek to aid you, if that is enough."

"It is more than I could ask. I would prefer friendship." She smiled. "I am not one for keeping staff."

"In you remains the only shred of a chance I have at a family who cannot leave me. Friendship it is." Zadok bowed, joining into the accord. "This will be interesting indeed. At least you are far more attractive to the eyes than our previous Master."

Walter kept himself from decking the Frenchman. Perhaps he would do so later. "What do you intend to do now, Miss Parker?"

She looked up at the moon overhead. "I think you should both go indoors."

Without having to be warned twice, he let his body dissolve into bats and head to the sky. He would seek shelter inside. He did not know what meant to follow such strange events. He mourned the loss of his friend. He grieved for Dracula. He would cry in silence and solitude this evening and likely many more to come.

But he knew his friend had needed rest. And he hoped he had found it at long last.

"Maxine?"

She shushed Eddie. She wasn't certain about what she was doing and needed to focus. It was as though she had been sat at a grand organ after taking a few lessons on a child's piano. There were too many switches, levers, foot pedals, strings, pipes —she knew if she hit the wrong key, she might ruin everything.

Power like an ocean flowed beneath her fingertips. She

could understand a little of why Vlad acted the way he did —as though the world around him consisted of only ants that now and then became interesting to him. That was what the world was to her now. Everything was…small.

She lifted her hand to the sky, gesturing to the red moon. She willed it to be free. She willed the city to be free. She commanded the cloud of miasma around her to *be silent.*

She held her breath—did she really even need to breathe now?—and watched as the moon slipped away and was replaced with the warm glow of the sun. She flinched and looked away. It had never been that painfully bright before. *Right. Yes. That.* "Ow." She laughed.

With the shadow of crimson that slid away, so went the twisted nightmares. Blood still stained the streets. The dead were still that. No tragedy was reversed.

The past could not be changed.

But the future was not yet written. Fate was not sealed.

She looked to Eddie. "Vlad is…dead and gone. Do you seek to kill me instead, hunter?"

"You saved my life." He sighed. "If I didn't kill that piece of shit incubus or Bella—"

"What?"

He grunted. "I spared them. She seemed happy, and he loves her, and—" Eddie sighed heavily. "She loves him. I can't fault them for that. For what they did to Al, sure, but… sounds like he got himself into that mess."

"Alfonzo." She cringed and shut her eyes. "I should go deal with him."

"I'm coming." She glanced up at him with a raised eyebrow. He coughed and cleared his throat. "I mean, I'd like to come with you, with all due respect, ma'am."

She laughed. She supposed she really was a ma'am now.

Curse of Dracula

She nodded and reached out to take his hand. "Come. I think I know the way."

Eddie hesitated but placed his hand in hers. She just *folded* into the nothingness and moved between places in the world. It was so easy now that she knew how it was done. Like a curtain being pulled back, it all made sense.

He, however, was of the same opinion that she was the first time she had experienced it. He doubled over and nearly retched as they reappeared in the stone corridor beneath the library. The curse from the city had lifted, but she kept this building under *her* control for the time being. There was business to attend to.

"I—oh—oh, my." The Chainmaster. It came out to greet its visitor, and seeing her, dropped to its knees. "I serve you, my Mistress."

"Free them all. All that can leave this place of their own will, you shall allow. Those who cannot be released are to be quickly and painlessly put out of their suffering. Leave Alfonzo. We are to tend to him. Do you understand?"

"Yes, Mistress," the demon purred. "Am I free as well?"

She furrowed her brow. "What do you mean?"

Its features creased in pain. "Master Dracula kept me here to punish me. I slighted him a long time ago, and he makes me serve. I miss my children. I wish to return to Hell. Do you wish to keep me imprisoned?"

There was always a context. There was always a reason behind the darkness. She shook her head. "You are free once you do as I ask."

The demon picked up the edge of her dress and kissed it and quickly left to make good on her command.

"Demons are weird," Eddie muttered.

"I find myself agreeing with you." She motioned for him to follow her as she walked down the hallway. She found

Alfonzo's cell quickly and opened the door but paused before she went in. She looked over to Eddie, who had lost much of the color from his face at the odor of the place. Of the stench of suffering and death. "I am sorry for what you are about to see."

"Walter told me what they…what they did."

"It's another thing to witness it." She pushed open the door and walked inside. She heard Eddie follow her.

There, in the center of the floor, was what remained of Alfonzo Van Helsing. His limbs were stumps. His right arm was longer than the others, extending down to a wrist, but the hand was gone. The charred remains of a hand lay on a tray by his head, chewed on, and bile soaked it.

They had made him eat his own hand.

She cringed and looked away, putting her hand over her mouth. No. She would look this cruelty in the eyes, and she would understand it. This was what she would become if she was not careful. She would keep this as a reminder of the value of mercy. She forced herself to take in every detail of what had been done.

Eddie had to leave the room, and she heard him retching in the hallway. She did not blame him. She walked over to Alfonzo's side and knelt in the blood. She did not care. The man was still alive. He was breathing, his eyes glassy and unfocused.

"Alfonzo…"

He moaned. The poor man still knew his own name. She tilted his head to her and stroked his hair gently. "It's all over, Alfonzo. I've come here to end it."

"Please," Alfonzo whimpered. "Please…"

"Al, oh, God…oh, fuck, Al—" Eddie finally came back into the room. He was weeping. He knelt beside Maxine, his hand resting on his friend's chest. "Al, I'm so sorry."

Curse of Dracula

"Eddie?" Alfonzo somehow managed to smile. "Is it really you?"

"It is. It is."

"Thought they...thought they'd kill you."

"No. I think I'm gonna live through this."

Alfonzo shut his eyes slowly, looking so tired, yet at rest with that news. "You're a good man, Eddie. Better than me. I let them win."

"But you tried," Maxine said gently, stroking his hair. "You tried, and that is more than most can say."

"What has...what has become of the monster?" Alfonzo squinted up at her and must have been strong enough to see the crimson in her eyes. "Are you like him now?"

"I've taken his place, I fear. A piece of his soul beats in my heart. It was enough to stop it."

Alfonzo laughed. It was weak. It was broken. But it was there. "You poor woman. I pity you."

He was bereft of his limbs. He had been eaten alive. But *he* pitied *her*. She shook her head and smiled sadly. Perhaps he could see her fate for what it was. An eternity of darkness and death, just as Vlad had suffered.

Alfonzo coughed. "Let it end, Miss Parker. Kill me. Please."

She nodded.

"I should do it." Eddie sat back on his heels and pulled his gun out of his holster. He cocked the hammer and held it close to Alfonzo's head. He hesitated, his hand shaking.

Reaching out, she took his other hand and held it.

"Do it, Eddie. Do it." Alfonzo kept his eyes shut. "Death is a gift. Goodbye, boy. It was an honor to train you."

"Goodbye, Al."

———

Maxine had held Eddie while he cried. The man wept like a child, and she did not blame him one ounce for it. She cradled him to her shoulder. They were sitting in the foyer of the library, and she could see the sun outside, streaming in. It did not hurt her, but it was indeed irritatingly bright. The streets were quiet. It would take a long time for the living to dare step out once more.

"Miss Parker?" Walter spoke from near her.

"Please call me Maxine."

"Ah. Yes. Forgive me." Walter bowed his head to her and glanced at the hunter. "What would you have us do now?"

"We should prepare to leave. We will go north, somewhere we do not cause so much damage." She eased away from Eddie, who was wiping at his face with his sleeves, looking embarrassed at being caught in a weak moment in front of the vampire. She smiled and stroked his hair. "Eddie?"

"I'm going. I can't wait to leave here."

"Are you going to be all right?"

He nodded. "I'll get through it. You?"

"I honestly do not know." She stood from the stairs and looked out at the sunshine beyond the door. It was something she did not belong to anymore. "I...I destroyed the man I love."

Eddie nodded again, weaker than before. "That's something I haven't had to do. That's why I know I'll be okay. If you can survive, so will I."

"I believe I no longer have a choice in the matter."

"Shut up. I liked my version better." He smiled and walked toward the door, plucking his long rifle from the steps and shouldering it mid-stride. "You cause problems like him, and I will hunt you down, though. I will stop you."

"I would sincerely hope so. Goodbye, Eddie Jenkin."

"Goodbye, ma'am."

And with that, the hunter was gone. Walter let out a sigh. "What a relief." She laughed. He raised an eyebrow at her. "I was not making any kind of jest."

"I know. I fear I still find it funny. I will need your help. I do not think I know where to begin."

"You have started this journey with compassion. That is a far better road to walk than any he ever chose." He placed his hand on her shoulder. "Come. There is much for us to do."

Yes. There was.

And it was time to begin.

EPILOGUE

EVERY DAY she spent by his side.

Every night she spent ruling in his stead.

It had been over a year since Boston had fallen to the Vampire King. It had been over a year since she shattered his soul inside his chest. Her existence had fallen into a pattern, if not a routine.

Walter had expressed confusion that his body did not dissolve into dust like all their ilk who died but remained as it was. Perhaps it was the age and power that had dwelled there that left it whole.

But it gave her a dangerous thing—it gave her hope.

Hope that he might return.

He had died a thousand times. Perhaps this was just one more.

More likely, he was forever gone to her.

But hope was a curse as insidious as the one that had taken her body. It refused to leave her. And she refused to part with him all the same.

She had taken them up to the woods of the far north and established their home there. It took the form of a large and sprawling mansion that was a far cry from the castles that Walter said Vlad preferred to summon for them. It suited her nicely. Zadok seemed quite pleased with the change, complaining that the castle had always been too big and drafty for him.

To her surprise, the two vampires stayed by her side. She came to rely on their guidance and their friendship in equal measure. Even Zadok, who was glad to have "been promoted up from the rank of court jester" under her reign. He was still nigh intolerable at times, but she resisted the urge to tear his arm off. Although she did threaten it from time to time.

They were not the only two who stayed.

Mordecai made the most adorable father she had ever seen. He was always bouncing the young winged girl on his shoulders or playing tag out in the rose gardens. Watching him and Bella together made her heart ache for the happiness she had known so briefly in another's arms, only to shatter it in her hands.

But she did not regret her choice. She could not let the suffering continue as it had. She had lived her life alone, and if she had to spend the rest of eternity in the same fashion, so be it. Such was her fate.

Now she had a family. Friends. She often spent her nights in the gardens, working to make the flowers and plants grow. Working to return a small manner of life to the world now that her dominion was only that of death.

She also had learned to feed. Mostly on animals, although Walter had seen fit to bring her out to hunt a local tribe one evening. He wished her to learn to fight, to fend for herself against an armed human. She understood the lesson, however she wished to shy away from its cruelty—she needed to learn to survive.

Walter had told her stories of Vlad's centuries of imprisonment, shackled and tortured at the hands of the humans who wished to contain the beast. The stories he told made her ill. But she did not doubt their truth.

Vlad had been a creature of his context. No darkness came without reason. She did not wish to let her heart grow cold, so she would learn to fight to protect herself from such things. She would learn to harness the strength he had once commanded.

Walter was an eager teacher. He seemed to take great pride in his new role as her confidant. She still thought him funny when he insisted that he was no such thing.

With her immortal curse had come more control over her empathic gifts. She now no longer needed to wear her gloves. It was a small benefit, but one she deeply enjoyed.

Her world of nightmares was not nearly as twisted as Dracula's had been, and her rose bushes were only rose bushes. There were no demons lying in wait or thorns ready to eat someone who happened too close.

And the moon overhead was always silver.

And each time the sun began to rise over the horizon, she went down deep beneath her home to where no light might reach. To a place where no doors or windows entered. To a place no one could find but her.

"Why do you sleep in a coffin, Vlad?" She had asked him that question twice. And now, she truly understood.

She stood at the side of the large black coffin that sat atop a center dais. The lid was closed, and it was emblazoned with a sigil of a warlord. She let her hand trail over the black painted surface before lifting it.

There he lay. Dressed in his finest, his arms crossed over his chest, and forever in repose. She climbed into the coffin beside him and curled up on her side next to his frame. He

Curse of Dracula

was exactly as he always was. Cold to the touch, but soft over the feeling of iron. Nothing in him ever decayed. His body was bereft of life and death.

And every day she whispered to him a command—"Come back to me."

And every day he defied her.

She would place a kiss on those lips she wished would return the favor, would swipe away the red tears that would escape her eyes, and she would lower the lid. She slept there at his side until dark.

And every day she returned.

Another year went by. And another. And several more.

She had sent a letter to Eddie via a messenger—a little imp that was more than happy to do her bidding. Eddie responded, and she discovered in him an odd pen pal. She told him of their home and promised she was not out to destroy the world. He told her of his new wife and his son. He vowed he was too old to hunt vampires now, but he'd be happy to make an exception for her if she stepped out of line.

And every day she commanded Vlad to return to her.

And every day he defied her.

There was a strange kind of contentment that came over her with enough time. Her home was a refuge for monsters —for those unfortunate souls that could not find sanctuary elsewhere, mortal or immortal as they may be. Scientists and demons alike. Every Thursday night, she took dinner with the Witchdoctor and discussed all matters of myth and science. Every Friday was spent at cards. She did her best to care for those around her. To tend to what they might need. It seemed that was more than enough to inspire their loyalty.

It was not joy. She watched the seasons come and go and watched them blur together.

And every day she commanded Vlad to return to her.

And every day he defied her.

Eddie passed away unexpectedly, but from natural means. She ventured to his funeral and paid her respects. She shed a tear by his grave and placed some of her red roses on the fresh dirt. A large sum of money was given to his widow and his young son. She did not stop to visit them.

The world was changing quickly. Another war was on its way. One that would span the continents, it seemed. It was a tragedy she did not know how to prevent. Walter had told her that mortal wars were for mortal men—immortals had no business interfering. It would only make matters worse. As he had seen nearly a millennium of them, she did not argue.

And every day she commanded Vlad to return to her.

And every day he defied her.

Each day she lay curled at his side, her fingers twisted into the lapel of his suitcoat.

And every day he defied her.

Until the day he did not.

Maxine must have been dreaming.

Fingers were curled into her hair, and she felt an arm around her, holding her close. She shifted, not wanting to wake from the illusion. Not wanting to wake from the dream she had wished to have every day for so many years.

A dream of him.

Sharp nails drifted over her scalp, and she purred. It was an inhuman noise. Something she had not known she could

Curse of Dracula

make until right that moment. She heard a dark and quiet laugh. The fingers caressed her cheek, tilting her head up. She did not dare open her eyes. She would not chase away this dream. Cool lips met hers in a tender, simple embrace.

That was enough to wake her.

She opened her eyes. The dream did not shatter. Lips grazed her forehead. The creak of a lid overhead, and firelight drifted into the coffin.

Propping herself up on one elbow, she expected to eviscerate whatever vampire thought to invade this space. It was likely Zadok. The cretin often tried to "cheer her up" in his own particular and perverted fashion. But instead, crimson eyes met hers.

"Vlad?"

"I believe so. To be fair, I have not been certain as of late."

She sat up, and before she could climb out of the coffin, he had grabbed her by her waist and dragged her atop him. She squeaked in surprise as she sprawled across his chest. He cupped her face in his hands and kissed her, bruising and intense.

He growled beneath her, and when she finally managed to push away from him, she found him smiling up at her. "Yes. That much I remember. I think I am indeed Vlad Tepes Dracula. Am I not?"

"What...how? I thought...I thought I—"

"I am not quite certain myself. I felt you there, tearing me apart. I think you rent my curse in half, my darling empath. You dealt me a grievous wound...but not a fatal one." He was watching her through lidded eyes, and he trailed his hand to rest his thumb at the hollow of her chin. "Look at you...your eyes. By the gods in Hell, you are beautiful."

"What do you remember?"

"I remember you riding me so wonderfully." He smirked.

If she could still blush, she was certain she would be. "After that, Vlad."

"I remember the moment I became as I am. I remember pain. I remember you tearing me apart. But it was too much for you. You left some pieces behind. It took me a long time to learn to exist again." His hand wandered to her throat, and the one at her hip shifted to pull her to him, pressing his hips up against her as she was straddling him.

She gasped and leaned up on her palms. "Please, let this not be a dream. Please. I have missed you so much—my life has been so empty."

"Oh, my Maxine. How I felt you at my side each day. I heard your call. I heard your command. I did not disobey you, but these things take time. You did not destroy me—you merely killed me as the hunters intended to do. But oh, if I had been ushered from the arms of death with such an angel of mercy at my side each time…" He pulled her close to him again as he pressed upward, teasing a dance she could not fight. "Perhaps happiness could have been mine far sooner."

"Vlad…" She moaned and shifted her hips to meet his. She wanted him. She needed him. She needed to feel his soul touching hers. All of it. "I love you."

Her heart began to beat. It lurched in her chest, and the cold of her body began to recede. It was such a bizarre sensation, even after so many years. She assumed she would become inured to it in time. And she had plenty of it now.

He dragged her down with a rough pull of her hair but did not steal the kiss she knew he was after. She went slack in his grasp, surrendering to him. He smiled, and his lips ran along her chin to the crook of her neck. She could feel how he was starving. His body was crying out for blood after it had lain dormant for so long.

She shifted, tilting her head to the side, her hand tangling into the hair at the back of his neck. She welcomed what used to terrify her so greatly. She would happily share herself with him. She let her eyes drift shut as his teeth scraped her skin. His sharp fangs descended in hunger, but not before he whispered to her in adoration.

"I love you, my immortal soul."

Fin.

ALSO BY KATHRYN ANN KINGSLEY

Harrow Faire:

The Contortionist

The Puppeteer

The Clown

The Ringmaster

The Faire

Immortal Soul:

Heart of Dracula

Curse of Dracula

The Impossible Julian Strande:

Illusions of Grandeur

Ghosts & Liars

The Cardinal Winds:

Steel Rose

Burning Hope

Cursed Opal

Frozen Dawn (Coming Soon)

The Masks of Under:

King of Flames

King of Shadows

Queen of Dreams

King of Blood

King of None

Queen of All

Halfway Between:

Shadow of Angels

Blood of Angels

Fall of Angels

ABOUT THE AUTHOR

Kat has always been a storyteller.

With ten years in script-writing for performances on both the stage and for tourism, she has always been writing in one form or another. When she isn't penning down fiction, she works as Creative Director for a company that designs and builds large-scale interactive adventure games. There, she is the lead concept designer, handling everything from game and set design, to audio and lighting, to illustration and script writing.

Also on her list of skills are artistic direction, scenic painting and props, special effects, and electronics. A graduate of Boston University with a BFA in Theatre Design, she has a passion for unique, creative, and unconventional experiences.

Printed in Great Britain
by Amazon